MURDER AT CLUSTER SPRINGS RACEWAY

A BRANDON HALL MYSTERY

JOHN THEO JR.

Print Edition

Published in the United States by CKN Christian Publishing, an imprint of Wolfpack Publishing, Las Vegas.

CKN Christian Publishing
An Imprint of Wolfpack Publishing
6032 Wheat Penny Avenue
Las Vegas, NV 89122

christiankindlenews.com

Paperback ISBN: 978-1-64734-970-7
Ebook ISBN: 978-1-64119-389-4

For my wife, Karin.
A clear example of God blessing me with a reality that exceeded my dreams.

SPECIAL THANKS TO

Dustin Francis, who patiently answered questions regarding Virginia law enforcement. Cathy Rice who gave me a crash course in racing, and Brian and Ashley Hall who were my go-to farming resource. And last, but not least, to all of Southern Virginia who have welcomed my family with open arms.

"Show me Your ways, O Lord;
teach me Your paths."
Psalm 25:4

MURDER AT CLUSTER SPRINGS RACEWAY

ROMANS 8:28

And we know that all things work together for good to them that love God, to them who are called according to his purpose.

On August 12, 2017 two activist groups converged in Charlottesville, Virginia in a clash of culture, politics, and world views. Many believe it was an isolated incident involving two fringe groups of society. One group, steeped in a history of racism dating back over a century and a half. The other, an amalgamation of progressive world views paraded in political correctness.
At their core both preached one thing…

Hate.

ONE

It always saddened me to put an animal down, but it was clear the two-week-old black Angus calf wasn't going to make it. The glazed eyes, lethargy, and inability to feed on his own were clear signs that it was only a matter of time before death came. I try not to leave the farm during the birthing season in case there are complications. This particular calf was born overnight and I didn't find him until early the following morning. He, more than likely, was deprived of oxygen during birth.

It wasn't the loss of money that upset me, but the fact that the animal had barely lived. I reminded myself that in two years he'd be off to the slaughter house. However, for those two years he would have lived a nice life on the farm, enjoying five hundred acres of green pastures, clean water, and beautiful views.

The animal looked up at me, his eyes focused for an instant, as if to let me know that he knew what was coming. I chambered a round of .22 into my son's lever action rifle. The animal closed its eyes.

"I'm sorry little fella," I said.

When I pulled the trigger, the small caliber round seemed louder than usual. A moment later the animal appeared as if he were sleeping rather than dead. I loaded the brass and walnut rifle into its sleeve on the front of the four-wheeler, and drove back towards the barn. I would need a tractor to dispose of the carcass.

The morning sun felt like a warm blanket, but the air had a clean fall smell to it. As much as I loved nice weather and clear skies, the farm was in dire need of rain. Passing by the large oak tree behind the house I spied two cute feet sticking out of the doorway to Emily's tree house. Flip flops dangled from the toes. I stopped at the base and ran up the ladder, knowing the exact scene I'd find. Emily lay on a beanbag with a book hovering over her adorable spectacled dark eyes.

"Whatcha reading, darling?"

She turned the book so I could read the title, *Little House in the Big Woods*. She had the same dark hair and light complexion as her mom. Without saying a word, she went back to reading.

"What's wrong?" she didn't reply.

"You heard the shot huh?" She put the book down and sat up. I could see that her eyes were red. Emily nodded clearly upset.

I sat down just inside the entryway. "I'm sorry sweetie. I hate doing that—"

"I know," she said. "I just can't stand it when something suffers."

"You got such a big heart. That's one of the things I love about you."

She got up and gave me a hug almost knocking me back down the ladder. "I feel so sad for the calf."

"We live in a broken world, sweetie. It's filled with sickness, natural disasters, and suffering. It wasn't like this at the beginning, and it won't be like this someday."

"What do you mean?"

I entered the tree fort and sat down. "The Bible says there'll come a day when there will be no more tears, or pain, or suffering."

"Until then we just do the best we can."

I gave Emily another hug. "Sometimes I wonder if your ten-years-old, or eighty." She smiled. "Love you, sweetie."

"Love you too."

Over her shoulder my gaze was drawn out the one small window in the treehouse. I had built the window to face southwest to get the afternoon sun, but in my haste to cut out the window I'd forgotten the view looked out over my ancestor's cemetery plot. It wasn't a big deal at the time as the headstones, and dates, were all ancient. That all changed a little over a year ago.

I left Emily with a kiss on her forehead and climbed down to go prune some of the dying mums on the newest grave. The entrance to the small cemetery was through a rusted knee high wrought iron gate. Every headstone was thin alabaster revealing ages from long ago. All the headstones except one.

This newer thick grey headstone read, *Jonah Hall, March 12, 2015-August 10, 2017. Beloved son and brother. Now resting in the arms of our Savior.*

Much of my heart was buried in that red clay cemetery plot. My son would never grow up on the farm. I would never be able to give him the lever action rifle when he became a teenager. He'd never date, marry, or raise his own children. My son would never bury his father in this cemetery, which is the way things should be. Instead the natural order had been turned upside down.

I used my stockman pocket knife to prune some of the

dead flowers. Fall in southern Virginia would stick around for a while longer, but winter would come and we'd replace the mums with some sort of greenery for Christmas. A subtle whisper of leather boots wading through dry leaves snapped me out of the trance. I didn't need to turn around to know it was my dad.

"I heard the gunshot from my porch," he said. "Lost another one huh?" I didn't respond. "You need help getting rid of the carcass?"

"I'm good, thanks."

His broad six-foot three inch frame towered over my smaller five foot nine. My dad used to say I inherited two things from my mother, her height and her disposition. It was obvious the latter was a compliment with the former being a dig. At thirty-five I was in good shape, but I'd still lose nine out of ten rounds with my fifty-six-year-old father. The old man worked out five days a week maintaining the same weight and waistline from his days in Desert Storm. He was a giant to me on many levels. Unlike my bearded face he was always clean shaven, another leftover from his routine in the military.

He kissed his right hand then rested it on Jonah's headstone. "I loved the way he chased after the chickens with his little skip run."

"I remember," I said.

He turned and walked away. Since the accident my father had retreated further into his already introverted stoic personality. I couldn't tell if he held us accountable or not. He never said, and I never asked. I was more focused on Annie and Emily to care. It had been just over a year since Emily's car was hit by a drunk driver on route 501. She walked away with a broken wrist, but Jonah died instantly from the t-bone collision.

My dad had to be dragged out of the courtroom when

they passed the light sentence on the drunk driver who killed Jonah. Slowly, over the following months he started distancing himself from everyone, and his passive-aggressive comments were starting to annoy me. Our family went back to the seventeen hundreds in Virginia, and the father-son legacy was more than likely going to end with me. I knew my dad loved his granddaughter, but I also knew that a male who carried on the family name was important to him.

Soon after the accident, he stepped down as an elder at our church to care for my mother who was having her knee replaced. It was a lame excuse as he started missing church services more and more, even after my mother started coming back to church. At some point I'd ask him what his problem was, but now wasn't the time. It had only been recently that I felt like I got the breath back in my lungs from the shock of losing Jonah. I needed to gain more strength before tackling the complex man that was my father.

"Not a day goes by I don't think of you," I whispered before leaving the cemetery.

The morning sun was already migrating from warm to hot. I shuddered at the thought of friends who worked in offices and cubicles. It was a good day to be a farmer. We owned five hundred acres in the small southern Virginia town of Nathalie. We named the farm TWENTY-THREE-ONE, after the Psalm of the same number. *The Lord is my shepherd, I shall not want*. The Lord had been faithful during both droughts and deluges, but the past year had been almost more than I could handle. There was a part of me that could see why my dad was mad at the world, but I knew it wasn't God's fault. I reminded myself of what I had just told my daughter. It was a broken world and man was a fallen creature.

As I drove the four-wheeler towards the barn I could see Annie out in the front yard wandering around in confused circles with her head down. I started up the small tractor and left the machine outside to warm up while I walked out front to check on her.

"Whatcha doing?" I said, stepping onto the front porch.

"Huh, oh look at this. We're in the middle of a drought, yet I'm ankle deep in mud." She lifted up one of her muck boots, which made a sucking noise.

"That ain't good."

"What do you mean?"

"You're standing in the leach field," I said.

"For the septic system?"

"Yup."

"What's that mean?"

"Somewhere along the line it's failed," I said.

"Just great."

"Why don't you go and hose your boots off, and tell Emily not to go near the front yard."

"How are we gonna fix it?"

"I'll call Bud from church. It's his specialty."

"Hopefully he can give us a family and friends discount."

I forced a smile as I calculated costs for a partial or full replacement of the septic system. The numbers that popped into my head were intimidating. A moment later my cell phone rang. The ringtone was set to Johnny Cash's, *Folsom Prison Blues.* It was the tone I assigned to the Sheriff who called me periodically for contract work.

I put it on speaker so Annie could hear in case I had to leave. "Brandon Hall speaking?"

"Hall, it's Tollers. Park Police got a drowning up at Buggs Island Lake. You available for a recovery?"

I looked at my watch. "I can be there by noon."

"Thanks. I'll have the Conservation Police pick you up at the boat ramp at Buffalo Junction. The accident happened a couple hundred yards offshore. Two jet skis collided. Body of a twenty-four-year-old male is still missing. And Brandon—"

"Yeah?"

"It was Bubba D'Angelo's kid, Jordan."

My stomach dropped. Everyone knew Bubba. He was the best auto body guy in South Boston. Everyone used him whenever they hit a deer with their car, which happened at least once to everyone in Halifax County. Bubba was involved in every school board, town meeting, and fundraiser known to man. He was a transplant from Long Island who loved southern Virginia more than any dixie family. I tried to remember what his twenty-year-old son Jordan looked like, but somehow images of my infant son's lifeless body raced in to fill the void. I hung up and immediately choked up.

Annie had her hand to her mouth. "Do you want me to come?" she said.

I collected myself and shook my head. "Stay with Emily. I'll be back soon."

I kissed her on the cheek and went to move the dead calf before I had to go recover the dead human.

TWO

Thirty minutes later I had my dive gear loaded in the back of my 1976 Ford F-250 Emily affectionately named, *Hazel*. Although we lived hours from the coastline I was the only one in the area who was a certified scuba diver. A left-over skill I picked up from my days in the Marines. Our farm income wasn't enough to support the family, so I did private investigating work and dive jobs on the side to supplement. The PI stuff was mostly insurance fraud cases, but the dive work was usually body recovery. It paid well, but I hated it. Ninety percent of the time I didn't know the families affected, which helped to compartmentalize the work. However, Bubba was basically the honorary mayor of South Boston, and a friend. This wasn't going to be fun.

I arrived in Buffalo Park an hour later. The satellite park was one of several that was situated on the largest lake in Virginia. Buggs Island Lake was a 50,000-acre lake with 800 miles of shoreline that spanned southern Virginia into North Carolina where it was known as John Kerr Reservoir. The employee at the gate waved me through and I drove down to the lake. Two small Boston Whaler Department of Game and Inland Fisheries boats floated just offshore with their lights flashing. Boat traffic in, and around, the launch had been halted. The beach was cleared and a dozen people congregated around picnic tables in the shade of the woods near the beach.

I backed Hazel down the boat launch to the water's edge. What was left of two jet ski's had been dragged onto the cement. The accident looked bad, and I started to envision what the body might look like. I waded out a few feet to meet one of the fish and game boats. I didn't recognize the two young Conservation Police in the boat.

"Thanks for coming out," one of them said.

"No problem," I said, handing him my tank.

I walked the rest of my gear out to the boat before getting in. The boat moved offshore and I proceeded to put on a two millimeter wetsuit. The air temperature was mid-eighties, humidity was moderate, and the water would be in the seventies. The only reason for a thin wet suit was if I had to go deep where the water temperature dropped.

"Did he have a life vest on?" I said.

"He did but it wasn't buckled. We found it floating nearby."

I sat down to put the fins and tank on. "What happened to the driver of the other jet ski?"

One officer snorted. "Guy was drunk and came away without a scratch. Police took him into custody before you arrived."

Yet another death caused by a drunk driver. It brought back the anger I struggled with toward the drunk driver who had killed my son. In the courtroom he had never acted contrite, nor asked for forgiveness when he was on the stand. Instead his lawyer talked about his abusive childhood and painted him as a victim who had zero control over his actions. Regardless of his lack of repentance, I needed to find a pathway to forgiveness. The Bible said to love my enemies and bless them that cursed me, do good to them that hated me. To pray for them which despitefully used me, and persecuted me. I had long since moved beyond hating the man, but I could not get to the point of loving him or forgiving him.

We reached the second boat and tied off. The boat under me shifted as the weight of someone stepped on board. A hand rested on my shoulder. I reluctantly looked up knowing it would be Bubba. He was shorter than me with dusty grey hair. The usual smile on his face was gone. In its place were bloodshot eyes and a lip that quivered. I placed my hand over his and squeezed it.

"You'll get my boy?" He said, in a hoarse voice.

"I'll do everything I can, Bubba."

The water visibility in the lake was only a few feet. It was clean, but murky due to all the clay sediment. There was a high probability I wouldn't find the body.

"You'll get my boy," he said again, this time it was a statement. Words of encouragement. The broken man was cheering me on.

I finished putting on the buoyancy compensation device and started to break down. Memories of Jonah assaulted my consciousness. I said a prayer for the strength to continue. A prayer for Bubba and his wife. A prayer for his boy's soul. Bubba was holding it together better than me. I dropped the mask down and rushed over the side.

As I floated next to the boat one of the Rangers shouted. "Below you is the last known location."

I gave the thumbs up, stuffed the regulator in my mouth, and deflated the air from the BCD. Murky water surrounded me. The descent brought me into cooler water which was the right temperature for the wetsuit. Visibility was almost non-existent. Even if the body was within twenty feet I'd still have a hard time finding it. I stopped and pinched my nose through the bottom of the mask and tried to blow out of it at the same time. This equalized the building pressure in my ears and allowed me to continue the descent.

At twenty feet my fin hit something. Before I could inflate my vest to stop the descent I drifted past the body. The lifeless eyes of the young man were wide open in terror. Bile rose in my throat and I forced it back down. Vomiting into a regulator while underwater would be devastating. I inflated the BCD and floated back to the surface.

"What's wrong?" one of the officers shouted?

I pulled the regulator from my mouth. "I found him."

There was silence. A moment later Bubba's wife buried her head into his shoulder and wailed. She sounded like a dying animal, but Bubba held it together.

"Brandon, bring me my boy," he said, devoid of emotion.

An officer handed me an OD green body bag tethered to a rope. A few minutes later I was at work on the body. I wouldn't allow myself to look at his pale face again. Instead I worked around the limbs and managed to cover him up from behind. After, I tugged on the rope and watched the bag go to the surface. I stayed down an extra five minutes not wanting to witness first contact between the body and people above. I was content floating in my protected underwater bubble. A minute passed and one of the boats fired up its engine. I surfaced next to the other boat. The moment they confirmed I had surfaced, the boat carrying Bubba, his wife, and their son, headed to shore where an EMT now waited with lights flashing. I was both relieved, and ashamed.

"You did good," one of the officers said, taking my fins.

"Some days I wish I never did this work," I said, climbing into the boat.

By the time we reached the shore Bubba, his wife, and the ambulance were gone. Driving back the sun was fierce. It was pushing almost ninety. Summer could be vicious in southern Virginia, and many times fall turned out to be an extension of summer. The consolation was usually mild winters.

Back in South Boston I stopped by my church to check on the playground being installed. I found fifty-five-year-old Pastor Dale outside next to a skid steer and freshly leveled ground covered with mulch. He leaned on a shovel and looked up towards the clear sky. In front of him was what looked like a trash pile of metal.

I parked the truck next to him. "You gettin paid by the hour or project?"

He broke into a wide grin. "Nice."

"What's so funny?"

"I didn't think God would answer my prayer so quick." He walked up to the truck and handed me a wad of papers. "Here's the assembly instructions."

"Oh no you don't."

"It's a divine appointment." He pointed to the pile of metal pipes behind him. "I've counseled wrecked marriages, overseen funerals, preached to prisoners, but assembling this play set is testing me."

I grabbed my work gloves and stepped out of the truck. The assembly instructions were in Chinese. I flipped the page and found Spanish, but no English.

"You hate me," I said.

He smiled. "Nothing but love for you, brother."

"Then you need to learn to love me less."

I texted Annie to let her know I was stuck at church and would see her when she showed up for Wednesday night service. The smell of fresh bark mulch on the bare playground brought back memories of my teen summers when I landscaped. It was an innocent time when my only frame of reference for sadness, and loss, was a broken heart from being dumped by a girlfriend. I had no idea just how painful life could be.

"How's your Dad?" Dale said, assembling a pipe.

I laughed. "Brandon senior has turned into a grumpy recluse."

"Think I should go see him?"

"I doubt it would do any good."

"You think it's more than the loss of Jonah?"

I huffed. "I think it's everything to do with my son's death. The guy seems to be taking it harder than me, and through some sick twist of irony I'm left walking on eggshells around him."

"We all grieve in our own way, Brandon. I'll give him a call and if he's receptive I'll go see him."

"Good luck with that."

Three hours later we had made progress. The slide and swings were up and the reminder of the play set would be easy. Cars started pulling in to the church parking lot. Annie showed up in her jeep with the top down. Emily jumped out of the back seat and rushed over to the play set.

Annie called from the jeep. "Emily, be careful there are cars everywhere."

Emily rolled her eyes. "She thinks I'm a baby. I can't even go to the bathroom without her checking on me."

"What'd I tell you honey?" I said.

"I know. Show her grace. I'm trying." She pointed to the play set. "It looks great." She stuck her nose near me. "Daddy, you stink."

"Pastor Dale's punishing me."

Annie approached with a tray full of chicken wings. My stomach growled at the smell of the buffalo sauce. I kissed Annie and lifted the tin foil.

"Don't you dare," she said. "This is for after church."

"Dale won't even give me a water break. Just let me take one wing, sweetie."

"Fine, but just one."

I took a wing and handed one to Dale. He scoffed it down.

"Your husband's been an answer to prayer with this play set," Dale said with a mouth full of chicken.

"Just don't break him. We need him on the farm." She turned to me, "How was earlier?"

I shook my head back and forth to let Annie know it didn't go well at the lake, and that I would fill her in later.

She leaned in to sniff me. "You need to go inside and take a shower before church?"

Emily laughed. "Told you."

"You guys are teaming up on me," I said, kissing Annie and taking another chicken wing on the fly.

"Brandon Hall!"

"Sorry," I said with a mouthful of chicken. "These wings are like your kisses. I can't just have one."

* * *

Dale's Wednesday night service was a bit more relaxed. He used mid-week sermons to talk about our culture, and how to navigate it from a Biblical point of view. This night he talked about the local elections and how we needed to hold candidates to a higher standard. Getting results while sacrificing character weren't good enough. He quoted Titus, Chapter One for qualities church leaders must have. He went on to say that we should look for these same qualities in politicians and worldly leaders, especially those professing to be Christian.

After the sermon I was first in line for the buffet dinner. Emily, Annie, and me sat next to Dale and his wife Sheila. The conversation was light and revolved around hunting season with me and Dale, and a shopping trip to the Raleigh Durham area of North Carolina for the girls. After dinner I stayed to help fold up the tables and chairs.

Before I left, Dale motioned for me to go into his office. "Can I talk to you for a second?"

"There's no one here but us, so why the cloak and dagger?" I said, entering the office.

"Don't know, I just feel like we need to have this conversation in my office."

"If this is about the funny pic I posted of you on the church's website I was kidding."

Dale grinned. "Nothin like that. Here sit down."

"I'd rather stand. You're making me nervous."

He took up a seat behind his walnut desk. The moment he sat down my easy-going friend seemed to leave the room and a sober Pastor took up residence. "I want to let you know I've been counseling Bud and his wife for the past month."

"Really," I said, sitting down. "I'm shocked. They've been married like twenty-five years?"

"The only reason I'm telling you this is I need your help."

"Name it."

"Obviously, what I'm about to say is confidential." I

nodded. “Sarah came to me claiming Bud is cheating on her.”

“What? I thought they were rock solid?”

“Don’t be fooled by facades you see on Sundays. The problem I have is, Bud says that Sarah’s mistaken. Bud did admit to surfing porn on the internet in the past and claims Sarah is still upset from that. Bud divulging this indiscretion leads me to believe he’s telling the truth. I’ve counseled a lot of couples over the years and I’m usually a good judge as who’s right, but I can’t read this one. You’re an elder and know Bud and—”

“And you want me to talk to him?”

“Do you mind?” Dale said. “Just see if you can get a read on him?”

I nodded. “Something’s up with my septic leach field and I already have a call into him. I’ll strike up a conversation when he stops by. Do you have any gut feelings one way or another?”

“None,” Dale said. “I’m at a loss. Sarah has been a bit melodramatic in the past with a couple of the women here, but I just don’t know.”

“I won’t mention that we spoke.”

Dale exhaled as if he’d been holding this breath. “I appreciate it.”

When I got home, Annie and Em were on the couch with a massive bowl of popcorn watching the movie *White Christmas* with Bing Crosby, Danny Kaye, and Rosemary Clooney.

“It’s a bit early to have this on don’t you think?” I said.

“I know, but I love Christmas.”

“I kissed her and took up a seat.

The movie characters were on a train heading to Vermont and were singing about snow. The very word was foreign to me. Living in southern Virginia I only experienced the white stuff a few times a year, and even then it was usually only a few inches and melted within twenty-four hours. This allowed me to keep a romantic view of snow. Compared to the way my day had started, an old Bing Crosby movie was a nice way to bring it to a peaceful end.

THREE

Saturday morning I was up at dawn sitting in front of an old computer in a barn office, which had been converted from an old horse stall. I ordered some organic feed for our chickens, and placed an order for the farm diesel tank to be topped off. Every year that passed it seemed like technology crept into farming more. I sometimes wished progress ended with the advent of diesel tractors, which were a game changer for farmers. With this much new progress comes frustrating things like email, and the need for farmers to be on social media.

It was also time to place my annual order for bull semen, a necessity if one wanted to grow their herd. In farming, there were very few glamorous moments, and impregnating cows and heifers surely wasn't in the top ten. Through the slow process of my two-finger typing I placed the order, grabbed another cup of coffee, and headed to the pastures to check on the herd. When I came back inside Emily was placing a wicker basket filled with fresh eggs from the chicken coop into the refrigerator. Annie held a pan of blueberry muffins she had just taken out of the oven. The entire house smelled like a bakery.

"Are the berries from our bushes?" I said.

"Yes, and no eating all the muffins in one sitting," Annie said. "You sticking around today or do you have to head out?"

"I'm gonna meet JT for coffee in downtown South Boston."

"How's he doing?"

"He's acclimating slowly. Between his New England accent, and rough demeanor, he's basically a fish out of water."

"I'm glad he's got you as a friend."

I smiled. "Doesn't say much if I'm your only friend."

Annie laughed and handed me a warm blueberry muffin rolled in a napkin.

I pulled her in for a kiss. "What you doing later tonight my dark-haired beauty?"

Emily turned from her book. "That's gross."

I went over and kissed Emily on her ear and nibbled it until her laughter turned to hysterical shouts due to my beard tickling her. Laughter had finally returned to the Hall homestead, and it was more than welcome.

The drive into South Boston, or Sobo, was quiet. The weather was such that I could still drive with the windows down. Up north, they already had a frost, but in southern Virginia the best season had just started. Fall had little humidity, and a warm temperature that generally hung between seventy and eighty-five. It was also when hunting season started, which added to every red-blooded male's excitement.

A half hour later I parked outside an old laundry facility that had been converted into a coffee shop. Inside, a solitary man sat at a round wooden table. He was my height, a bit chubby, and wore a Boston Red Sox cap over his bald head. Although JT dressed like a sloppy college kid no one would know that he was an MIT grad with a hi-tech background. At one point he was a big-shot in the tech industry up north but went through a nervous breakdown when his wife up, and left him, for one of his business partners. He punched out of the rat-race, threw a dart at a map, and moved to South Boston to purchase a small self-storage facility on Webster Street.

We met a few months back when I accidentally cut him in line and he shouted at me with a thick Boston accent laced with expletives. As angry as he was, I found the accent both disarming and hysterical. I apologized and bought him coffee and struck up a conversation. After learning his story I mentioned God and was happy to hear that this northerner was open to the idea of God, and even had questions. Since then, I met with him for coffee every few weeks to discuss little things like life, death, suffering, pain, and what the purpose of life was.

I patted him on the shoulder as I passed by to go to the counter. "Sorry I'm late. I'd have called or texted, but you don't own a cell phone."

"I own as little technology as possible these days, brotha," he said in his Boston accent.

"Want another coffee?"

"I'm all set, thanks."

Two minutes later I sat across from JT with an iced coffee. "So what's the good word?"

"Oh, I don't know," he said, putting down a newspaper. "Economy's in the crapper, terrorist attacks and school shootings are so common they don't even make the front page anymore." He paused. "Want me to keep going?"

I held up my hand. "It was a rhetorical question."

"Oh, my bad. I gotta stop following the news huh?"

I nodded. “So my dear MIT professor, what’re you pondering this week?”

JT pulled out a piece of wrinkled paper from his jeans and spread it out on the table with his hands. To say he was eccentric was an understatement. “I can’t get beyond this suffering thing,” he said. “I know I keep beating this into the ground but—”

“Don’t you dare apologize,” I said. “I know you’ve been through a lot. Fire away and let’s figure this out together.”

He exhaled and seemed to relax. “The last time we spoke you made a solid point about how man can make choices to do evil to other men, which causes suffering. I get that. The problem I now have is, when man’s not involved and there’s suffering.”

“Like?”

“Like natural disasters, earthquakes, tsunamis, mudslides, you name it.”

I took out my cell phone and started scrolling through my bible app. JT cringed like a vampire faced with a crucifix.

“Big brother’s watching your every move with that thing.”

“I got nothing to hide,” I said.

“Famous last words all the people, or sheeple, say. Trust me I’ve done work for most of the big government agencies. They’re watching.”

“Here,” I said, turning the cell phone to face him. “Read it.”

“Romans eight twenty-two,” he said. “For we know that the whole creation groaneth and travaileth in pain together until now.”

“Man isn’t the only thing affected negatively by the fall,” I said.

"So what are you saying? That the earth is broken as well?"

"Exactly." I scrolled over to Matthew twenty-four and read, "For nation shall rise up against nation, and kingdom against kingdom: and there shall be famines and pestilences, and earthquakes, in divers places. All these are the beginning of sorrows." I put the phone away. "The Bible predicted this type of suffering a very long time ago."

"Gee, how very uplifting," he said.

"I agree. It's not very hopeful, unless—"

"Unless you believe in God," he cut in. "I believe there's something out there; otherwise I wouldn't be meeting with you, but don't you think it's arrogant to say Jesus is the only way?" Before I could respond JT held up his hand. "Hear me out, brotha. What if there's a group of people in a pitch-black room feeling around an elephant. One person has the trunk, one grabs a foot, another a tail. If you asked each one what the elephant looked like they'd tell you exactly what they held onto. What they knew. And from their point of view they'd be speaking the truth."

"JT, the arrogance is on the storyteller's part."

"How so?"

"You tell the story from a macro level.

"Huh?"

"You've acknowledged that you, the storyteller, are the only one who can see the entire elephant. The reality is everyone is feeling in the dark."

He pondered what I said for a moment. "So how do you know you're right?"

"I've personally seen miracle after miracle in my life that defies both logic and probability. Times when very specific prayers were answered very specifically. There's no other way to explain it."

"Give me an example?"

"I have several," I said. "A few years back I ran a 5k with my dad. He was adamant he could beat me. Well, he did beat me, and proceeded to collapse at the finish line and have a heart attack. Turns out the guy who finished just ahead of us was a cardiologist. My old man literally fell at the feet of a heart doc. The doctor tore through a nearby first aid kit and went to work on my dad. Had this doctor not run the race, my dad would have died."

"Cool," JT said. "Well, not cool that he had a heart attack, but you get my point."

"There's more," I said. "My pastor, Dale, was part of a gang in Danville in his youth. After he came to Christ he tried to leave the gang and let's just say they wouldn't let him."

"What happened?"

"He was beat up and stabbed multiple times. The knife cut one of his kidney's in half, hit his spleen and pancreas, broke a couple ribs, and punctured a lung." JT winced at the rough description. "Dale was rushed to the hospital and bled to death twice."

"As in—"

"As in he bled through all the plasma the docs gave him. Turns out the hospital in Danville was hosting a one night only medical summit of all the top surgeons in the world, so Dale ended up having the top docs pulled from the meeting. About five surgeons worked on him throughout the night and saved his life. Had they not been there for that meeting, at that specific night, he would have died." I waved my hand in the air. "There are many more instances of my prayers being answered on the farm, in life, and when I was deployed overseas that defy all probability."

"Wow," was all JT said. "Just wow."

"JT, every Bible believing Christian you meet will have stories like mine. Maybe not life or death stories, but the mathematical impossibility stories will be there." I finished my iced coffee and watched the brainiac's wheels turn. "Besides answer to prayers, everything you throw at the Bible works," I continued. "History and archeology all support the book. Every day science discovers something new the Bible already spoke of thousands of years ago. So many people throughout history have gone on crusades to disprove the Bible and ended up believers. The bottom line is He's been faithful to me."

JT winced. "Even through the death of your boy?"

"Especially through the death of my boy," I said. "I wouldn't be here talking with you were it not for Christ seeing me through that dark time."

"I'm not trying to offend you."

"I'm not offended," I said. "Behold, I stand at the door, and knock: if any man hear my voice, and open the door, I will come in and sup with him, and he with me." JT didn't respond so I continued. "I know you've been through a lot with your wife, but just know that He's knocking."

There was a long pause. JT was clearly upset at just the mention of his ex-wife. He got up without a word and went to the counter to order another coffee leaving a half-filled cup on the table. I knew he didn't want me to see him upset. A minute later he returned with a new cup of coffee and his composure intact.

"You going to Cluster Springs Raceway tonight?" He said.

I knew this meant he didn't want to discuss theology further. "Sure am."

"Good, I'll look for you at the same spot we sat last time."

The conversation continued on a few minutes with Nascar, the weather, the lack of Dunkin Donuts in South

Boston and JT's beloved Red Sox. We parted with a promise to find each other at the race later.

I left the coffee shop and went across the street to an antique store. The building was over a century old and had tall ceilings and chipped plaster walls. Every square inch of the massive three-story structure had something for sale. From expensive paintings, antique furniture, down to old big band era records and dollar knick knacks. The elderly woman behind the counter smiled when she saw me.

"Come to pick up your layaway, Brandon?"

"Yes, Ma'am." I handed her the last forty bucks from my wallet.

"Wait here a moment." She disappeared into a back room and returned carrying a mid-sized cardboard box. "Your wife is gonna love this set."

"She's always wanted a china set, and she loves the blue on white colonial patterns. Very farm-like." I opened the lid to find dishes, bowls and cups with blue and white designs. Old farm scenes were laid out across the lip of the bowls. Horse drawn carriages and sleighs. A simpler time when our country was young and seemed innocent.

"Here's your receipt," she said. "Happy anniversary."

On the ride home I kept one hand on the box. The truck's lifted suspension made for a stiff bumpy ride. The rest of the morning I drove the pastures with Emily checking on the herd and marking fence posts that needed replacement. Annie met us near the large pond for a late lunch. The sky was clear and the temp was eighty with very little humidity.

"I think I have the best job in the world," I said, tossing the crust of my turkey sandwich into the pond. Within seconds a group of fish attacked it.

"You definitely have the best office," Annie said.

"So who's coming to the race with me tonight?"

"I am," Emily said.

"I was gonna meet up with a couple ladies from church." Annie said.

"What, you don't think eating funnel cakes and watching cars race around a track is romantic?"

"C'mon mom," Emily said. "It's the last race of the season."

"I was thinking we could celebrate our anniversary tonight?" I said.

"Nice try," Annie giggled. "We're still going to Cherry Hill Tuesday night, and you're going to wear a tie. And before you ask, no you can't wear your camo tie."

Annie left with a kiss. Emily helped me work in the garden for the remainder of the afternoon. We kept a small quarter acre vegetable garden that still had pumpkins and squash that needed to be picked.

FOUR

Around seven p.m., Emily and I entered the town of Cluster Springs. It was a sleepy hamlet near the North Carolina border. It had less than a thousand residents, but was strategically located along route 501 between Virginia and North Carolina. A perfect spot to pull racing fans from both states. The old raceway was just off the road and overlooked a small duck pond. The sun was just about to set leaving the sky a dark crimson over the old white wooden stadium. The five acres of grassed parking lots were littered with trucks draped with American flags and NRA stickers. The temperature had cooled, but the long sleeve shirts we had on were more than enough. JT found us off to the side of the bleachers where lawn chair seating was allowed next to the handicap seating. He was just finishing a funnel cake.

He opened a New England Patriots folding chair and turned to Emily. "You excited for the race?"

"Yeah. Drew Schilling's favored to win."

"I have no idea who that is."

I leaned over. "He's a nineteen-year-old kid that all the girls around here are ga-ga over."

"How does a nineteen-year-old stumble into this?" JT Said. "I know it's not the level of the cup races, but it must still cost a small fortune to get a car in these races?"

I rubbed my fingers together to signify money. "It's what you do down south when you don't go to college and daddy has coin."

"Ahh, I get it."

An adorable girl, around Emily's age, came out onto the track with a microphone. We all rose as she started to sing the national anthem.

I turned to JT. "Unlike the NFL, you won't see anyone at a race take a knee for the national anthem."

A nearby mid-thirties man in a wheelchair wearing a US Semper-Fi shirt with his hand over his heart turned to me. "Right on. I'd kill to be standing right now."

The first race was quick and uneventful. The main race was set to start just after eight o'clock. The late model cars rumbled as they waited for the flag. They sounded like diesel trucks without mufflers. From our seats you could feel the vibration from the idling engines. Everyone closest to the chain link fence overlooking the track wore ear protection. The flag dropped and the explosion of sound could have loosened a kidney stone. For fifty laps Drew Schilling held on to second place just behind a red car sponsored by Bubba's Performance Center. Although the track was on the smaller end, the drivers still hit 100 miles per hour on the straightaways in the late model race cars. Emily screamed every time Drew came around the corner in his white Diesel Tractor sponsored car.

JT pointed to Emily and shouted over the noise to me, "This is only gonna get worse when she's sixteen and the boys come sniffing around."

I shouted back, "That's why I own a shotgun."

JT laughed and gave me a thumbs up.

A caution flag went up and a disabled car was towed off the track. Minutes later the race resumed. Twenty more laps and Drew had gained first place. Em's voice had not given out. In fact her enthusiasm was starting to wear off on me as I was starting to root for the kid as well. On the next lap Drew's car passed by and moved into the blind spot of the bleachers followed close by Bubba's Performance car and the pack.

There was a sickening sound of an explosion followed by a ball of fire rising up from the track. I immediately knew it was Drew's car. All the cars slowed to a stop as people on the bleachers rushed to leave their seats.

I couldn't tell if the explosion hurt anyone in the crowd. My only thought was Emily. In one motion I flung her up to my chest. Her arms instinctively wrapped around my neck like they had done many times before. Only this time it wasn't for fun. JT was already beside me as we moved to leave.

I looked back at the veteran in the wheelchair. He waved us on. "I'm right behind you, Hoss."

Another explosion went off on the track. The crowd rushed the main gates, which were becoming congested. People had started pushing on one another. Even from this distance I could feel the heat coming off the tracks. There was no way the kid survived. Emily was crying and almost choking me. I motioned JT to follow as I moved back towards the direction of our seats.

"Where we going?" He said.

"Follow me."

I bumped into people who were rushing past us towards the main entrance. Behind our seats were a playground and a massive locked gate. I handed Emily to JT.

The sirens from emergency vehicles on the track were loud enough that no one would hear a gun go off. I took out my Smith and Wesson Shield from my appendix holster and fired it at the gate's rusted padlock. The lock exploded and fell to the ground. I re-holstered the gun and took Em back from JT. The wheelchair bound vet rolled up with a couple more people in wheelchairs as I kicked the gate open.

"Nice shooting, Hoss." The vet didn't seem at all phased at what I had just done.

Once at the safety of my truck I plopped Emily on the tailgate and looked her over. The only marks on her were from tears running down her cheeks.

"You okay baby?"

She nodded.

"JT, watch Em for a second?"

He sat next to her as I got out a couple bottles of water and the medical kit I kept in the truck cab. In the distance the flames on the tracks were above the top of the bleachers lighting up the dark night sky like some ancient pagan ceremony. The flames looked like tentacles trying to reach the stars above in a jealous rage.

I gave Emily a close exam to make sure she was okay before I texted Annie to let her know we were both safe. No doubt she would hear about the accident on email and social media.

"You good if I take off?" JT said. I nodded. "I'm outta here then."

"Be safe."

"Never seen anything like this," he said, walking towards his car. "That poor kid."

For fifteen minutes we sat in a traffic que waiting for the police to let us out of the parking lot. Emily was quiet. I was worried she was in some sort of shock.

"Talk to me, baby?"

She unbuckled her seatbelt and crawled up next to me to lie down. Normally, I would have told her to put the seat belt back on. Instead I put a hand on her head and stroked it.

At home, Annie pulled into the driveway the same time we did. She rushed over to the truck. I put my finger to my mouth to let her know that Emily was sleeping. I stepped out of the truck happy to hug the warm body of my wife.

"You okay?" She whispered. I nodded. "I heard on the radio that Drew Schilling died. A couple other cars were totaled but no one else was hurt."

She started crying and her sobs started to morph into hyperventilating. I walked her over to the porch and sat down holding her hand. "It's okay. We're fine, Sweetie. Take a deep breath."

She took several breaths and wiped her cheeks. "Brandon, After Jonah—" she stopped. "I'd die if something happened to you two."

"Nothing did, and we're fine."

She looked up to the star-filled night sky. "Thank you Lord for keeping them safe." She dropped her head. "I pray this Schilling boy knew you, and you bring comfort his family."

"I've never seen anything like that explosion," I said.

"How so?"

"People have died in racing but it's mostly from collisions, not explosions."

"I'm just thankful you and Emily are okay."

We prayed together and sat on the porch until Annie calmed down. I carried Emily inside and placed her on the couch covering her with a fleece blanket. Our bedroom was on the first floor and I wanted Emily to sleep near us in case she woke up with any nightmares. I couldn't imagine what it was like for her to witness a death like that, let alone it being a young boy she had a crush on. Emily had already lost a baby brother. My heart ached for her. My heart ached for the Schilling boy's family. I said another prayer for his family before going to bed.

The next morning was Sunday. At breakfast Emily was quiet, but said she still wanted to go to church.

Before we left for church Annie said, "In all the excitement I forgot to tell you that Bud stopped by yesterday afternoon just after you guys left for the racetrack."

The conversation with Dale rang in my mind. "I hoped to talk to him. What did he say?"

She pulled a pad of paper off the top of the refrigerator. "He said our entire leach field was failing. If we had a localized break it would only be wet in one area but our entire front yard is wet."

"Ugh. Did he put a price on it?"

"No, but he did say it would be a time-consuming project. We're gonna need to tap into our savings for this aren't we?"

"We'll be fine," I said, trying to convince myself as much as my wife. "As long as we do our part, God has always been faithful."

"Keep telling me that."

Annie held onto my hand the entire drive to church. It was tense and I stroked the top of her hand with my thumb and forefinger trying to get her to relax. At church, Bud was nowhere to be seen, but his wife was there. Early that morning Dale had scrapped his entire sermon and did one off the cuff regarding the traumatic death of Drew Schilling, which was all over the local news. Dale talked about time and love being the only currencies we had on this planet, and how we must not waste either. He preached from James, Chapter Four and Ephesians,

Chapter Five on the subject of time and from several different passages on love.

After church Emily stayed on the couch all afternoon watching DVDs. She was an old soul and liked black and white shows like Andy Griffith. I sometimes wished we lived in Mayberry. Annie and I traded off sitting with her. When either of us tried to bring up the accident Emily changed the subject.

The next morning I was out of the house at sunrise. The sky was clear and temperature cool. It was perfect flannel shirt weather. As much as I wanted to rip up the scuba bill for the recovery of Bubba's kid I sent the email with the invoice attached in to the police. The septic repair bill would be big. When I came back inside for breakfast Emily seemed better, but was still quiet. I made sure to remind her how much I loved her, and to let her know I'd be working on the fence line if she wanted to grab a four-wheeler and come out to join me.

The traffic on the roads around the farm was mostly neighbors and logging trucks, so when a black limousine drove by I took notice. I didn't even know where someone could rent a limo in Halifax County. The vehicle drove the neighborhood slowly, like someone who was lost. I continued on with the fence repairs. Fifteen minutes later, the limo returned and slowed to a stop a few feet from where I worked. A window lowered from the back seat and someone cleared their throat.

"Excuse me, I'm looking for Brandon Hall?"

I took off my leather work gloves, and approached the shiny vehicle. "How can I help you?"

The man got out from the vehicle. He was tall, at least six two and dressed in an expensive grey wool suit. I recognized his salt and pepper hair and tan complexion. Senator Gregory Schilling was a four term senator from

Virginia. His roots went deep into southern VA, but he now resided in the wealthy Alexandria area just outside DC.

"I'm—"

"Senator Schilling," I said, taking his hand. "My deepest condolences for the loss of your son, Senator."

His eyes started to fill up. "I'm in Halifax County to collect Drew. I'll never forgive myself for not being there the other night."

"There's nothing you could have done had you been there, sir."

"You were there?"

"I was."

Hesitantly, he asked. "Do you think my boy suffered?"

"I don't think so." I paused not sure what else to add. "It was quick."

He pulled out an embroidered handkerchief and wiped his face. A moment later he'd collected himself. "I need your help, Mr. Hall."

"Anything, sir."

"I had my staff pull all your files. Your reputation as a soldier, a man of faith, and as a private investigator are impressive. I believe that our ancestors even crossed the Dan River together?"

"I had no idea," I said.

The Senator looked skyward. "Mr. Hall, I'd like to engage your services."

"Like I said, anything you need, sir."

He turned to face me, now clear-eyed. "I'd like you to investigate my son's murder."

FIVE

"Murder?"

The Senator waved his hand as if to cut the pleasantries. "There's no way a race car just explodes. I know my son was murdered."

"If that's the case," I said, "why don't you let the state police look into this?"

"They're running an investigation, but as of now it's considered an accident. It could be weeks before it gets flipped into a homicide case, if ever. I also don't know who I can trust."

"But don't you think—"

"I'm not a patient man, Mr. Hall. Bottom line is I want to run my own parallel investigation. Every second that goes by the person responsible crawls deeper into their hole. There could be a lot of people involved in this, but I want you to focus on one aspect of this. Find the trigger man. Someone had access to my son's car and tampered with it. I want you to find this person."

"Senator, let me back up for a second. Why would anyone want to hurt your boy?"

He walked away from the limo and I followed. "You know the uranium mining that's been the talk of the state who the past few years?"

"Yeah."

"I have been openly opposing it in Congress. I've received threats over this and I believe Drew's murder is in retribution for my actions."

"From who?"

"The Russians, people in congress, anyone who stands to benefit from uranium being mined in Virginia."

"Sir, that level of investigation is above my pay grade—"

"I understand. Like I said, I just want you to find out who's involved on a local level and let me take care of the high-level stuff. I'm begging you for your help Mr. Hall."

There's no way I could say no to this grieving man. I stretched out my hand. He took it with an iron grip and pulled me in close. "Find the demon the killed my son, Hall. Find him, so I can give his mother some peace."

"I'll do everything I can, sir."

Before he got back in the limo he handed me a business card. "Send your bills to my personal assistant, Jane. Whatever cost you see fit I'll approve. Anything else you need to help with the investigation, she can get you."

Inside the limo he tapped on the front glass to let the driver know to leave. As the tinted window went up I could see the senator's head drop into his hands. The man was barely holding it together.

Annie drove lunch out to me on a four-wheeler. I told her about the interaction with the senator and the new side job.

"I'm impressed. You're working for a famous senator," she said. "Couldn't have happened at a better time with our leach field issue."

"Tell me about it."

After lunch I finished up the section of fence I was working on before checking the herd. There was only one heifer who hadn't given birth yet. Her due date was coming up soon. The sky had only a few wisps of what could pass as clouds and showed no signs of giving up any moisture. All the smaller ponds I used for watering the herd were nearly dry. Fortunately, I cut hay in September before the drought kicked into overdrive, so the winter food supply was solid. Water was now the primary concern.

At the end of the day I found Emily and Annie in the tree house. Emily had always wanted to have a dinner picnic in her tree house and my sweet wife had made a roast chicken and brought everything up to the fort. We said grace and ate crossed legged in the cramped space. A breeze wafted in from the pastures keeping the tree house from becoming stuffy. Outside the window my boy's tombstone reflected the setting sun like a dark beacon. My thoughts drifted to Bubba and Senator Schilling who would both experience moments like this. I shut the calico curtain and returned to the girls.

* * *

A LIGHT RATTLE woke me at five thirty am. I found my dad brewing coffee in the kitchen. The old man was decked out in full frontier getup. He had on moccasins, buckskin leggings, breeches, and a long hunting frock. In his belt were a long knife and a tomahawk. A leather possibles pouch hung over his shoulder one way with a powder horn crossing the opposite. His black powder Kentucky long rifle leaned up against the counter. I forgot we were supposed to go hunting. He handed me a tin cup filled with black coffee, just the way he liked it.

"We're burning daylight," he said.

"Sorry," I said, doing everything I could to keep from pointing out the window at the stars still in the dark sky. "Been crazy around here lately. Give me a minute."

I crept back in the bedroom and snuck out with my jeans, boots, flannel shirt and hunting vest. I scratched a note for Annie on the kitchen table because my dad banned cell phones on our hunts. My father was on the porch swing when I came outside carrying my eighteenth century matching long rifle he'd made for me years ago. In an army surplus rucksack I brought along fruit, water, my hunting knife, ball and powder. Through the trees at the far end of the east pasture I could see a sliver of light starting to show up. The slight chill of the morning would be gone soon.

"Gonna be a good day for hunting," I said.

"Indeed," he replied.

Without a word he strode off the porch in the direction of the forest. We entered the family cemetery. Passing by my son's headstone my dad kissed his hand and rested it on the stone. He whispered something before exiting out the far gate towards the forest. I stopped and simply touched the stone. I remembered Jonah as a ball of energy. When it was time for bed, and his batteries were empty, he'd finally rest his head on my shoulder and I'd sing him a hymn in my off-key voice. I remember the warmth that ran down my body as he held onto me. It was the simplest form of love from a child. What I wouldn't do to hold him one more time.

"I love you," I whispered to my son, before I rushed to catch up with my dad.

In the early morning light the giant in front of me looked like he stepped from the pages of a history book. We were both fans of US history. My favorite era was the late nineteenth century wild west, but dad was stuck in the eighteenth century. He claimed we could trace our lineage back to some of Daniel Boone's kin. As a child he would tell me stories about the early frontiersmen. People like Boone and Simon Kenton. Stories about the discovery of Kentucky, and the small period of quiet before the inrush of people through the Cumberland Gap into the west.

Regardless of firearm or muzzleloading season my father only hunted with his black powder rifle, and always wore era appropriate clothing. Although he appreciated modern firearms he only owned flintlock rifles and pistols. Even his patch knives, tomahawk, and belt knife were authentic 18th century replicas with hammer marks still on the metal. The old man refused to hunt from a blind or stand and always hunted on foot. It was less efficient, but the spot-and-stalk approach was the only way I was ever allowed to hunt.

For the next hour we walked trails through the farm's wooded forty acres, pausing for long periods of time so he could observe tracks, wind direction, and check for signs like droppings and half chewed acorns. My father moved like a deer making very little noise. Me, on the other hand, snapped twigs like it was my job. Each time I could see his shoulder's wince. I was impressed he hadn't said anything yet. The sun was mid-way in the morning sky, but it barely punctured the heavy foliage of the mature forest. I had been offered thousands of dollars for the timber rights to this section of the farm, but my father wouldn't hear of it. He liked the ancient trees, which were rare in the heavily-logged area of Virginia we lived in. I agreed they were beautiful, but bills kept coming that tempted me to cash in on the easy money.

A short while later he stopped to take a sip from an

antique gourd canteen. "Heard about the raceway," he whispered. "Shame about that kid."

"We were there. Emily was traumatized."

"I didn't know," he said. "Anything I can do?"

"Just give her some extra attention the next time you see her."

"I always do."

"I meant extra affection."

"What's that supposed to mean?"

I paused, knowing I should let it go, but I wasn't a morning person and gave in to the whim to jab him. "I think you know."

He re-corked the canteen. "Son, I worked intelligence while in the military and speak fluent Arabic, but I don't speak chic."

"Never mind," I whispered. "Let's keep going."

"No, you got something to get off your chest, then spit it out."

"Forget it—"

He stood to his full height. "Speak up, son."

I was a grown man who had fathered two children and seen action overseas, but my father was still the most intimidating figure in my life.

He stuck a long finger towards my chest. "Speak boy."

"You're different," I said. "You're closed off. Since Jonah's death you've turned into—"

"A what?"

I knew this conversation wasn't going anywhere good and tried to notch it down. "Just forget it."

"A what?" he repeated.

"A grouchy old man."

"What you call grouchy I call survival instinct." He pushed his finger into my chest. It felt like a piece of oak hit my sternum. "Life's tough, and kids need tough love to survive the horrors they're gonna see in the harsh world. You think I want to see a repeat of what happened to my grandson happen to you, your wife, or my granddaughter? Man-up, son."

"Gee, how uplifting."

His voice turned into an annoying version of itself. "Are you sad that daddy didn't give you enough hugs when you were little?" He changed back to his husky voice. "You think that's the only way to show someone you love them?"

"Up yours, old man."

"Wow, nice response," he said, not seeming to care about the rising octave of his voice, and how it could ruin the hunt. "You're acting like a spoiled brat."

"What are you talking about?"

"I gave you the farm when you came back from deployment, which is more than ninety percent of the people out there are given in life. And here you are feeling sorry for yourself."

"Then take the farm back," I shouted. "I don't care."

"I don't want it," he said. "I wanted you to have it, and carry on the family name.

"Is that all you care about? Family lineage and land?"

"Absolutely not. I care very much that my son eventually grows up."

"Are you serious?"

"As a heart attack."

I stood on a nearby rock so I could look him in the eye. "Where were you mister tough guy when I was up with my wife night after night trying to console her about the loss of our son?" I pushed my finger into his chest, but it felt like I hit a granite wall. "I sat there with her every night, dad. I sat with my wife like a real man as she wept, and hyperventilated until she vomited in the toilet. Then I'd wipe her chin with the sleeve of my shirt and continue to hold her until she ran out of tears."

I could tell by the angry squint of his eyes that he'd barely heard a word I said, so I doubled down my assault. "You want something off my chest then how about this. Not once since Jonah's death have I heard you say to Annie, to my wife, that the accident wasn't her fault. Not once have I heard you say to me, your only son, that it wasn't my fault. I didn't make that drunk driver hit Annie's car you jerk. Your tough-guy approach to life may work for the military but it fails with family. You've turned into a miserable old man with zero sympathy."

Still no response from my father. I cocked the hammer on my rifle and fired it into a nearby mound of dirt. The boom echoed throughout the forest guaranteeing any animal within miles would scatter. The hunt was over. I stormed back towards the farmhouse.

"How mom ever put up with you is beyond me," I called back to him.

"Most common sense thing you said all morning," he shouted back.

"Up yours," I repeated.

Back at the house Emily was at the kitchen table doing homeschool work while Annie sat in front of a laptop. She had a paying gig as a blogger writing about life as a Virginia farm wife.

"Why you back so soon?" She asked. "You guys always hunt at least a half day?"

I mounted the rifle over the fireplace mantle. "Two words, my father. From now on I'm referring to that man simply as your father-in-law."

She giggled. "Wanna talk about it?"

"No," I said, coming back into the kitchen and grabbing a box of cereal. "The man is infuriating." Annie pointed to

Emily who was listening. "Emily, I love your grandpa. I just want to run him over with a tractor right now okay sweetie."

Emily smiled revealing her dimples. "Don't worry. I'll talk to him."

I kissed her on the forehead. "Give him a time-out and put him on the naughty step when you do."

Annie gave me a hug. She was the one person who could laugh at me when I was mad and somehow get me to smile. It worked again.

"What can I do to help?" She said.

I leaned into her ear, "Uhm how about a little one-on-one time—"

She slapped my shoulder and whispered my full name as if to scold me. She moved her eyes toward Emily. Before I left the room I heard Annie say the word, "Tonight."

SIX

THAT AFTERNOON I DROVE OUT TO THE CLUSTER SPRINGS Raceway. There was a closed sign on the ticket gate, which was unlocked. I entered the property and sat in the bleachers right behind where the accident happened. That portion of the asphalt track had been dug up and already repaved. In the center grassed area, where the racing trailers would be parked, sat two torched cars. Caution tape surrounded the vehicles.

"Can I help you?" came a husky voice.

I turned and saw a gray-haired man walking down the aisle of bleachers towards me. He had on navy blue Dickie's shirt and pants and an unfiltered cigarette dangled from his fingers.

I stood up. "Horrible what happened here the other night."

"Never seen anything like it," he said.

"How so?"

He stopped. "You a reporter?"

I laughed. "Uh, no." I handed him a business card. "I've

been asked by the Drew Schilling's father to look into the accident."

The man's eyes widened. "Senator Schilling? Really?" He read my card. "A private investigator?"

"The Senator is understandably broken up over this."

"He's not the only one. My names Gerald Lawson. My lawyers told me not to talk to anyone about this."

I shook his hand. "I'm Brandon Hall. And Mr. Lawson, I assure you this isn't about blaming you guys. The boy knew the risks.

"Then why are you here?"

"To be honest, the Senator asked me to uhm poke around the accident a bit."

"So he thinks the car was tampered with?" Gerald said.

"I'm not so sure—"

"So do I."

"Really?" I said. "Why'd you say that?"

"Way too many safety measures in place for an explosion like that to happen."

"Well if it makes you feel any better, the Senator has me looking down rabbit holes that have nothing to do with your track?"

The man straightened as if a giant weight had been lifted off his shoulders. "Mr. Hall, this racetrack is the only thing I have to pass down to my children, and grandchildren."

"Can you help me out?"

"What do you need?"

"I'd like to go look at the car?"

"Can't."

I pointed to the two charred vehicles on the field. "But—"

"It ain't there," he said. "Those two caught fire from the blast. Schilling's car has been taken offsite."

"Where?"

"No idea. State Police came in the middle of the night and took the car away. They had all the right paperwork. I assumed it was due to the fact the Schilling's dad was a Senator?"

"Can I go and look at the other cars?"

"Be my guest," he said.

We descended the bleachers to a metal gate in the chain link fence overlooking the track. Gerald unlocked the gate and we descended a staircase and crossed the steeply-pitched asphalt track to the leveled grassed area. The two race cars were unrecognizable.

I whistled. "Drivers got out okay?"

"Yeah, one of them had minor burns but he's fine. Shaken, but okay. I took out my phone and took pictures of the vehicles.

"What you looking for?" He asked.

"Not sure," I said. "Can you show me how they laid out on the track."

"Yeah," he said. "This first car was behind Schilling's and was blown into the wall. The second one skidded to a stop right behind it. They both ended up catching fire."

I started typing notes on my phone. "Who had access to the track and vehicles?"

"Each team can bring whoever they want in the grassed area known as the infield, but pit row does have some security."

"Did Drew bring a lot of people?"

"Schilling always brought an entourage. After races, they'd party on the roof deck of the trailer he used to haul his race car in."

"Video Cameras?"

"None. Teams are paranoid about other teams spying. We're a small town country track that race late model stock cars, nowhere near the Cup Series you see on television."

"What about safety checks?"

"There's a tech inspection when the teams arrive. It's held in the infield."

"If someone were to tamper with a car when, and where, would be the time?"

"After the tech inspections before they go to pit row."

I put my phone away. "I appreciate you letting me see this, Mr. Lawson."

We left the track and headed toward the main entrance. Gerald motioned for me to follow him inside. "C'mon, I have some pics of Drew Shilling's car I can give you."

We passed through a gift shop littered with, hats, t-shirts, and hundreds of toy cars for sale. I recalled how Jonah used to run around the house with toy tractors and matchbox race cars. He would have loved this gift shop. I thought of his toothy smile and the deep blue of his eyes. It was getting harder to remember.

A voice brought me back to the present. "Mr. Hall, are you okay?"

"Huh, yeah. Sorry. I lost my infant boy last year to a drunk driver and I couldn't help but think he would have loved your gift shop."

The old man teared up, as if he could relate. I wondered what losses he'd experienced in his life. "I love seeing little kids come in here for the first time," he said.

We went up a wooden staircase to a messy second floor office that overlooked the raceway. Gerald rifled through a couple folders and selected a half dozen eight by ten color photos.

"I need to keep some of these for insurance but you can have these copies."

"This is all very helpful," I said, shuffling through the

pictures. Drew's car reminded me of vehicles I'd seen overseas that had been hit by IED's. Senator Schilling's concerns echoed in my mind. The evidence I thought would point to an accident was looking more and more like foul play.

Gerald photocopied a piece of paper and handed it to me. "Here's the receipt the police gave me for Drew's car."

The paperwork contained very little information, which led me to believe Drew's car would never be found. I'd pass the paperwork onto Senator Schilling to see if he could uncover anything. I left Gerald with a handshake. I needed to take the pictures of the car to an expert, and I knew just the man.

Passing through South Boston I stopped in at Bubba's Auto and Performance Center. Inside the showroom was a mint cherry-red 67 Chevelle and an early 70's navy blue Camaro. I whistled and dared to touch the gloss paint of the Camaro. It felt like thick glass.

"That's Esther." I turned around to see Bubba. He looked older and skinnier than I remembered. He pointed to the Chevelle. "That's Ava."

I shook his hand. "How you holding up?"

"Each day's a struggle. I'm just trying to put one foot in front of other and not look too far ahead otherwise I'd crumble."

"I'm sorry, Bubba."

"I always thought asking God for my daily bread meant necessities like food and money. Never thought it could mean strength to simply breathe."

"I don't know what to say."

He didn't let go of my hand. "I'm glad it was you, Brandon. It means a lot to my wife and me to know you were there. We'll never forget it what you did for our boy."

"I did nothing," I said.

He tightened his handshake and pulled me in close. "It was everything to me."

I thought back to Jonah's death, and how much it meant that Dale stopped by to check on us every couple of days. During tragedies, little things did matter.

An elderly lady entered the showroom. "Bubba, your accountant is here to review Q4 projections?"

"Tell him I'm in an important meeting." He turned to me. "How can I help you, Brandon?"

I lifted a manilla folder up that held the pictures from the race track. "I wanted your expert opinion on something, but I can come back. I shouldn't have just showed up like this."

"Nonsense, let me see what you have."

He led me over to a glass display case full of expensive after-market parts like mufflers, nitrous kits, and LED lights. He put on reading glasses and started to look over the color photos.

He whistled. "Is this the Schilling boy's wreck?"

"Yeah. His dad asked me to look into it."

"Senator Schilling huh?" He said without looking away. "I'd do the same if I were him."

"What do you mean?" I said.

"If he's hired you then he thinks there was foul play right?" I didn't respond, curious to see what else Bubba could decipher. "These types of accidents rarely happen."

"Types?"

"Full on explosions."

"Assuming you're correct," I said. "What do you think happened?"

"I know cars but—" he stopped, as if he were embarrassed to say anything further.

"Tell me what you think, Bubba?"

"I'm speculating here."

"So."

"Well look at this," he said, pointing to one of the pics.

"What am I looking at?"

"This," he said, pointing to a spot near, what appeared to be, the rear end. "See that slag?"

"Yeah."

"That portion of the chassis is melted. That type of steel would melt around 2500 to 2700 degrees Fahrenheit."

"And?"

"And racing fuel burns at less than half that. No chance it could have melted this?"

"What about it burning for an extended period of time and weakening the metal?"

Bubba shook his head. "Fire and EMT's were on the scene within minutes. That vehicle didn't burn very long. It was a flash of extreme heat that did this."

"You mean an explosive?"

"You're ex-military. Do you know of any explosive that burns that hot?"

"Thermite off the top of my head, but I'm sure there's more."

Bubba closed the envelope and handed it back to me. "I'd say the Senator was right to hire you. Not sure what his boy was into, but someone wanted to make sure he was dead."

"Thanks Bubba. Keep this on the down-low okay?"

"Of course." He pulled me in with another handshake. For a small guy his grip was like iron. "Come by and see the wife okay?"

"Will do, and thanks again."

The few remaining doubts I had about foul play were all but gone. The next thing was to find motive and then suspects. A monumental task.

On the way home I called the number the Senator had given me for his personal assistant.

A female answered the phone. "Jane speaking?"

"This is Brandon Hall, Senator Schilling gave me your number."

"I've heard all about you Mr. Hall. How can I assist you?"

"I'm going to email you a copy of a receipt that was given to the racetrack owner to authorize the removal of Drew Schilling's car. The Senator's resources might help to discover where it went."

"Of course. Is there anything else?"

"I'd like to have access to Drew Schilling's apartment."

There was a pause on the phone. "Of course. During race season he stayed at the family town home in Charlotte. During the winter he was at the family compound in Palm Beach. He rarely stayed at their Clarksville manor, and only went home to his parents' residence in Alexandria for the holidays.

"Then I'm assuming his personal effects are in Charlotte?"

"I would assume so," she said. "Which property would you like access to?"

"Charlotte please."

"I'll text you back at your number with directions, access code, and key location."

SEVEN

When I got home Annie was waiting for me in the kitchen. She looked beautiful. Her dark hair was up in a high pony tail and she had on a grey silk dress with a matching shawl.

"Our anniversary!" I shouted, acting as if I hadn't forgotten.

"I didn't mention it to you earlier because you were so upset about your dad—"

"I didn't forget."

"Sure," she said, smiling.

I looked down at my jeans and untucked shirt and moved past her. "I'm getting dressed as we speak. I need five minutes."

"Uhm I can smell you from here, so take a shower. I can wait."

A minute later I shouted from the master bathroom shower. "You're gonna love what I have planned."

I could hear Annie picking up some dishes in the kitchen. She said something but I couldn't hear. Ten minutes later I came out in khakis and a blue dress shirt. I carried my cowboy boots and three ties for Annie to choose from. She picked a simple yellow and blue pattern, and proceeded to lick her hand and fix my hair before kissing me on the cheek.

"Thanks for not getting upset," I said. "You look stunning by the way."

"After the past year it's gonna take a lot for me to get upset over something stupid like being late for dinner."

"Dinner?" I said. "This ain't no dinner. This is our eleventh anniversary."

"Twelfth," she laughed.

"This is our twelfth anniversary," I corrected, without missing a beat. "And it's gonna be extra special."

"What do you have planned?"

I finished putting on my boots and got up to pull her in close. She smelled of peppermint from the organic soap she used. "How does a horse drawn carriage ride through the countryside sound?"

"Seriously?"

"Uh no, but we are going to Cherry Hill for an awesome dinner just like you wanted.

She giggled. "Good enough."

"Where's Emily?"

"I walked her over to your parents a little while ago."

I was happy to see Annie had let go of the reins a little. "Are you okay with that?"

"I'm a nervous wreck, but I think I'll make it."

"God's in control. We can't hold on too tight, sweetie."

"I know, but if something happened to her I think I'd die."

"She'll be fine," I said. "I just hope my old man is in a better mood."

"He's putty in her hand."

"He's like broken glass in mine," I retorted. "Can you believe he—"

She stuck her index finger to my lips to shush me. "No talk of him tonight. We aren't going to talk farm business, bills, or any other day-to-day stuff."

"How about we talk about dessert?" I said.

"Ooh. They have this strawberry dish that's to die for—"

"No, I meant after that."

It took her a few seconds to get the innuendo. "I did wear matching lingerie."

My heart rate tripled. "Maybe we should have dessert first and—"

Annie dragged me by the hand outside. "Later, sport."

* * *

CHERRY HILL WAS an old plantation that had been converted into a resort. They had an old pub with a juke box and pool table, but also a formal dining room along with overnight accommodations. We chose to eat in the formal dining room. It was nearly empty as it was a week-night, which made it feel like we were royalty. We sat at an antique wood table surrounded by old pictures of George and Martha Washington and oil paintings of southern plantations. The ornate room had tall ceilings and massive antique true-pained windows.

I made sure to tell Annie to get anything she wanted from the menu while at the same time mentally tracking the cost. We started with caesar salads. Annie ordered seafood while I ordered the roast chicken and baked potato. The dinner conversation was tough. Every time I brought up the farm, my work, or my dad Annie would hold up her index finger reminding me to get back on track with only fun topics.

I did whatever she wanted. It had taken such a long time for her smile to return after losing Jonah. It was as if she forgot how, and had to retrain both her brain and body. For months she barely ate, and wasted away to a hundred pounds. She finally had her curves back and a nice glow to her skin. Part of me wanted to place her in a crystal room to protect her from ever being hurt again. I knew it wasn't realistic and remembered my words to her earlier. God was in control.

I watched as she checked her cell phone for the sixth time. "Mom would call if there were any problems with Emily," I said.

She put the phone away. "Sorry, I know. This is just something I'm struggling with."

"It's okay," I said, "check as much as you need to." From my pocket I removed a wrapped saucer from the china set and slid it across the table.

"What's this?"

"Happy anniversary."

"I thought we weren't getting each other anything," she said.

"I lied."

She hesitated for a moment before unwrapping the saucer. "You are too—" her hand went up to her mouth.

"The rest of the set is back home," I said. "We have six place settings." Annie said nothing. "I promised when we got married that someday I'd get you a china set. I searched high and low and knew you liked the old-fashioned pattern." Annie still said nothing. "You like the pattern?"

She nodded and wiped her eyes with a napkin. "It's perfect."

After dinner I went to the men's room. The ornate

bathroom had a carrara marble sink that was a throwback to the 1920's. In the antique mirror my beard had gone from brown to a dusty looking color. Convinced it was dirt rather than grey I washed my face, but the color remained.

On the way back to the dining hall I passed by a couple small private dining rooms. One was empty, and one had a couple in it. I noticed a familiar black cowboy hat on a peg in the back of the room. Upon closer look I saw fifty-year-old Bud sitting across from a young blonde. Both were dressed up and both were laughing. He had let his dark mustache grow into a full goatee and he wore an item of clothing I'd never seen on him before, a tie. Bud hadn't seen me pass by, and I was able to watch their reflection from a mirror across from the room entrance. Bud reached across the table and took the blonde's hand in his. A moment later he lifted it to his lips and kissed it, thus confirming they were more than friends. He had lied to his wife Sarah, and Dale. My thoughts went to Sarah and the pain of what she was dealing with.

Back at our table Annie noticed something was off. "What happened? You get sick in the bathroom or something?"

"Dale had asked me to look into something at church and I just found the answer to my question."

"Confidential I take it?" I nodded. She thought for a moment and shocked me with the word. "Bud?"

"How did you pull that out of thin air?"

"Sarah had asked a few of us women to pray for her and Bud. She didn't get into it, but I got the impression it had to do with something in their marriage. Presently, we are at dinner. Whatever it was you stumbled across was dinner related, or hotel related. Dinner and hotel problems related to marriage nine times out of ten mean infidelity. I put two and two together."

"Maybe you should be the PI?"

Annie got up. "You know, I might go give Bud a piece of my mind."

I got up and blocked her. "It's not our problem to solve, sweetie. Let me talk to Dale."

"What are you going to do, give Bud a locker room pep talk? You better drop the hammer." She huffed. "Oh, you men."

"Calm down. I'm not the enemy. The church will confront him."

"And if he doesn't confess or repent?"

"He's not going to be given a pass if that's what you mean."

She took a breath and relaxed her shoulders a bit. "Sorry, but there are people suffering all over the place. Look at what we went through. It drives me nuts when I see suffering that's unnecessary, and easily preventable."

"I know."

Dessert arrived. After the waitress left I whispered, "Let's just enjoy the night. It's our anniversary. Bud's problem isn't going to be fixed tonight."

Before leaving the restaurant Annie made me pass by the private room again and promise to say something if Bud were still there, but the room was empty. On the way home we drove through South Boston and passed by Bud and Sarah's house. His truck was missing from the driveway. In the window of the living room a single light was on. A shadow of someone, I assumed was Sarah, paced back and forth.

Annie started to cry. "Brandon, we have to do something."

I did, and dropped the jeep into first gear and headed in the direction of home.

"I could throw up," she said. "What is wrong with you men?"

"Us men?" I said. "Don't group me in with Bud."

"If you ever did that I'd—"

"Trust me sweetie. I love you, and I fear you."

She giggled at the joke and reached out for my hand. "Sorry, I'm emotionally fragile from the past year."

"I understand."

Just beyond our farmhouse was a hidden gravel driveway. I drove down the long path which led up to my parents' two-bedroom single level log cabin. My dad built it decades ago knowing he'd one day hand the farm over to me. He never gave me an option and told me the property had to stay in the family. He helps on the farm part time when I need him and I, in turn, take care of the entire property and give him a stipend. I offered him half the farm profit, but he said due to his military pension he only needed a quarter share. The man was as generous as he was difficult. When we pulled up dad and mom were on the porch in their rocking chairs with Emily sitting in dad's lap. The smile on my dad's face vanished and he got up to go inside. Emily was oblivious and came running down to the jeep.

"How was it honey?" I said, getting out of the jeep and twirling her like a dance partner.

"It was a blast. Can I stay over? Nanna said it was okay?"

"It's up to your mom," I said, placing her down. She ran on to Annie's side of the jeep. I approached the porch and my mom. "How's it going?"

She got up, all five foot three inches of her and gave me

a kiss. Her brown hair only just now had a few grey streaks in it.

"Don't you look handsome," she said, giving me a hug.

"You should see my wife," I said. "I felt like I was taking a college undergrad out to dinner, ma." I made sure Annie heard it.

"How's grumpy doing?" I whispered.

"Your father is your father."

"Did he tell you about our hunting trip?"

"No, why?"

I gave her a quick debrief. She listened and shook her head. She pulled a shawl tight around her shoulders. When I finished she said, "You know your father loves you?"

I grinned. "Maybe, but does he like me?"

"Of course he does."

"How that guy gets in my head is either genius, or evil."

"I'll talk to him sweetie." She walked over to the jeep and leaned in to kiss Em who was sulking in the back seat. "No sleepover tonight huh?"

"She's got school in the morning," Annie said.

"I'm homeschooled," Emily whined. "I can be late."

Ma looked at me. "I can bring her back over first thing after breakfast so she can start on school and—"

"Next time," I said, winking to let her know Annie wasn't ready to let go of Emily just yet.

Ma nodded. She understood. She always understood.

EIGHT

THE NEXT MORNING I WAS THE FIRST ONE AWAKE. I PUT THE coffee on and took a tour of the property in the truck. It was a quick once-over to make sure everything was okay before I headed out for the day. The last heifer still hadn't given birth yet. When I entered back into the kitchen Annie and Emily were eating eggs and turkey bacon.

"Can I come with you today, Dad?" Emily said.

"Ah, sorry sweetie I gotta head offsite."

"So."

"Not today," Annie said.

Emily slammed her fork down on the plate and stormed off upstairs.

"Don't you act like that," Annie shouted up the stairs after her. She turned to me. "Am I doing that over-protective thing again?"

"Maybe," I said, "but I gotta go investigate this Schilling death and I don't want her exposed to the case anymore." I called up to Emily, "I gotta go to North Carolina and won't be back until late. Next time sweetie." No response and I didn't press it further. Annie looked at me clearly confused. "Drew Schilling's apartment is in Charlotte. I need to go check it out."

"You should take my jeep if you're gonna go long distance. Your old truck Hazel might not make it."

"Thanks sweetie."

I packed a bag with some extra clothes in case I had to stay overnight along with a cooler full of fruit, snacks, and water. I went upstairs and kissed Emily on the top of her head. She wouldn't talk, but I reached in to nibble her ear.

"Stop it," she said, trying desperately not to laugh

"I love you," I said. She didn't respond. "I love you," I repeated.

"Love you."

"No, you don't," I said, jokingly.

"Yes, I do."

"No, you don't," I said again.

"You are so annoying," she said, finally smiling.

"I have that effect on women." I left her with another kiss and a reminder that I knew she did, in fact, love me.

Once on the road I decided to call Dale. When he answered I said, "Pastor Dale, are you sitting down?"

"Oh no. What?"

"I think I have an answer for you on Bud." Dale listened to my recap of seeing Bud at Cherry Hill with his mistress.

"He lied to my face," Dale said. "I can't believe I fell for it. I feel horrible that I doubted Sarah. I'm so mad at Bud right now."

"What do we do?"

"I'll confront him," Dale said.

"If he doesn't confess and repent?"

"Then according to Mathew eighteen, I'll take you with me and we go back to try again."

"This is gonna be awkward. I've never had to do this before as an elder."

"I have, and it's not fun. I'll confront him after the service on Sunday. And if he's a no show then I'll go to his house."

"Roger that. Glad you're the point man on this."

The last thing Dale said before hanging up was, "I hate this part of my job."

It was midday by the time I entered Charlotte, North Carolina. The temperature was easily ten degrees warmer than home. There were flowers blooming everywhere and a humidity that reminded me of summer. I pulled up to a gated condominium community.

The armed elderly guard at the gatehouse walked out to greet me. "Can I help you?"

"I'm here on behalf of Senator Schilling," I said. "I'm heading up to his townhouse. I have a guest code to punch into the gate."

He smiled as if he had heard that before. "What's your business?"

"I'm sorry it's confidential," I said.

He smiled again as if he had heard that before as well. He grabbed a clip board from inside the security shack and walked around the jeep like a K-9 dog sniffing for hidden drugs. He took down the jeep's plate number.

"Your name?" he said as he came back around.

"Brandon Hall. Am I on the list?"

"ID?" he said without answering my question.

I handed him my license and he wrote down my information. "You said you had a guest code to punch in?"

"Yes sir."

"Then drive up to the keypad and let me see you punch it in." I drove up to the keypad and punched in the code. The moment the steel gate moved aside he handed me back my license and his tone was much friendlier. "Sorry,

Mr. Hall, but there's been some weirdo's around here lately. Have a nice day."

The first thing I passed was an enormous pond with a fountain in the middle. A couple small children fished off a wooden bridge with an elderly man in a cowboy hat. The complex was massive, stretching at least twenty acres with large brick buildings liberally spaced apart. There were a half dozen balconies on the back side of each complex. Golf carts driven by elderly couples passed by in a marked lane.

Beyond the pond was a metal building with glass windows lining the sides. Through the windows I could see people working out on precors, ellipticals and treadmills. Behind the building was a pool that was being covered by staff. Although the weather was still warm enough to swim not many people would show up due to the start of school, and football season.

I found building number eight and pulled into a guest parking spot. There was a small patio out back of the first-floor units rather than a balcony. The key was under the tray of a terra cotta potted palm tree just where Schilling's assistant said it would be. The key got me into the back door and I punched in another code to silence the chirping burglar alarm. Inside, the condo was open concept and high-end. The floor was all white marble. Stainless appliances filled the massive kitchen and the three bedrooms were outfitted each with their own full bath.

The Senator's master bedroom was clean and looked like no one ever stepped foot in it. The daughter's room was clean and had pictures of a random boy band and male celebrities lining the walls. Drew's looked like a car dealership had blown up. The room was a mess with helmets, parts and Nascar framed pics. Drew was in many of the pictures. I used my cell phone to snap photos of the pictures to keep track of faces. On a cherry desk was what I was looking for, his laptop.

It was password protected, so I put it in my ruck sack with the power cord. The rest of the home was what I expected. Clean, fancy embroidered towels, sparse food in cabinets, fun vacation romance books on the bookshelf, and antique paintings on the wall of what looked like old Virginia. The master bathroom revealed very little. Aspirin, toothbrushes, floss, and other toiletries. The only thing I flagged in the Senator's bathroom was an out of date medication for high cholesterol and a strange smell.

I stuck my nose in the shower and found the source of the scent. When showers were not used the water in the below-grade pipe called the p-trap dried out allowing sewer gas to creep back up into the home. It takes a bit of time for the water to evaporate thus confirming the bedroom was rarely used. A simple fix was to run the water for a few seconds to fill the trap back up, thus recreating a barrier against the sewer gas. I ran the water and the bathroom vent fan and the smell dissipated within minutes.

Drew's bathroom was messy but offered nothing out of the ordinary. I found a couple empty nips in the trash can. It was clear he used this as his home base when he raced up and down the east coast. For a young guy who liked to party it was a palatial bachelor pad. It was a top end condo with a pool, a gym, and probably affiliated with a golf course or two. I assumed it was rent free as well.

I spent another hour documenting items in drawers. There was mostly warm weather clothes in dressers, what little food was in the kitchen was organic and non GMO. In an office desk I found high-end vodka along with a box of Cuban cigars. With nothing else to note I re-armed the alarm and left the key back where I found it under the potted plant.

Back in Virginia a few hours later, I pulled into a self-storage facility in South Boston to find a light on in the small business office. JT was on the phone when I entered.

"Guy, I don't barter," JT said. "You haven't paid in three months." He looked at me and shook his head in frustration. "I don't care if the shotgun you're offering to trade me is worth ten times your rent. I can't pay the bills with buckshot, buddy. I need something by Friday." After he hung up he said, "I feel like Pa Ingalls here working on the barter system. What's up?"

I held up Drew Schilling's laptop. "I need your help. I'm working on a case and need to get into this."

"I'm done with technology, brotha." He pointed to his immaculate desk. "You see any computers here? I run this place old school. Pen and paper, baby."

"It's regarding Drew Schilling," I said. "His father, Senator Schilling, asked me to look into this. He thinks there was foul play at the race track."

"Foul play as in murder?" I nodded and JT whistled. "I didn't know the kid's father was a senator."

I nodded again. JT clasped his hands together and looked skyward. I wondered if he was praying or just thinking. Something in JT's mind snapped when his wife up and left him back in Massachusetts. He now associated technology with his former life and the pain of his divorce. What I was asking of him was going to cause discomfort on some level but I had no one else to turn to.

"I wouldn't ask you unless it was important. The boy's parents want closure and I'm not the best with technology."

JT exhaled and motioned with his hand to give him the laptop. He took a deep breath before turning it on. Once it fired up his fingers floated over the keys the way a concert pianist would tickle the ivory. Five minutes later he was past the login and into the computer.

"How?" was all I could say.

"I'm wicked awesome," he said.

The few yanks I came in contact with had a sense of humor that was paradoxical. They would brag, but in a strange way that was self-deprecating. A hilarious contrast.

"What's daddy looking for?" JT said.

"Daddy?" I said.

Without looking up he said, "Third person persona I take on when I'm in the zone." He patted his big belly. "Unlike you, my fit friend, my football field is virtual, and I'm Tom Brady. Problem is there's no cheerleaders for my sport."

"Yeah, but you nerds always get the last laugh making all the money."

"So what's daddy looking for?"

"Well Daddy," I said, "I'm looking for clues as to why someone would want to hurt Drew. Email is the best place to start."

JT typed at a speed I didn't think was humanly possible. After a few minutes he let out a strange exhale. He continued, and after another minute, let out another similar exhale. As if he was stumped.

"What's up?" I said.

"Well, I can't find any emails. Most people cache passwords and after I log onto gmail, yahoo, etc. they auto populate, which his email accounts did, but nothing is opening up. It's as if he deleted all his email accounts and the stored passwords no longer work."

"He's the only one that could do that right?"

"No, anyone that had his passwords could do that from any location." JT typed for a few more minutes. "Okay, the stuff I did find on the hard drive seems to be normal for a nineteen-year-old knucklehead."

"Such as?"

"A couple action movies were streamed on here. A lot of music?"

"Type?"

"Techno, dance, metal, and some country. A real renaissance man. He's got pics, lots of pics."

"I'll need those," I said.

"I'll put them in a folder for you. It's labeled Brandon Hall owes me." He continued to type. "There's no word docs, or anything weird. Hold on a sec."

"What is it?"

"Huh," JT said. "I got something I can't open." He typed some more. "Weird."

"What?"

"It's encrypted with some high-tech software. Not something a nineteen-year-old kid would have."

"What do you think it is?"

"No idea." He continued to type some more. "Hold up, daddy's got something else." A few moments passed before he said, "I thought you said he didn't go to college?"

"I didn't think he did."

"He's got a lot of college activity to groups up in Charlottesville."

"Such as?"

"Young socialists, and AFA."

"AFA?" I said.

"It's an acronym for Antifa. AFA lets them legally slither onto college campuses under the guise of a non-threatening leftist group."

"I don't get it," I said. "His father's a Republican Senator. Why would he join these radical leftist groups? Teen rebellion?"

"Hall, you're getting ahead of yourself," JT said. "The real question is why would he travel all the way up to Charlottesville. There are plenty of these leftist chapters much closer to this area."

"I take it you have an answer?"

"Answer hasn't changed since time immemorial my friend."

"That being?"

JT stood as if he were giving a profound speech with arms open. "The species known as female," He sat back down. "Women are the only force of nature that can do this to a guy. Trust me, I speak from experience."

I dialed Schilling's personal assistant and left it on speakerphone. She picked up on the second ring. "Hi Jane, this is Brandon Hall again. Could you tell me when Drew Schilling attended college and what classes he took?"

"Drew never went to college, Mr. Hall. He started racing right out of high school."

"Did he have a girlfriend?"

There was an awkward pause. "Drew was a good looking guy and a partier. Combine the two with his minor celebrity status and you can imagine he had numerous women he uhm associated with."

"No special someone though?"

"Not that I'm aware of," she huffed, as if I brought up a sore spot.

I assumed Drew and her had a past so I cut the conversation short. "I'm sure I'll have more questions. "

"Sure thing Mr. Hall."

After I hung up JT smirked. "Females dude. They'll do it to ya every time."

I pulled a chair up next to JT. "Show me the pics."

"Here," he said, sliding the computer over.

I spent the next hour scrolling through hundreds of

pictures while JT made phone calls to tenants about overdue bills. There were a lot of pictures of Drew partying with large groups of people. I tried to make a note of consistent faces. There was a red head kid with a beard that stuck out as he seemed a bit older than most of the nineteen to early twenty-year olds. There were a lot of pictures of pretty girls. Drew was in a lot of drunken positions with different females, but nothing that said he was dating them, nor even hooking up. I found pics of Drew with four serious looking chubby bearded men, dressed in matching racing uniforms. They were clearly his pit crew.

Finally, I came across a picture of Drew and a young dark-skinned brunette kissing. I found more of them together in what appeared to be dating pictures. There were scenes of them at dinner, at a fair, and on a pontoon boat, which confirmed they had a relationship of some kind. I kept scrolling and found a folder labeled P. I opened it to find Drew and the same brunette in racy sex pictures. There was video, and more pics which I didn't click on. The timestamp on them: Charlottesville, Virginia a month earlier.

JT looked over. "Daddy's surfing some porn is he?"

I shut the laptop. "I think I found a lead."

"I'd say you did."

"Daddy's gotta go up to Charlottesville," I said. JT laughed at my joke. "What do I owe you for your help?"

JT laughed. "It's on the house."

"No. I'm paying you something."

He waved his hands. "You'd soil your pants if you knew what I used to get paid back home. Least I can do for all your therapy sessions."

NINE

I made it home by eight thirty. Annie kept a plate of chicken and a baked potato in the oven for me. Emily had on one her favorite movies, *Anne of Green Gables*. I ate on the couch and watched as the girls gushed over Gilbert and Anne's back-and-forth relationship.

The girls inhaled as the movie reached a romantic crescendo between the duo. I quietly took the remote and changed the channel over to a cable station that played old Westerns.

"Dad!"

"Brandon!"

I just want to see what's playing," I said. "Oh look, John Wayne. Who doesn't love a good John Wayne movie?"

Emily grabbed the remote from my hand and put *Anne of Green Gables* back on. "You're so rude. You ruined the moment."

Annie smirked. "You are rude. And cute."

My cell phone rang. I answered laughing, "Brandon Hall speaking?"

"Brandon, it's Dale. I'm heading to South Boston Hospital to meet Sarah."

"Hold on a sec" I said, getting up to walk through the kitchen so I could stand outside on the back porch. Annie must have known something was wrong and followed. Once outside I put the phone to speaker. "What happened?"

"Bud's been in a car wreck," Dale said. "He was with his girlfriend and they were drunk. She was behind the wheel and drove off the side of the road flipping the truck. Bud was passed out in the passenger seat, which is probably why he survived."

"The girl?"

"Dead on impact."

"Sarah?"

"She's there now and called me in hysterics. I guess it's bad. They don't know if Bud's gonna make it."

"I'm on my way."

I hung up and turned to Annie who started to cry. "That stupid man. That foolish woman."

She pounded her fists into my shoulders. It didn't hurt, so I let her continue. Memories from my son's death at the hands of a drunk driver came up like bad food. I imagined Annie was thinking the same.

"It's not Jonah's accident," I reminded her.

"I know," she said, collecting herself. "I just can't believe how careless people are. Bud's cheating on his wife, lies to the church, and now someone's dead and he could die as well. I'm so mad at Bud right now."

"He may pay with his life," I said. "We need to pray."

"For what? For him to get better so he can go sleep with another woman other than his wife."

"Annie—"

She buried her face into my shoulder. "I'm sorry. I just

feel so bad for Sarah." She collected herself again. "Don't you ever—" she cut herself off. "It's a fate worse than death for a spouse. You understand?"

"I do."

Emily cleared her throat. She was at the screen door. Tears on the verge of breaking. "Daddy, what happened?"

"Everything's okay, sweetie. A guy I know was in a car accident and your mom's upset."

"Is he gonna die?"

"I don't know baby. Come here. We need to pray."

Emily came out onto the porch and the three of us hugged. I thanked the Lord for seeing us through our terrible times, and prayed for the people affected by the accident.

* * *

I ARRIVED at South Boston hospital around nine p.m. Dale was in the waiting room by himself. He was reading from a pocket-sized Bible. It looked as if he'd been crying.

"Bud?" I asked.

"Surgeons saved his life," he said putting the Bible into a coat pocket, "but he'll never walk again? They're finishing up in surgery."

I slumped to the nearest chair. "Sarah?"

"She's pulled it together. She's an amazing woman."

"If I were Sarah I'd have thought about telling the surgeons not to save Bud's life."

"Trust me," came a female voice. "I thought about it."

I turned to see Sarah. Her hair and clothes were disheveled, and her eyes swollen and red. Not the woman I saw at church on Sundays.

"I'm sorry, Sarah. That was out of line—"

Sarah held up her hand. "Don't you dare apologize,

Brandon. You're right. That jerk put me through hell and now I'm left dealing with his bad decisions."

I gave her a hug. "I want him to get better so I can punch him in the nose for what he's done to you."

She laughed. "Take a number."

For the next hour Sarah kept coming out to keep me and Dale up to speed. Each time she entered the waiting room she looked more resolute as if she were getting pep talks in the back room. Bud made it through surgery, but his legs had been broken in numerous places, and his knees were junk. If he ever walked again he was going to need assistance. His life as a plumber and contractor were over.

At midnight Sarah came out to say that Bud was awake but in a lot of pain. He'd confessed to everything and asked her for forgiveness.

"What are you gonna do?" Dale said.

"I don't know," she said. "The ironic thing is I don't love him anymore. He's whimpering like little boy in there who needs his momma, and all I want to do is say, tough."

"We're here if you need anything," I said.

"Thank you both. You can go see him if you'd like."

Dale said he would go in while I made up an excuse about needing to get home. Sarah looked at me with a sympathetic expression. It was as if she knew that if I looked at Bud I'd have seen the drunk driver who killed my son. I had a lot of prayer ahead of me before I would approach him. At this point, sympathy for him was non-existent in my world. I knew that was wrong. His sin had nothing to do with me, or the man who took my son's life.

When I got home Annie was up in bed reading the Bible. I gave her the debrief on Bud's situation.

"Doubtful he'll walk again," I said. "He confessed to everything."

Annie huffed. "Bit late for that."

"It's never too late," I said.

"Tell that to the dead woman he was sleeping with."

I had no response for the rude, but accurate, comment so I changed the subject. "Sarah's a strong woman."

"I'll reach out to her when I calm down," Annie said. "Sorry, I'm having a hard time compartmentalizing this, Brandon."

"Remember this has nothing to do with Jonah."

"Keep reminding me of that."

I reminded her of what I told myself about praying before we interacted with Bud. I felt like I had run an emotional triathlon resulting in mental, physical, and spiritual exhaustion. I slept like the dead that night.

* * *

THE NEXT MORNING Annie woke me at eight with a cup of coffee.

"I can't believe I slept in this late," I said.

"Clearly you needed it," she said. "Dale texted and said that Bud wants to confess publicly to the church after he's discharged."

"Time will tell how repentant he is."

"That poor girl. Dead—"

I held up my hand as if to warn Annie she was descending a rabbit hole that would lead to a myriad of wrong thinking.

"I know. I know," she said, completing my unspoken rebuke. "So, what's the plan today?"

"Gonna check the herd and then go follow another lead on the Schilling case."

After breakfast Emily took a break from her homeschooling to ride the property with me in the diesel UTV.

I pointed to the clear sky. "Isn't it nice to be out here while all your friends are in school?"

"Best classroom in the world, Daddy."

After the rounds, I took a dirt trail which led to my parent's house. My dad's truck was missing, but we found my mother tending to the pumpkins and squash in their garden. Her hair was up under a blue handkerchief and she wore her gardening khakis. She was the only person I knew who could work in a garden and never get dirty. She gave Emily a kiss and asked her to check the chicken coop for eggs. A moment later my daughter disappeared around the cabin where the coop was located. I knew mom did this to get me alone.

"Am I gonna get a lecture?" I said.

"No lecture. I just want to check and make sure you're okay?"

I leaned over and kissed her forehead. "How'd that grumpy old man land someone as nice as you?"

"He's a proud man, Brandon."

"He's a prideful man," I corrected her. "He deserves a kick in the rear end."

"I don't disagree with you. He's getting older and starting to slow down, which I think is making him grumpier."

"Is that even possible?"

She smiled. "Maybe you should show him some grace—"

"Hold on a sec," I said. "How's this about him? How's it always about him? We Hall's must genuflect in front of the patriarch is that it?"

"That's not it—"

"Do you have any idea what my wife and I have been through this past year?" I stopped myself. "I'm sorry, mom. Of course you know. You've been there for the three of us every step of the way. I hope you know how much I appreciate everything you've done, and that I'm not mad at you."

"I know, baby." She hugged me around the waist. I could never imagine my life without this woman.

"I just think dad doesn't get it," I said. "He's so focused on the loss of the family name, and land, and lineage and all that crap."

"You're wrong. He's been grieving in his own way."

"That's funny."

"Brandon, I think you should know—"

"It's fine." I waived my hand in the air as if to wipe the conversation away. "Just forget it." I made sure to kiss her again as a reassurance that my frustration remained with the man she married, and not her.

After I dropped Emily at home for lunch I went outside on the porch to make a phone call.

Gerald Lawson seemed happy to hear from me. "Been thinking about our meeting," he said. "What can I help you with?"

"Can you tell give the address to Drew Schilling's garage? I'd like to go check it out."

"Let me see here." In the background I could hear the shuffle of papers. "I got a PO box to send bills to his dad's firm, but I'm sure I have something with the shop address. Oh here it is. D.E. Schilling Race Team. It's an address in Virgilina."

TEN

It was late afternoon when I entered downtown Virgilina. It was aptly named for the two states it bordered, Virginia and North Carolina. If someone blinked they would miss the small post office and pizza shop which made up the entire downtown. About a mile beyond Main Street I found a dirt driveway. At the end of a quarter mile I reached a semi-rusted corrugated windowless two bay garage. It was a drab forty by forty prefab metal building. I remembered Drew wasn't in the big leagues with racing, and was likely self-funding the majority of his racing via his father.

I walked the perimeter and found a small junkyard of abandoned car parts along with a port potty that was in desperate need of being picked up. There was a frost-free water spigot with a hose that ran up to the garage. Both roll up doors were locked along with the single pass door. The shiny brass doorknob on the pass door stuck out against the weathered building. It was brand new. A closer look revealed that the doorjamb was cracked. It was as if someone had broken in and then replaced the door knob.

I pushed on the locked door and, with a crack of splintering wood, it opened. The jam was busted and could barely hold back a breeze. I felt along the wall of the dark garage and found a light switch. Nothing came on. I took out a pen light I kept in my pocket and looked for another light switch as I tripped over tools. The next light switch also gave no results. Between the penlight and open doorway I still had enough light to poke around.

Tool cases were opened but all the wrenches and tools seemed intact. There was a shell of a backup race car on the far side of the room. Dust outlines showed where pictures had been removed from the walls. There was a rusted two drawer metal file cabinet that was empty. Whoever had been in here cleared out every piece of paper.

Outside, I made sure to close the door with a handkerchief. When I turned around I gazed into the barrel of a twelve-gauge shotgun. The bearded young man holding the gun had dip in his mouth and wore jean overalls with no shirt underneath. Behind him an old chevy truck covered in primer was parked nose-to-nose with my truck, blocking its exit.

The young man spit onto my boots. "You better have a good reason for being in that garage, or you're gonna meet the almighty."

I raised my hands and took a gamble that he was an overprotective local. "I'm working for Senator Schilling regarding the murder of his son."

"Murder?" He said, not moving the shotgun. "I knew it." He spit again.

"I'm gonna reach into my pocket and get you my card okay?"

He didn't lower the shotgun until after he had looked at my business card.

"A real PI, just like on TV," he said, dropping the gun to his side.

"Do you mind if I ask who you are?" I said.

"Name's Colt. I was part of Drew's pit crew. "

He held out his hand and I took it. "Why'd you say you knew it was murder?"

"Cars rarely explode like that in racing, sir."

"So I'm told," I said. "Any idea where the car is?"

"I tried to track it down but it's a ghost."

I pointed back to the garage. "What can you tell me about the break in here?"

"Just that I came to the shop the day after the accident to find it had been broken into. Whoever did it replaced the knob to make it look like it hadn't been touched."

"Did you report it to the police?"

"Yeah, they told me they'd get to it when they get to it."

"Really?"

"Let's just say I don't have the best relationship with local law enforcement in Halifax County."

"Mind if I ask why?"

"Some of my kin have been moonshiners goin' on three generations," he said, "but I don't partake in that anymore."

"Were you and Drew friends?"

"Yes, sir," he spit again and started to choke up.

"So the cops never came out to fingerprint the garage?"

"Far as I know they haven't. I've been watching the place hoping whoever broke in the first time would come back."

"Any idea what they'd be looking for?" I said.

"I was hoping you could tell me?"

"I don't know much yet," I said, pointing to the garage. "They did take all the files and pictures. Any idea what was in the file cabinets?"

"Nothing important. Old bills and orders for parts."

"Any other guys from the pit crew I should meet?"

"The pit crew's made up of me and my three brothers. Wesson, Wynn, and Moss."

I chuckled. "Your names are Colt, Wesson, Moss, and Wynn. Seriously?"

"Yeah, daddy liked firearms."

"So Moss is short for—"

"Mossburg."

"And Wynn is Winchester I assume?"

Colt smiled. "Yep."

"What do you know of the people Drew hung out with?"

Colt seemed hesitant to answer. "Drew and me hadn't hung out much outside of work lately."

"Why's that?"

"My brothers and me got baptized back at Staunton River State Park last year and have repented of that lifestyle."

"That lifestyle?"

"Partying, Mr. Hall. We used to raise cain with Drew during race season, but apparently I'm not much fun since I've been washed by the blood of Christ."

"Know anything about people he parties with now?"

"Nope. There've been a lot of new faces at the track this past season. Me and my brothers just focused on the job then went home after the races."

"Anything else you can give me on these new friends?

"If I were a betting man I'd say most of em were yanks."

"Why do you say that?

Colt huffed. "Some had northern accents, and you could tell they were educated the way they treated the rest of us. No idea what Drew saw in them."

"Anyone stick out?"

"Some guys, but there were a lot of pretty girls. None of 'em talked to me or my brothers though."

I took out my phone and showed him a pic of Drew and the brunette. "Know her?"

He huffed. "Kinda."

"Does she have a name?"

"No idea. She only recently started coming around. Made it to the last couple of races."

"She and Drew were a couple?"

"Yeah. They couldn't keep their hands off one another."

"Was she there the night Drew died?"

"No idea. It was chaos that night, Mr. Hall. My brothers and me showed up late. Drew's new friends hung out on the roof of the trailer on the infield and we were in pit row, so I didn't get a chance to see much of anyone. Do you think she had something to do with his accident?"

"No idea." I put the phone away. "Drew say anything that night that was off or a red flag?"

"Drew looked tired. Like he hadn't slept. I asked him if he was up for the race and he said he had no choice if we wanted to move up in the circuit. Not like him."

"How so?"

"Drew was a competitor. He raced with injuries, hang-overs, sicknesses. Very out of character for him to sound indifferent on racing."

"Thanks for your help, Colt."

He spit again. "How we gonna catch the scumbags that did this?"

I laughed. The guy was serious. "Colt, this ain't the old west."

"Mr. Hall, us rednecks may not be the smartest, the most well-spoken, or well dressed, but we're loyal folk."

"I respect that, but I can't get you involved. I suggest

you just focus on your family and move on with your life." He sneered. "What's so funny?"

"Drew was my friend. You don't get it, Mr. Hall. We don't abandon our friends, even in death."

Colt tossed the shotgun in the cab of the truck before he got in. The vehicle started with the sound of a glass-packed muffler. He threw it in reverse and sped back out the driveway flinging dirt and rock. I felt bad for offending him. Colt's loyalty was admirable. One thing was clear; it was time to head up to Charlottesville to visit Virginia State University.

At home, dinner was roasted chicken and potatoes with a caesar salad. Annie and Emily gave me a debrief on a science field trip they took to Edmund's Park and the Tobacco Heritage Trail. Emily could now correctly identify the difference between oak, hickory, pine, cedar, birch, Elm, and beech tree leaves.

"But can you tell the difference between black oak and red oak?" I said.

Emily looked at me for a moment, her beautiful dark eyes squinting as she tried to figure out if I was joking or serious. A smile formed on the corners of her mouth followed by the dimples I loved.

"I'm just playin," I said. "I'm happy you got your mother's brain."

"You're too hard on yourself," Annie said.

"Oh don't get me wrong," I said. "She got her good looks from me."

Annie laughed. "Tell me Mr. Hall, do you think she got your modesty as well?"

* * *

Early the next morning I stood in front of the mirror in the master bathroom. Below me was a mass of grey and brown hair in the sink. I hadn't seen my full face in years. In the mirror, a few lines appeared where there was once smooth skin. The lines almost looked like scars. The question was, could I still pass as a twenty something undergrad? My hair was now a light brown, almost a blonde. I had left the hair dye in too long. Regardless, the mission was accomplished and the handful of grey hair was now nonexistent. I pulled on a sports hoodie and swapped my cowboy boots out for workout sneakers before entering the kitchen.

Emily screamed when she saw me, which scared Annie into dropping her coffee mug in the kitchen sink. "What did you do?" Annie shouted, and laughed.

"Mid-life crisis," I said.

"Daddy, you look funny."

I kissed Emily and nibbled on her ear forcing her to giggle. "Daddy's got to head up to Charlottesville and try to blend into the college scene. We used to do this when I was deployed overseas, but we went a shade darker with the hair dye over there." I did a twirl like I was showcasing a new outfit. "So, do I look like I could pass for an early twenties undergrad?"

"I think you can," Annie said, still laughing. "How long will you be gone?"

"At least today. I'll call if I have to stay overnight."

Annie walked with me onto the porch. She pulled her bathrobe tight around her. "I'm not sure I like this. I forgot how handsome you were under all that scruff."

"Oh, be quiet."

She grabbed my chin and turned it to face her. "Don't you dare talk to any undergrad girls."

“Unless it’s for the case I won’t even look,” I said. “Can I take your jeep again, Ma?”

She kissed me. “Only if you promise to be careful?”

“I promise.” I pulled her in close and kissed her again. “You know I could delay leaving for a half hour if you want to—”

She smiled and pushed me away. “When you get back, stud.”

“Roger that.”

I jumped into the jeep and started singing Beyoncé. “All the single ladies.” As I drove off I sang the chorus and waved my hand in the air, “Oh oh oh, oh oh oh.”

In the rear-view mirror Annie was hysterical. Over the past few months I had acted like a court jester doing anything I could to get her to laugh. I said a prayer of thanks that her precious smile had returned.

ELEVEN

IT TOOK ALMOST THREE HOURS TO REACH VIRGINIA STATE University in Charlottesville. Compared to the sparse population of Halifax County the place was bustling with people and cars. My first thought went to JT. If this small Virginia college town made me claustrophobic then I could only imagine how I'd feel in the metropolis of Boston, Massachusetts. JT told stories of spending a half an hour in congested traffic just to go five miles to reach a store. I couldn't wait to get back to the farm where I could breathe again.

I found parking behind an outdoor mall. I reluctantly left my gun in the jeep. If I were stopped walking around campus without a student ID I'd be asked to leave, but having a firearm in an unconstitutional gun free zone like this campus would complicate matters exponentially. I hadn't been to the area since I was eighteen when I visited for the weekend to scope out the school. The restaurants and coffee shops had changed but the young hip latte ambiance hadn't. I took up an outdoor seat at a pub and ordered a burger.

Across from me was a theater with ads for an off-broadway version of Le Miserables. On the steps a young guitarist played for street change. The twenty-something man shredded an acoustic guitar. His hands moved up and down the neck at a rapid pace and the sound coming out of it was more like a violin than a guitar. The song wasn't anything I recognized but I was mesmerized by the boy's talent. In front of him a young heavily-pierced girl in a ragged skirt with new doc martins on her feet twirled in circles. Her black t-shirt had yellow letters that read, *I heart zombies*. The burger arrived and it was phenomenal. The menu had stated it was local grass fed beef. Being a cattle farmer made me a beef snob, so I was pleasantly surprised at the quality of their food. After the meal, I ordered an iced coffee at a small kiosk and headed up to the campus.

The plan was to find the groups Drew had visited and collect some data. The ultimate piece of intel would be if I could find, and speak with, the brunette Drew had dated. All the student government offices were in one building, which made my job easier. I entered the campus and passed by dozens of kids dressed in similar outfits as mine. Jeans and hoodies were the staple for most of the boys and most of the girls were dressed casually as well. However, I felt like everyone could see through my disguise. I threw on a pair of shades and tussled my hair a bit. The messier I looked the more street credibility I'd get.

The student government building was a three-story brick structure with swipe card access. I waited outside the entrance pretending to check my smart phone. A moment later a group of girls exited the building. One of the girls was nice enough to hold the door open for me.

"Thanks," I said.

"Anytime stud," she responded.

Social rules of college had changed a lot since I had

been an undergrad. Inside the building a young female student sat behind a welcoming desk. She scrolled through her phone oblivious to the people walking around. Next to her was a directory. I snapped a pic of the directory, and moved out of her range of vision to look closer at the picture. Drew had attended meetings for the young socialists, and an Antifa front group called AFA.

I started with the Young Socialists. Their office was on the first floor. It was located in between the student Republican and Libertarian rooms. A young female sat at a desktop computer working alone. I stuck my head in and saw Bernie Sanders pictures plastered on the wall along with pictures of socialist countries like Norway and Sweden. There was a picture of Sydney, Australia with a caption that read, *Another beautiful day in Australia with no mass shootings*. An homage to their gun purge.

"Can I help you?" The girl said in a bit of an aggressive tone. When she turned I read the phrase on her t-shirt, *free healthcare and free education is a right.*

"Just checking out what you guys are all about." I said.

"Have you been living under a rock, dude?"

"Huh?"

"You don't know what we're about?"

"Not really. I'm thinking of transferring in from Virginia Tech and I'm looking for people to meet."

She grabbed a few fliers and walked over and slapped them into my hand. "Education and healthcare are a right, not a privilege. Climate change is settled science. These are core principles. Other stuff that's a deal breaker are women's reproductive rights and DACA. If you disagree with anything I just mentioned then you don't belong here."

"What if—"

"I'm not done," she said. "No less important, is the fact

we're pro-vaccine and want to promote small farms and non-GMO. It's all there in the pamphlets."

I stared at the pamphlets which contained pictures of a lot of angry young people. "I like the non-GMO and local farm ideas."

She had a look of disgust. "Seriously? That's it?"

"When do you guys meet? Maybe I can sit in on one of your meetings."

"We meet once a semester. Next one is in January. "

"What do you guys do the rest of the time?"

"Go to school and work, like most students. Once a month we have an event where we boycott certain activities on campus."

"Like?"

"Like the lighting of the school's Christmas Tree. We lobbied last year and had it downgraded to a holiday tree. This year we're going full force to take it out completely."

I thanked her for her time and tucked the paperwork into my back pocket. I gleaned two things from the young socialist. The first was she bought into my disguise, and second, their group didn't seem to roam into the criminal realm as of yet. On the top floor were glassed spaces that looked like they were R&D rooms at NASA. Each room was lined with smart technology boards and computers. The nicest room was the Young Democrats. There was an Islamic group, an interdenominational group and the last room was AFA. It was obvious all of these spaces were heavily funded. Each room had swipe access to get in. There were a handful of students within each.

I stopped in front of the AFA room. The posters and papers lining the outside walls were advertisements for rallies, open boarders, and littered with anarchist symbols like the Guy Fawkes mask. The Russian communist flag was hung from the ceiling and pictures of burning American flags surrounding it. Inside the room were a small group of white males with one female. They all worked at different computer stations in pairs. Everyone looked angry. A few of them saw me outside the glass fishbowl and gave suspicious stares. I was shocked young kids could be this intimidating. One of the skinny white males got up and approached the door. He had on flip flops, baggy pants and a t-shirt, but it took all my willpower not to laugh at his dirty blond dreadlocks.

He stuck his head out the door. "Can I help you, guy?"

I pointed to the literature on the glass. "I'm just curious is all."

"You look like a narc, dude." I looked down at my hoodie and jeans and realized I looked more like a jock than a rebel without a real cause. "You a narc dude?" He repeated.

"Huh, no I'm just not sure where I stand politically. I kinda just woke up."

"Bull," he said.

I doubled down. "I gotta be honest. I'm pretty disenfranchised with the last DNC convention I went to, and I'm seeing what's out there for options."

"Socialist group's on the first floor," he said. "Why don't you get a Ben and Jerry's ice cream cone and go sit cross-legged with them and chant or something."

I held up the pamphlets from the socialist girl. "Already checked them out. Some people think Antifa should be labeled a terrorist group."

"We're AFA?"

"Like I said. Many people believe Antifa should be labeled a terrorist group."

"They're idiots," he said, not correcting me this time. "We're doing real work in here."

"Define real work?"

"Gonna change the world." He gave me a suspicious look then shut the door in my face. Inside the room he spoke to a couple other males and thumbed his finger my way.

I figured my cover had been blown and decided to grab as much intel from the notices and pamphlets outside the room before someone called security and I got the boot. One of the colored sheets of paper noted there was a rally that night in a random outdoor quad. I made a note of the time and location and turned to leave. That's when I bumped into a young female holding a latte.

She jumped back making sure not to spill the latte on her expensive blouse. "Watch it."

"I'm sorry," I said, recognizing the pretty face as Drew's brunette friend.

She swiped a card and the door clicked open. "Out of my way."

I grabbed the unlocked door. "Here, let me get that for you."

"I don't need a male to hold a door open for me."

"Sorry," I said, continuing to hold the door. "Least I can do for almost making you spill your coffee."

She huffed and walked past me into the room. "Okay, listen up everyone," she shouted.

Everyone turned around and gave me a combined angry stare which said, *shut the door*. I complied and moved off to a nearby couch pretending to check email on my phone. This girl was some sort of leader. I checked the handful of Drew Schilling's pictures I kept on my phone and confirmed it was the same girl.

Periodically, I looked up from the phone to view the activity in the room. The girl did a lot of finger pointing and yelling. The males in the room cowered in front of her.

The dreadlocks dude looked like a lap dog who was both in love, and terrified, of his master.

An older black janitor walked by with a cart. He looked at me and smiled. "G'day young man," he said in a southern accent I placed somewhere in Georgia.

"Hi," I said.

He moved over to the Antifa room and took out a bottle of glass cleaner from the cart. He sprayed the area of the glass not covered with propaganda. Something about the man struck me as odd. His dark blue Dickies pants and shirt with the school logo looked normal. His worn black shoes weren't out of place either. It was his posture. The only place I'd seen perfect posture like that was in the military. The leader girl stared at the janitor from within the room before walking up to the window and snapping the venetian blinds shut in his face.

He chuckled before turning to me. "You belong in there, son?"

"Nah, not my scene."

"Buncha spoiled kids who need Jesus if you ask me." He held his hand to his mouth like he had just said a cuss word. "Did I just say that?"

"Amen," I said.

He looked at me as if he wasn't expecting my affirmation. A moment later he started whistling Amazing Grace. He finished cleaning the windows and winked at me as he moved on towards the other meeting rooms. The glass on the Antifa room was streaked and looked dirtier than before he cleaned it. The whistling janitor continued on down the hall neglecting several candy bar wrappers strewn on the floor.

Unable to get into the AFA room I decided to walk each floor of the building with my cell phone in the palm of my hand recording video of all the rooms. With nothing else to do I decided to scope out the quad where the meeting was to be held later that night. There was a portable stage set up on the far end of a brick courtyard. An employee from the college was setting up a mike stand on the stage. I found an area under a maple tree where I could sit and have a clear view of the students attending. I decided to head back to the jeep to take some notes, and call Annie to let her know I'd be home late. I scribbled down on a pad of paper the website and location of the meeting. How many kids I saw in the room, their descriptions and the equipment in the room.

For dinner I decided to be lazy and go back to the same pub. This time I ordered a chicken sandwich which came with thick cut beef fries. I washed it down with a sweet tea. Annie texted me pics of Emily on the tractor. She had hitched up the mower and was cleaning up around the big pond where we fished. She knew I liked the grass cut low, which allowed us to sit right at the water's edge to have picnics while we fished. I knew Annie was using the excuse of sending me pictures, so she could watch Emily closely while she was on the tractor.

Another glass of sweet tea was placed in front of me. "I'm good, thank you," I said to the waiter.

"It's not for you," a voice said.

I looked up and saw the black janitor from campus. He had changed out of his school uniform, and now wore an Atlanta Braves baseball cap and an expensive dress shirt tucked into jeans. He sat down across from me without being asked.

TWELVE

"Hi, again," I said.

"Hi yourself, Brandon Hall," he said, taking a sip of sweet tea.

"I knew you weren't a janitor."

"What gave it away?"

"Your posture, you're clearly in phenomenal shape." He perked up at the compliment and smiled. I didn't know if he was friend or foe, but it never hurt to break new ground with a compliment. I also liked his carefree smile. "And you're a horrible janitor. That glass window you left was a mess." He laughed at himself. Another good trait. "Who are you? Homeland security?"

"Something like that," he said, taking another sip of tea.

"Antifa, is that big a threat?"

"They are," he said.

"I thought they were a bunch of spoiled skinny white kids who are angry at the world."

"They are," he said again. "However, we have reason to believe they're starting to get organized and are researching tactics of other radical groups."

"Like the weather underground from the sixties?"

"Worse," he said.

"Like?"

"Like I've told you too much," he said. "Now I have a problem, Mr. Hall."

"What's that?"

"My peers want me to arrest you."

"For what?" I said.

"You were trespassing on campus."

I tilted my head as if to let him know that was a weak angle. "That's a bit thin don't you think?"

He nodded as if he knew I would call his bluff. "Don't worry," he said. "However, I do need to ask why you're here? I know your ex-military and work as a farmer and a PI. I'm assuming it wasn't the farming that brought you here?"

"You assume correct. I was thinking of going back to get my Master's Degree."

It was his turn to tilt his head and smile. "That's also a bit thin don't you think?"

"Okay," I said. "I'm investigating a case."

"I have to press you on that, Mr. Hall."

"I'm sorry, I can't discuss it."

"That ain't gonna fly."

"It's all I can give you, unless you want to do a little quid pro quo?"

He sat back in his chair and looked over my shoulder and shook his head. He was calling someone off. "I can dance a little, but not much. However, before we start, please consider that not everyone in my company is as nice as I am."

I nodded. "Understood, Mr?"

He smiled. "Woodstock."

"Okay Mr. Woodstock," I held up my fingers to make

air quotes to mock his obvious fake name. "What I can tell you are facts that are self-evident. Yes, I'm here on a case. Yes, I live in Southern Virginia. That area of Virginia is not a wealthy area. My rates are such that very few people off the street can afford my services."

"Based on that I'd say that your clients are, for the most part, insurance companies and local law enforcement?"

"Correct," I said. "And those cases are mostly relegated to Halifax County."

"So you're outside of Halifax County, which means this is a private case. And the only people who can afford you are high profile elites who probably live outside of SoVa?"

I nodded again. "Yup."

He leaned back in his chair looking up at the tin ceiling of the pub as he pondered the riddle. His eyes widened and he snapped his fingers. "Senator Schilling's son's death?"

I was shocked at how fast he pieced it together. I lifted up my shoulders and smiled not willing to answer the question.

"I thought police ruled it an accident?" He said. I didn't respond. "He doesn't think it was an accident?"

"That's what I'm trying to find out," I finally conceded.

"His son was into this Antifa stuff?"

"I didn't say that."

Woodstock laughed. "If he wasn't, then you spent an awful lot of time scoping them out in the student government building."

"You guys were observing me the entire time?"

"Of course we were."

"I've given you a lot," I said. "Now we get to see how honorable you are."

"Shoot."

"My client thinks this could be in retribution to the Virginia uranium mining he's opposed to in congress."

Woodstock pursed his lips. "I don't know."

"Don't lie to me."

"I'm not," he held up his hand in an open-palmed peaceful gesture. "But I'll look into it."

"Good. It's above my pay grade anyway. I was hired to find the Southern Virginia trigger person and that's it. I shouldn't even be here, but this is where the evidence led."

"I could help if you let me see that evidence," he pleaded one more time.

"I'll wait to hear from you on the uranium intel. You prove to be a stand-up guy then I'll consider giving you more."

"I could pull you in and force you to give me what you have," he said.

"You won't," I said, getting up to leave. "My gut tells me you're an honorable man. I'm rooting for you Woodstock." Before I walked away I said, "I'm assuming you don't need my card?"

He laughed. "I already have everything I need on you, Mr. Hall. Have a good night."

I passed by two agents standing by the exit. They blended in with their casual attire but stuck-out due to their middle age. I nodded to both. One nodded back and the other gave me an angry grin, like an animal trying to bear its teeth.

I was a few minutes late for the rally. The skinny white dude with the dreadlocks was on stage. He was shouting obscenities into the mike. The kids in the large crowd, most of them white males, shouted back at him like they were in some sort of anarchist mosh pit. Campus police circled the crowd on slow moving Segways. A lot of the kids were calling them obscenities and holding signs that read things like, *the only good pig is a dead pig.*

A man stepped on stage to take the mike from dreadlocks. He was the red-haired guy from Drew's pictures. He was late twenties, either a grad student or not a student at all. He wore combat boots, green camo pants and a dark t-shirt that barely covered his large belly.

"How serious are you guys?" He shouted. The crowd cheered. "Are you willing to sacrifice?" The crowd responded with cheers. "To effect real change we're gonna have to take this up a notch." He turned towards the campus cops. "There's gonna be a time and a place we deal with you, pigs."

Again there were hoots and hollers. I was convinced most of the kids were high, or drunk. Behind the red-haired man appeared the brunette, Drew's ex. She typed away on a cell phone like she was in the middle of a texting fight with someone. I thought how easy my job would be if I could just walk up to her and snag her phone. Two more male speakers got up, but everything they said was either vague or cryptic in some way.

Make sacrifices, change the world, solidarity, oppress the oppressor, fight fascism. Nothing concrete came out of their mouths. It was if they were debriefed on what they could, and could not, say. They walked up to the line where the call for violence was almost spoken, but then walked it back. It was genius. Insane, but genius. I snapped pictures of all the speakers and emailed myself notes on their descriptions.

Over the next half hour more college age kids got up on the small stage shouting profanity and incoherent sentences. They reminded me of children throwing temper tantrums. I had never seen a group of people so full of rage. I snapped a few more photos and got up to leave. Someone grabbed my phone. I turned to find the blond dreadlocks kid from earlier looking at my phone screen.

"I knew you were a narc," he shouted, holding up my

phone in victory. He screamed over the crowd, "I told you, he's a narc!"

As he turned to run away with the phone I stuck my foot in between his legs tripping him. He fell flat on his stomach. I twisted his arm behind his back and easily retrieved my cell phone from his hand.

"Let go of my arm, narc."

"You need a brush up on your manners. And a visit to a barbershop wouldn't hurt?"

He turned his head, and when I looked down there was nothing in his eyes. It was as if he had no soul. He couldn't have been more than a hundred and thirty pounds, and would probably lose a fight with a comatose patient, but something about dreadlocks scared me.

A campus cop came over. "I saw what happened," You're not at fault. You want to do anything?"

"Such as?"

"Charges?"

I held up my phone with my free hand. "I got my phone so I'm good. I was just leaving. This ain't my cup of tea."

"You and me both," he said. "Be safe."

As soon as I got off dreadlocks he jumped up to rush me. "You're a piece of—"

The cop grabbed him by the sleeve of his t-shirt and flung him to the ground. "Where you going?"

"Get your hands off me, pig." One of dreadlocks flailing hands slapped the cop in the side of the head.

The cop smiled as he put a knee into dreadlocks back. "You just struck a police officer, son."

The commotion drew students who started to surround the cop and dreadlocks. The situation was getting precarious. Even though they were young skinny kids, if enough of them piled on they could do real damage. I moved back to help the cop.

"Just get out of here," he said, taking out his handcuffs.

"Are you sure?" I shouted over the noise of the temper tantrums.

"Go," he said, as he handcuffed dreadlocks.

Kids were now in the cop's face. A bunch of additional campus security rushed in and started throwing kids aside. The students were shouting, blowing whistles, using air horns, anything to provide a chaotic environment.

"You're gonna burn," one of them shouted at the cop who was now marching dreadlocks off.

A tomato hit a female campus cop in the face. I tried to push my way through the crowd but I'd already been flagged. Kids started to surround me. A moment later someone hit me in the back with what felt like a water balloon filled with warm water. It only took a second for the smell of urine to hit my nostrils. Someone punched me in the ribs and ran off. I was surprised that the hit actually hurt. I felt like I was in the middle of a shark feeding frenzy.

A scrawny male with a bullhorn blocked my path while shouting profanity. I grabbed him by the shirt and used him as a battering ram to push through the rest of the zombies. He cussed me out until the wind was knocked out of him by a petite girl trying to rush me. I tossed him aside when I was free of the pack.

A muffled explosion went off somewhere behind me followed by smoke. Someone had released tear gas. Before I rounded the corner I looked back on the chaotic mess that was modern day student activism. The brunette was still on stage pointing in my direction as if to tell her minions to come and capture me. Someone grabbed my upper arm and tried to twist it behind my back while at the same time push me against the corner of a stucco dorm. I instinctively rolled out of the move and came face-to-face with the chubby red-haired bearded speaker.

"You think we're a bunch of amateurs don't you, pig?"

He swung a beefy tattooed arm at me and I ducked. His fist struck the corner of the building with a pop. He bent over and cried out in pain.

"I bet that hurt," I said, doing everything I could not to counter punch him.

I left the hunched over guy and turned the corner to leave. The noise and chaos faded away as I blended into a massive crowd of students heading towards a gymnasium for some music event.

An undergrad male in workout gear in front of me turned to his friend. "Dude, you smell like pee."

Back at the jeep I took out a clean shirt and used some wipes Annie kept in the car to clean myself. I couldn't believe the kids would launch water balloons filled with their own urine. I was disgusted with what the college world had turned into.

I left Charlottesville and was tailed by a dark SUV for the first half hour. The breadth of government law enforcement was both comforting and scary. As if to remind me of the scary part of big brother, I looked up at the red light in front of me and noticed at least five street cameras on this one intersection light.

Around one a.m. I pulled into my gravel driveway. The dark palette of the night sky was littered with massive amounts of star light. The air was cool but not cold. I shut the jeep off and thanked God for the life I had on the farm with Annie and Emily and asked him once more to give me strength to get through another day without my son.

"Lord, please tell Jonah how much I love and miss him."

I stepped out of the jeep as a sliver of moon came out from behind a cloud diluting the surrounding star light.

The smell of decomposing leaves blended with the crisp clean fall night air. Beyond Emily's tree there was a rustle in the leaves. I wondered if it was a deer or even a bear. I'd placed my gun back in the appendix holster after leaving the campus, so I wasn't worried either way. I took out my pen light and walked past Emily's tree. The noise came from the family cemetery. As I approached the noise morphed into what sounded like a low moan.

A noise only a human made.

THIRTEEN

I ENTERED THE LOW WROUGHT IRON GATE INTO THE SMALL cemetery. The small flashlight cast strange shadows on the ancient alabaster headstones. Something moved near the end, near Jonah's headstone. There was another moan. My hand dropped to the appendix holster. A large dark form leaned up against Jonah's stone. I started to pull the gun. In the dim light my dad's face came into view. My foot snapped a twig and he perked up wiping his eyes.

"Oh, it's you," he said, holding his hand up to block the light.

"Sorry to disappoint," I said, shutting off the flashlight and standing over him like a parent. "Is there a reason you're sitting on my son's grave in the middle of the night?"

He started to say something then stopped as if his voice left him. He started again, but nothing came out. It reminded me of the story of Zechariah in the Bible. When Zechariah didn't believe the angel Gabriel and was struck dumb, unable to speak. My father tried to speak a third time and this time a groan came out. It sounded like an electric motor that was dying. Within seconds the noise turned into a sound I had never associated with my father, a sob. The crying turned into wails and he buried his face in his hands. I had no reference point for dealing with my dad like this, so I just stood there dumbfounded.

"It's my fault, Brandon."

"What is?"

He jacked a thumb back at Jonah's headstone. "The night he died I kept playing with him knowing Annie had to leave for an appointment. If I only gave him over to your wife sooner he'd be here. Your son would be alive. My grandson would be alive."

A sliver of my subconscious wanted to latch onto what he just said and be mad at him, but I had dwelled in the past for too long. "You can't do that to yourself. That man who hit Annie was drunk and speeding. The fault lies entirely with him."

"I keep telling myself that," he said, "but it doesn't help. I can't let go of this anger I have towards that murderer," he said. "I'm mad at the world, I'm mad at myself."

"You don't think I went through a litany of emotions too?"

He waved his hand back and forth as if to tell me I wasn't getting what he was trying to say. "You're missing the point. I felt so bad for you, that I took it out on you. How insane is that?"

All the frustration and anger I had towards this man disappeared in an instant. I had been reading him all wrong.

He continued, "Seeing what you went through killed something inside of me and I became so angry. I didn't know how to deal with watching you suffer through this. I wanted to hurt someone. To kill the one responsible for hurting my son, and killing my grandson. In the end I only hurt the people I loved the most."

"Daddy I—"

He continued to cry. "I failed as a father but I had hoped I could make up for it as a grandfather."

"You didn't fail."

"I'm a man of few words and even those words aren't enough to express how much—" he choked up again, "How much I love you."

Another figure came into focus from the darkness. My mother stood off to the side in a wool coat. She looked like an angel under the heavens. She was crying and motioned for me to go to my dad. I reached down and helped him up.

"C'mon, we gotta get you home."

"You forgive me?" he pleaded.

"Of course I do."

He put his arm around my shoulder and leaned down to kiss me on the head. "I loved that boy."

"I know you did," I said, starting to tear up. "I know you do," I corrected. "We'll see him again, Daddy. It's what helps keep me going."

My father's weeping resumed. "I love you."

I stretched my arm around his broad back. "I love you too, old man."

"I'm sorry," he said again. "For everything."

"It's okay."

We stepped over the low wrought iron fence and my mother took my dad's arm from me and draped it over her shoulder. He didn't even ask why she was there. It was at that moment I realized she had done this before. Maybe my father had been out to Jonah's grave dozens of times in the middle of the night without me ever knowing. Mom led him off onto the trail that led to their cabin. Once they were away I dropped to my knees and looked skyward thanking God for resolving the issue with my dad.

* * *

The next morning I woke to the scent of strong coffee. Annie stood over me with two cups in her hand.

"What time is it?" I grumbled, taking the cup of coffee.

"Eight thirty." She put her hand to my forehead. "You feeling okay, sweetie?"

"Yeah, just a long day, and emotional night."

"What happened?"

I spent the next twenty minutes recapping my time up in Charlottesville and then the encounter with my dad. Annie was relived, and we spent a few minutes reading from Roman's eight and praying together.

Around nine thirty I patrolled the property checking on fence lines and the herd. The final heifer still hadn't given birth yet. She was nearing her due date. If she didn't go into labor soon I'd induce her. I made a mental note to confirm there was still dexamethasone in the animal medical cabinet I kept in the barn office. In the sky, the gray clouds taunted me as if they held back water over my property on purpose.

"Lord, I could use some rain," I said. "But you know this already." I was shocked how unrelenting my sin nature was. It had been all of twelve hours since God had resolved a problem with my dad, and here I was already worried about the next problem. I finished my prayer with the words. "Teach me to trust you more."

After lunch Annie, Emily, and me finished picking the remaining pumpkins and squash in our garden. The scare-crow in the back corner looked ominous with the grey sky behind it. Like a dark angel waiting to pounce on a victim.

As if to counter my thoughts the sun broke through the clouds with a wave of warmth that felt like an embrace. The scarecrow seemed to shrink in the presence of the light. Staring down at the spent garden, my thoughts drifted ahead to Christmas. Soon, we'd drive out to the deep woods of the property to cut down a pine tree. It would be bitter sweet celebrating our second Christmas without Jonah.

The sun burnt off the remaining clouds in the afternoon sky and it warmed up enough to take off my flannel shirt and work in a tank top. After the crop was in, Emily and I cut out of work early to go fishing. Annie was making her famous fish tacos and needed us to catch some largemouth bass. I had stocked our largest pond with a variety of sunfish, crappie, perch, and bass. It was a perfect day to fish with the weather around seventy-five, and just me and my baby girl.

"As much as we need the rain," I said, "I'm glad it's another nice day."

"Me too," she said, finishing baiting the hooks with worms. "Here's your rod."

"You'll make an awesome farmer one day." I said, "That is if you still want to be a farmer?"

"I do. But Daddy, why do you always say I'll be a good farmer. What if I want to be a farmer's wife?"

"You'd make any man proud to be their wife," I said tossing my line in the water. "Shame though."

"Why's that?"

"Cause you ain't ever gonna date. Like ever. So you won't be getting married."

She rolled her eyes. "You think I'm gonna live with you forever don't you?"

"You used to tell me you would."

"Daddy, I was like five years old."

"So."

Her pole moved, then mine did as well. The worst part of the day turned out to be the fish were biting too quickly. Within a half hour we had a stack of bass with the biggest being two pounds.

My phone rang just as we finished putting the fish into the back of the pickup. "Brandon Hall speaking?"

"Mr Hall," came a familiar smooth voice.

"Agent Woodstock, nice to hear from you."

"It's actually Agent Drake."

"You have a real name," I said.

"I've done enough background checking to trust you with that piece of info."

"Any other info you want to trust me with?"

"That's why I'm calling. I'm a man of my word. And per our discussion in Charlottesville, I searched the uranium mining rabbit trail to its end."

"And?"

"It's a nothing-burger."

I motioned for Emily to start up the truck while I walked a short distance to talk further. "What do you mean?"

"What happened is a couple low brow DNC staffers in Washington were playing tough guy with Senator Schilling. They were hoping to pressure him to move in favor of uranium mining in Virginia. As we speak their getting a wakeup call that's gonna ween them off their momma's breastmilk mighty quick." There was a pause on the other end of the phone. "I'm assuming you know this already?"

"I suspected it would be a dead end," I said.

"So you're back to the Antifa conspiracy with his son's murder?"

"I don't think it's a conspiracy," I said.

"Care to share what you have then?"

"I'm not sure what I have."

"I'd like to see what it is and make that decision for myself."

"I need to talk to my client first."

Emily was now revving the truck. I motioned for her to wait a minute, but she kept revving. I put my hand over the phone. "Hold on a sec, honey."

"That your ten-year-old daughter?"

"How'd you—"

"It's my job, Mr. Hall. Can I share something with you?"

"Sure."

"Off the record, we're now looking into this Antifa connection with Drew Schilling as well, and if this boy's death gets re-opened as a homicide case then my friends are gonna come down there and put a world of hurt on you for sitting on evidence."

"My dear agent Drake, are you threatening me?"

"Trust me. I'm looking out for you. If you don't believe me then try to call me back on this number when I hang up. You won't even get a voicemail."

"What do you mean?"

"I'm calling you on a burner phone. That's how far I'm sticking my neck out for you."

"Why are you doing this?"

"Because I know you're a fellow believer, and I like you."

"You like me?" I laughed.

"Yeah, the wife says I don't have enough Christian friends. You know, the whole iron sharpens iron thing from the Bible. I'm thinking of making you my friend."

I laughed again. The man was charming to the point of disarming. "I've got to go. Call me soon and I'll talk more."

"Oh, I will."

I let Emily drive back to the house. She sat in between my legs and drove and shifted while I operated the clutch, gas, and brakes. It was small moments like this that I hoped she'd remember. Annie and I couldn't afford to give Emily much more than love and memories as an inheritance. I hoped it was enough.

For dinner, we ate on the back porch facing the open pastures. After dinner, we moved our three rocking chairs onto the grass next to a small rock pit so we could toast smores. I kept the garden hose close by in case the parched grass caught fire.

A short while later, Emily and Annie went in to shower while I put out the fire. A text came through on my cell phone. It was Senator Schilling's personal assistant, Jane. The Senator was going to be at the family estate in Clarksville tomorrow and asked for an update in person. I had a lot of thoughts, but nothing definitive yet.

I went inside and opened Drew's computer again to look at his pictures. I recognized the white kid with dreadlocks in some of the group photos.

I listened to confirm and Annie and Emily's showers were still going before I re-opened the folder labeled P, which held the dirty pics of Drew and the brunette.

All the time stamps showed a ten-day period of time a month earlier in Charlottesville. The bedroom they were in was fancier than a dorm room with high-end furnishings, which meant the girl had money and an off campus apartment. I organized the pics according to type. When I did this, all of the videos were grouped at the bottom as mp4's. I hadn't clicked on any of them and didn't want to. They were all labeled p1, p2, p3, etc. All except one, which had the title *d*.

I reluctantly clicked on the mp4 expecting more bedroom sports from Drew and the brunette, and instead found the brunette in bed with an old man. It was a different bedroom furnished with a dark wood four-post canopy bed. It looked like a setting from a Dicken's novel. The time stamp on the video also read four weeks ago in Washington DC. The word betrayal started to make sense. So the brunette was two-timing Drew with an old man.

"What's that?"

I turned around to see Annie in her bathrobe with a towel on her head. "Huh?"

"You better have an excuse for bringing that crap into the house Brandon Hall."

"Oh, this," I said pointing to the video. "Sorry, It's Drew Schilling's computer. I need to find out who these people are."

"Seriously?" She leaned in. "Is that an old man with a teenage girl?"

"This girl and Drew dated, or had a relationship. Based on the time stamps on the files I think he found out she was also dating this old man for some weird reason. Maybe he loses it and threatens to expose them, but that wouldn't mean murder would it?"

Annie leaned in closer. "Move out of the way." She replayed the video. "I can't believe I'm looking at this crap. I want to vomit." She paused the video and snapped her fingers. "That's the old guy we saw on the news a while ago. The billionaire guy who manipulates markets, wants a one world government, open borders. Gaspar something—"

"Schultz?"

"Yeah."

"I can't believe I missed that," I said, looking at the stilled image.

"You think he had something to do with Drew Schilling's death?"

"Maybe," I said.

"He'd kill someone over a video of him and a girl in bed being released?"

"No," I said, trying to piece this into some scenario that made sense. "But maybe he'd kill over a video of him in bed with a national leader of Antifa, especially if he had something to hide.

"Like?"

"Like, maybe he's funding it."

Annie snapped her fingers again and pointed to the kitchen door. "Good. Case solved. Now if we're done please get this evil computer out of my house and go put it in your truck or something." As she walked back into the bedroom she said, "I think I'm going to take another shower. I feel dirty."

FOURTEEN

THE DRIVE INTO CLARKSVILLE ALONG ROUTE 58 THE NEXT morning was peaceful. The scenic road passed very few stores and endless farms giving the sky unparalleled dominion. The skyline was dotted with clouds. I hoped some of them contained rain and found their way over to my place as the farm was rapidly turning into a dustbowl.

The small town of Clarksville overlooked a massive expanse of Buggs Island Lake. The town was perfectly situated as a tourist destination but never took off due to the majority of the land surrounding the lake being owned by the Army Corp of Engineers.

Senator Schilling's plantation style estate was located a few blocks behind Virginia Drive in downtown. The long gravel driveway was lined with magnolia trees. The white antebellum home had Georgian columns at the entrance. Senator Schilling sat in a rocking chair on a second story balcony talking on his cell phone. He waved and got up to go inside. By the time I parked he was on the front porch waiting. The Senator looked like he stepped from the pages of The Great Gatsby dressed in a fancy beige three-piece linen suit.

"Good to see you Brandon," He said, shaking my hand. "You shaved your beard?

"Long story."

"Well, come in."

Stepping into the house was like being transported back into multiple eras at the same time. From the 1800's up to the 1930's. The foyer ceilings were at least twenty feet high and the floor was a bright white marble. A wrought iron elevator ascended through the middle of a grand spiral staircase up to a second story landing.

"This summer home has been in my wife's family for five generations."

"Summer home," I laughed.

"Sorry, I'm sure that came out wrong," he said. "In the circles I walk Mr. Hall I'm considered poor by their standards, so I have no problem talking matter-of-factly. I admit the house is palatial, but we only have five acres left from the family's original forty-five. It's getting a bit cramped for my taste.

"I can relate to that point, Senator."

"Ah, your farm. It is beautiful. Try to learn from our family mistakes and never subdivide your property if you can help it."

We entered a library that looked like a museum. It was lined with dark floor to ceiling bookcases packed with leather bound antique books. All of Mark Twain's catalogue along with other authors like Tolkien, Dickens and GK Chesterton. I assumed some of them were first editions. A brass ladder was linked to a track above the bookcases, which allowed you to reach the ten foot height of the top bookshelf. Bronze busts of old men lined a mahogany table. The only two I recognized were Robert E. Lee and Stonewall Jackson. The Senator led me out to the back porch and on to a clamshell path.

We started walking and I started the conversation. "Did anything come from the receipt I sent you from Drew's car being picked up?"

He huffed. "The car's gone, which solidifies my point it was no accident." He stopped to pull a weed from middle of the pristine bleached clamshell trail. "How's progress on your end?"

"I've made headway but everything I uncover leads to more questions. It's a tough situation you hired me for."

"If it's more money you need—"

"Of course not," I said. "I'm sorry if it came out that way. What I mean is, you've kind of tied my hands behind my back.

"How so?"

"I was hired in a compartmentalized capacity. You wanted me to find a trigger man in southern Virginia, but we both know this goes outside the community. It's hard for me to find one link in a chain without needing to uncover more."

"What are you saying?"

"I've found some more evidence outside of southern Virginia."

"Well then spit it out."

I stopped walking and tested him. "I'm assuming you knew this had nothing to do with uranium."

The Senator's face darkened and the default soft smirk morphed into a tight-lipped feature. "What are you implying, Mr. Hall?"

"The threats that were sent to your office were traced out and they turned out to be duds. As in low level DNC staffers in Washington. Not pranks I'll give you, but nothing serious." I pressed him further. "But you know this already don't you?"

"No, I didn't know. And for you to imply otherwise I find offensive."

I held up my hand to stop him. "My sincere apologies, Senator. Part of me thought you might have me going on a wild goose chase."

"I've had a five hundred dollar an hour firm in DC looking into this and, as of yesterday, they've turned up nothing. How'd a small-town sleuth come across this information?" I couldn't tell if he was impressed or annoyed.

"I came into contact with some government people the other day."

"What? Homeland security?"

"Uhm, I'm not sure."

"You're not sure?" he huffed, "And you trust them?"

"No, but I have no reason not to trust them."

"That's not convincing. You don't even know who you spoke with?"

"They could have fed me no information rather than going out of their way to give me this feedback."

"You don't think they're trying to pull you off the trail?"

"It's possible." I paused trying to make sure my tone was even. "Senator, I don't think Drew's death is a conspiracy involving uranium."

It was as if he picked up on my softened rebuke and, in turn, relaxed. "If what you're saying is true, then I've been wearing a tin foil hat chasing monsters where there aren't any."

"Of course not. There was something to the threats, but I don't think it's tied to Drew's murder."

"You said the word murder? So you do think there was foul play?"

"I do," I said.

"Please tell me you have something else then?"

"What do you know about the friends Drew kept?"

"I knew some of them," he exhaled as if I had discovered a dark family secret. "They liked to party a bit too much. Why?"

"How about girls he dated?"

The Senator's head slumped a bit further as if I found another weakness he wanted to protect. "Like I said, he liked to party. His mother warned me about this, but I didn't listen. We were married young, and for some stupid reason, I thought it was a right of passage for Drew to sow his oats."

I pulled up a picture of the brunette on my phone and showed the Senator. "Do you recognize this young lady?"

"Pretty girl, but no." He handed the phone back. "Am I to believe this girl was involved in my son's murder?"

"Yes."

He stopped. "I was being facetious, Mr. Hall."

"Drew got involved in some serious groups, Senator. I think this girl sucked him into one up in Charlottesville."

"Like?"

"Antifa. This girl's a leader in the anarchist group. I believe Drew attended some of their meetings because he'd fallen for her."

"This doesn't make sense? Why—"

"Here me out," I said. "They dated and I believe he discovered she was using him."

"For what? Drew's inheritance hasn't kicked in yet so money's out of the question."

"I came to the same conclusion from a different route."

"That being?"

"I believe they have more than enough funding. I'm confident you've heard of Gaspar Schultz?"

"The billionaire ex-Nazi sympathizer? Of course."

"I think he's at the end of the line," I said. "Ultimately, I think he had Drew killed."

The Senator's hands went to his forehead like he was fighting a migraine headache. "Why would you say that?"

"Drew discovered something on him."

"Like?"

"He found out this girl had a relationship with old man Schultz and was using him. I believe Drew was going to expose evidence he uncovered tying Schultz to Antifa, which is why he was murdered."

The Senator shook his head back and forth. "What you're saying doesn't make sense. If she wasn't using Drew for money, then what was she using him for?"

"The only scenario that makes sense to me is the girl, Schultz, and Antifa, were courting Drew to get access to his father." The Senator said nothing, his mind clearly racing. "I believe he was going to expose them to protect you, Senator."

The Senator slumped to the ground in his thousand-dollar suit. His head fell into his hands and he started to cry. I sat down next to him and waited for the wave to pass.

"All the while I thought my son was a spoiled brat who only cared about himself. But to think, for even a second, he was trying to protect me, just makes me ill."

I placed my hand on his shoulder and whispered. "We need to take Schultz down."

The Senator chuckled through his tears. "You're a funny guy, Mr. Hall."

"I'm not joking."

"You have no idea who this man is." The Senator got up and started back towards the house at a brisk pace, and I followed. “I appreciate all that you’ve done. I’ll take it from here.”

I rushed to keep up with his long strides. “Keep in mind this isn’t a hundred percent, but I do believe the girl could have been the one who planted the explosive on Drew’s car.”

“Send your final bill into my assistant and I’ll get you a check.”

“Senator, did you hear what I just said?

“I did.”

“Do you mind if I ask what you’re gonna do?”

“I can’t let any of this get out?”

I stopped walking and the senator stopped. “What? Why?”

“It’s not for what you think,” he said. "I don’t care about my political career.”

“Then what?”

“I have another child, Mr. Hall. A daughter.”

“You can’t let Schultz get away with murder.”

“You don’t understand,” he said. “This man owns Washington. Senators, Congressmen, even presidents aren’t protected from his reach. It makes perfect sense he was courting Drew to get to me. That’s his M.O.”

“So your son died in vain.”

“That’s enough,” he barked. “I don’t need you to lecture me about the death of my only son.” He stopped himself. A moment later he was the composed Senator again. “My apologies. I know you lost a son as well. It’s just that this is so raw.” He took out an embossed handkerchief and wiped his eyes. “Tell me you wouldn’t do anything to protect your remaining child?”

He hit me where it hurt the most. I had no response because I agreed with him. As much as I wanted to see justice I had no comeback.

"So we're done?" I said.

"We're done."

I walked off as the Senator called after me. I was mad at him for not stepping up for his dead son, mad at Schultz for the vile life he lived which involved murder, and mad at the man who took my son, but it was no longer my problem. I entered back into the library and exited out the front door. Outside on the front porch sat a woman who looked like a twin sister to Raquel Welch. She was dressed in a fancy pant suit with a straw hat protecting her wrinkle free skin. She held a martini in her hand.

"Mr. Hall," she said in an old Virginia southern accent. "Have you found the people responsible for my son's death?"

"I've given your husband my update."

"And?"

"You'll have to talk with him ma'am."

"I'm talking with you." I didn't respond. "Speak boy, speak."

"I have some solid leads but the Senator wants me to stop."

"My husband's weak," she spat. "I want you to ignore him and to continue with your investigation."

"Your husband's afraid for your daughter's safety."

"It's my understanding that you also lost a son?"

"Yes Ma'am."

"I'd be willing to stake my family fortune that his mother, your wife, was broken in a way you didn't think was humanly possible."

I didn't respond, not willing to admit she was right.

"I want God's vengeance to descend upon the one who did this to my boy, Mr. Hall."

"Good day, ma'am."

As I walked to the truck I heard the shattering of

martini glass as it was thrown onto the porch. “Do you hear me, Mr. Hall!”

I did. Loud and clear. Resting my hand on the truck door I said, “I’ll look under one or two more rocks to see what I find, but I can’t promise anything.”

She collapsed back into the chair and started to cry. The effort of our conversation having drained her of any semblance of strength, or self control.

FIFTEEN

ON THE WAY BACK FROM CLARKSVILLE I STOPPED IN SOUTH Boston to visit JT. I pulled into Cozy Cavern to find the light still on in the office. JT was at his desk working on a laptop.

He looked up for a moment then back down to his work. "You looked better with the beard."

I laughed, not sure if he was busting my chops or serious. "I'm shocked to see you using an actual computer."

"I got the itch after you made me touch that other laptop. I'm thinking of getting back into programming on the side."

"Good for you."

"For too long I've associated computers with my past life. I'm not gonna let my ex steal my joy."

I sat down in a red leather chair across from his desk and took Drew Schilling's laptop out of my rucksack. "You still part of those libertarian websites?"

"Yeah, but I haven't logged on in a long time. Why?"

"I need to get some news out that will be picked up by alternative media."

"I can get it out there, but I can't guarantee it'll get picked up. That said, if it's the Schilling boy then it shouldn't be a problem as he was a high-profile kid?"

"It is, but I need it released in such a way that it can't be traced back to Senator Schilling."

"Why?"

"He's not on board with this and has a lot of weak points that could be exploited." JT smirked as if I were feeding him a line of bull. "It's more than his political career at stake. He's concerned about his other child's safety."

"Okay, so give me the rundown."

"I believe the guy behind Drew's death is Gaspar Schultz?"

"The one-world-order dude?"

"Yeah."

"He's bad news, brotha. Guy has an endless bank account and endless resources."

I exhaled. "You're the second one who's shown fear at the mere mention of this man?"

"Not fear, respect.

"For what?"

"For what he can do."

"Do not be afraid of those who kill the body but cannot kill the soul," I said.

"Let me guess," JT said, "The Bible."

"You should read it sometime."

"I know, I know. Just give me some time dude."

"Tomorrow's not a guarantee," I said. "At least think about it?"

"I will." JT snapped his fingers and held out his hand. I passed him the laptop and he went to work.

"Come over here and tell me what to release," he said. "I want to put descriptions with some of this stuff."

We shuffled through a myriad of horrific pictures of the girl and Schultz in bed. In one of the pictures I noticed, for the first time, a faint blood red pentagram above his bed. I hated the fact that I had to look at this stuff to solve a case. It was both vile and sad. This young college girl was someone's daughter. I thought of my precious ten-year-old and prayed God would protect her, and one day lead her to a man who would treat her like a queen, not a prostitute.

In the end we chose eight screen shots of Schultz and the girl to release with the nude parts redacted. Then we chose pics of Drew and the brunette in social settings clearly showing them to be in a relationship. These pics would be released later.

"How much more do I have to look at this crap?" I said, feeling the need to wash my eyes out with saline.

"Quiet, daddy's thinking." Five minutes later he shut Drew's laptop. "Done."

"It won't be traced in any way to Senator Schilling right?"

He giggled. "If it's traced, it'll go back to Wayne Rideout's company.

"Who?"

"My former business partner back in Boston."

"You mean?"

He grinned. "The dude that's sleeping with my ex-wife."

Before I left, JT handed me a flash drive. "Here's another present."

"What is it?"

"Remember that one doc on here I couldn't open. Well, I kept a copy of it and figured out how to open it."

"And?"

"I have no idea," he exhaled clearly frustrated. "Bunch of garbled code and transactions. Whatever it is, you'll need a cypher to unlock it further. Nothin more I can do."

"Thanks," I said, placing the zip drive in my pocket.

* * *

Two hours later the pics of Schultz and the girl were all over the web. It was clear this tied Schultz to this girl with the hope that the public, and media, would then tie Schultz to Antifa. Later that night I texted JT to release the pictures of Drew Schilling and this same mystery girl. The evidence would show two degrees of separation between Schultz and Drew Schilling. Drew's death would be drawn into the picture organically, and the media could piece everything together. By doing this I made the investigation open-sourced, and expanded my resources a thousand fold. Reporters from around the world were now on the case. People with far more time, money, and skill than a small-town sleuth.

By dawn there was chatter of Drew Schilling's death being reopened as a potential murder. Throughout the morning JT texted me video clips of camera's following the brunette and other Antifa people around the campus Virginia State University. Her name turned out to be Rebecca Shaw, a privileged white girl from New York who dyed her hair black and wore heavy makeup to give the appearance of foreign descent. Someone stuffed a microphone in her face asking why she altered her appearance from her college ID. In a moment of weakness she screamed into the camera that she identified as Indo-African and had every right to alter her appearance. On social media Schultz was being accused of a myriad of crimes. From rape to terrorism. If he never went to prison, at least his life was going to be uncomfortable.

I felt like there was some closure to the case. I sent the final bill into Senator Schilling's assistant and decided to go for a drive around the farm on a four-wheeler to celebrate the end of a case. The farm is where I relaxed the most. When I reached the main fishing pond I found my dad on horseback. He was about to rope a steer that had broken out of the fence and was standing near the middle of the pond. We didn't let the cattle near this specific pond otherwise we'd have water infested with bacteria from bovine dung, and any fish we caught wouldn't be healthy enough to eat.

I drove up and shut the four-wheeler off. "You need help?"

He pointed to the split rail fence posts that had fallen down. "Just put the posts up when I get him back inside."

"Roger that."

He swung the rope over his head as he had done a thousand times before. After a few seconds he threw the open lariat around the steer's neck from the shallows of the pond.

"Nice throw."

"Your old man still has it," he said wrapping the rope around the horn of his saddle.

With a nudge, his horse Savannah, backed up like a diesel truck with a winch. The steer slowly came out of the watering hole. I waded in and helped push her in the direction of the fence. Once she stepped back into the pasture I repositioned the split rails back in place.

"The best job in the world," my dad said, coiling the rope.

"Agreed," I said, happy to see a smile back on my dad's face. He was in a better place. We were in a better place. God was good.

After lunch I sat at the kitchen table with a yellow pages open in front of me. With Bud out of the picture, I had to find someone to fix our failing septic system. I called six different septic companies. Of the four companies I spoke with, all of them were booked out at least a month. I hoped the two I left messages for would have better news.

"Anything?" Annie said, entering the kitchen with a basketful of eggs from the chicken coop.

"Nothing. We're gonna have to start rationing showers and laundry until I can get the leach field fixed. We're on borrowed time."

"I wish we knew what the cost was so we could figure this out."

"The Schilling case will cover a portion of whatever it is."

"Yeah, but what about—"

As if to remind us both of how insignificant the problem was I said, "Romans eight twenty-eight."

Annie spoke a portion of the verse, "He works for the good of those who love him, who are called according to his purpose."

"That's right," I said, gettin up to hug her around her waist and kiss her neck. "Have I told you that I happen to have the prettiest wife in the world."

"You won't be saying that if I go a couple days without a shower."

* * *

My dad once told me that nothing good happens after midnight, and from my experience he was right. So when my cell phone vibrated at twelve thirty am, I knew it couldn't be good news.

"Brandon Hall," I whispered, getting up to leave the bedroom so as to not wake Annie.

"Brandon?"

"Yeah?"

"Sorry to bother you so late.

"Who's this?"

"Tollers."

"Park police need a recovery this late?" I said.

"No, I wanted to give you the heads up. I just heard that one of your buddies was attacked tonight. Jason Tayler."

"Who?"

"He owns a self storage place on Webster Street."

"JT? What happened?"

"Someone came into his place robbed, and stabbed him. We don't know who it was."

"Is he—"

"He's in surgery now. Should make it though."

"Do we know anything?"

"Nothing yet. Whoever it was, stole his security DVR as well."

"Thanks for the info. I'm heading to the hospital now."

"That's not the reason why I called." There was an awkward pause. "Sobo police need you to come down to make a statement first."

"Why?"

"When the police got to the crime scene JT had written the letters *B-r-a-n-d* on the wall of his office in his own blood. It appears he was forming a word, or name, before he passed out."

"And what, Sobo Police I had something to do with this?"

He answered my question with a question. "Annie can corroborate your whereabouts tonight right?"

"Of course."

"Then go down, make a statement, then go to the hospital." Before I hung up he asked one more question. "Why would he write your name in blood?"

"I'm not sure."

I emailed Annie an outline of my conversation so as to not wake her. If she woke up, and didn't find me next to her, she knew to check her email. On the way to the police station I ran through a myriad of scenarios. Could this have been a random robbery? But then why would JT write my name on the wall? It had to do with Drew Schilling's case and what he did on the computer. Someone must have traced the information we released back to his office on Webster Street. I arrived at the police station a little after one AM. Tollers was outside in civilian clothes wearing a Sheriff's baseball cap. Jim and I grew up playing baseball at Halifax County High School. Tollers received a pitching scholarship to Duke where he proceeded to blow out his arm sophomore year. He dropped out and came back to become a Sheriff. He was still referred to as fast-ball Tollers by most of Halifax County guys my age.

He greeted me with a handshake before smacking my clean shaven face lightly to acknowledge my new look. "Sorry to do this to you in the middle of the night."

"It's fine," I said. "You didn't have to show up."

He waved his hand like he had nothing better to do at one AM. "Once you pass through this door I want you to say the least amount possible."

"I have nothing to hide," I said.

"Still, only say what you need to."

After we entered the building Tollers escorted me to a back room where a young officer sat at a table with a laptop and pad of paper.

"My name's Sergeant Richardson," he said without looking up or shaking my hand. He thumbed a finger toward a wall-mounted camera. "This is being recorded."

Richardson proceeded to read me the obligatory Miranda warning which put a knot in my stomach.

"How long is this gonna take?" I said.

Richardson ignored my question and started typing at the laptop. "Why did your friend write your name on the wall of his business in blood?"

"Was it my name?"

Richards looked at me for the first time. "The quicker you tell me how you're involved, or not involved, in this the quicker I can help you."

"I'm not sure involved is the right term?" I said. I looked to Tollers who nodded his head to continue. Rather than dance around the subject I told Richardson the truth. "You know that big news story about Gaspar Schultz, that young girl, and Antifa being connected?"

"I heard something about it," Richardson said.

"My friend JT broke that story over the Internet."

"And?"

"And I think he was attacked by people associated with those groups. That's the only reason he'd have written my name on the wall that I can think of."

"I'm confused. Why would he write your name on the wall?"

"I fed him the information." Richardson said nothing. "I'm the one who discovered the intel while working on a case as a private investigator."

"What case?"

"I can't talk about it right now."

In the back of the room I could see Toller's hand go up to his forehead.

Richardson exhaled. "This is going to be a lot of paperwork."

There was a loud click. Richardson stopped typing and, for the first time since I entered the room, he showed emotion in the form of a wince.

A moment later the door opened and another older

officer stepped into the room. "You're gonna lose your PI license and go to jail if you don't talk," he said.

"And you're officer?"

"Officer none-of-your-business. Now you're gonna talk or else I'm—"

"Or else nothing," Tollers said, stepping between us. "This law-abiding taxpayer is in here voluntarily, Lewis." The old officer grimaced. "Keep up your rude bedside manners and he'll get lawyered-up, which means you'll get nothing from him for weeks."

"What he did was criminal."

"He didn't break any laws posting that info on the internet and you know it," Tollers said. "If you knew anything about the new thing called the internet you'd be smart enough to not say such gibberish."

Lewis moved towards Tollers, but Richardson rose up to block him. "Get out of the room. I can handle this."

Lewis left the room and slammed the door. A moment later there was a loud click again as the light on the wall-mounted camera came back on.

"Nice guy," I said.

Richardson resumed his position at the laptop and whispered, "Try working with him."

I spent the next forty minutes filling out paperwork and making statements. The only positive that came from the meeting was Tollers persuaded Richardson to position an officer outside JT's hospital room for the night. Tollers escorted me out of the station like I was his personal security detail. Officer Lewis waited for us at the front door trying his best to give us a feral dog grin. I did everything I could not to laugh.

Outside I shook Toller's hand again. "Thanks for having my back in there."

He grinned. "Third shift cops can be testy."

At two thirty AM I entered Halifax regional hospital. JT had been out of surgery for an hour. I was told he was sedated and asleep. I knew the officer stationed outside JT's room from church. Roger Bates had a son who was the same age as Emily. He was hesitant to let me into the room though.

"Rog, I want to go pray over my friend," I said. "Just come in with me."

He looked left and right. "Okay, Brandon, but do it quick."

Inside the room JT looked like a different man. His face was swollen and bruised and his chest and stomach were wrapped in bandages. Tears formed against my will. I had done this to him. No, evil did this, but it didn't change the fact that had I kept JT out of the case he would be healthy.

I placed a hand over his. "Father, please stay with JT and heal him. My friend doesn't know you yet, Lord." I continued in a whisper. "Forgive me for bringing this on him." Roger and I said *Amen* at the same time.

I stayed a few more minutes before leaving. As I walked down the hallway familiar voice came from one of the second-floor rooms.

"What time is it?"

"I'm sorry to wake you," a female voice said, "but I need to take more vitals. I'll be quick."

"It's okay," Bud said.

I stopped in front of the open door. Bud turned to me. It seemed to take him a moment to register seeing me at this hour in the night. "Brandon, what are you doing here?"

I started to say something, but turned and walked away. Bud called after me, but I rushed out of the hospital. I wasn't ready to see him yet. I kept thinking of the man who killed my son.

It was around five AM when I pulled into our gravel

driveway. I sat in the truck blurry with exhaustion, but managed to type an updated email for Annie to read for when she woke up. When I crawled into bed she stirred, and mumbled something. I whispered for her to go back to bed, and that everything was fine.

I knew it was anything but fine.

SIXTEEN

It seemed a moment later a strong cup of coffee was placed next to me. The aroma of my wife's coffee was like smelling salts. A blurry figure of Emily slowly came into focus next to me on the bed.

I took the coffee from her. "Hey sweetie, what time is it?"

"Eleven," she said.

Memories of JT's near lifeless body rushed back, along with the accompanying guilt. I placed the coffee mug down and Emily proceeded to jump up and down on my gut. Like me nibbling on her ear, this was her thing she did to annoy me. I flipped her over onto Annie's side of the bed and started to tickle her. My daughter's laughter was the remedy I needed.

"It's all over the local news?" Annie said, entering the bedroom.

"What?" I said, holding Emily down with one arm.

"JT's attack."

"Not fair," Emily said from under my arm.

"Any word on his condition?" I said.

"I called Jessie from church who's an ER nurse. She said he's stable and will be released in a day or two."

I turned to Emily, "Can you go in the other room, sweetie?

"Adult stuff?" She huffed.

"Yeah, work related. Not for little ears as cute as they may be." After Emily left the room I said, "I think JT was attacked because of my case."

"What?"

I gave Annie the debrief on how JT hacked Drew Schilling's computer and how we released the Schultz info onto the web.

"Are you sure the two are connected?"

"Not a hundred percent, but I don't believe in coincidences. JT was in the process of writing my name on the wall in his own blood. He was trying to get a message to me. From now on just carry your gun please."

"Even around the house?"

"Even around the house."

For the first time since we'd been married I asked Annie to check the herd for me. I went straight into Cozy Cavern Self Storage. Police caution tape wrapped around the entrance to the office. I didn't go in but put a sign on the door stating business was closed for a week and to call my cell number for any storage needs. Out front, a shiny blue BMW X5 slowed down to a stop on the street. I stared at the car trying to see who was driving but the window was tinted. I shut the door to my truck and started to walk towards the small SUV. It took off before I could get a license plate number. The rest of the property was secure so I headed back into the hospital. The police detail was gone from outside JT's room. Someone had made the call that JT wasn't important enough for South Boston's limited resources. I entered the room to find JT awake and wearing a Boston Bruins baseball cap.

"Hey buddy," JT whispered, in a hoarse voice.

"How you doing?"

"Feel like I got run over by a truck." He winced as if speaking was painful. "Come to find out I was only beaten and stabbed."

"Tell me this had nothing to do with the computer hack you did for me?"

He shook his head back and forth. "I think we woke a sleeping giant."

"How could I be so stupid?"

"Forget it, dude." He clenched and unclenched a fist. "Were I not so fat and out of shape I'd have at least tried to fight back with more than sarcasm."

"Did you ID any of them?"

"It was four kids, couldn't have been older than twenty. All white males but all of them had on masks. I gave them what I had in my wallet, but it was clear they were there for something else."

"How do you know?"

"Because one of them was dumb enough to ask where my computer was." JT coughed and his eyes teared up. It was clear he was in pain. "I didn't have my laptop with me, which they didn't believe, and proceeded to rough me up."

"You were stabbed," I corrected him. "I'd say it's a bit more than roughing you up. I feel sick to my stomach that I brought this on you."

"You didn't do this. I should have put more backdoors into the info I launched."

"I thought you covered your steps?"

"I did with the Schultz info," he coughed and winced again, "but I forgot to do the same when I sent out the pics of Drew Schilling later on." He held onto his stomach.

"Brotha, I held out for as long as I could." He coughed and winced in pain again. "They beat me for an hour before—" he trailed off. "I knew why they were there and confessed to what I did, but told them it was a PI from Richmond who brought the computer in that I hacked into."

I placed my hand over his. "Don't worry about it."

"You don't understand, Brandon. They found my security DVR and took it. It's a matter of time before they break into it and find out it's you, and not some dude from Richmond." JT started to get choked up. "You gotta watch yourself, Brandon."

I lifted my shirt to reveal the Smith and Wesson in the appendix holster. "I'm fine."

JT wiped his eyes. "Loyalty's a big deal where I come from. You're my only friend—"

He broke down. I could tell it was more than physical pain, or the trauma from the night before causing this. The mental torture of his wife's infidelity, and abandonment, compounded everything.

I patted his hand. "I'm blessed to have you as my friend."

He composed himself and wiped his eyes with the sheet of the bed. "Sobo police called a few minutes ago and are coming in to take my statement."

"Just tell them the truth," I said.

"Okay, but just a heads up I was visited by a couple Feds just before you came in."

"Really?"

"I told them nothing. I wanted to speak with you first. They're gonna come back with legal pressure though, and at that point I'll have to talk. I'm sorry I couldn't do more."

"Are you kidding? You've done more than enough."

"Brandon, I—" he started to cry again.

"It's okay," I said.

He shook his head back and forth. "I thought I was going to die last night. I was scared."

"Anyone would be."

He wiped his eyes again. "Just as they stuck the knife in my gut, I called out to God."

The sick feeling of guilt that I felt lessened, ever so slightly, as I waited for JT to continue. "And?"

"I cried out, forgive me and remember me, Lord." The tears now fell down JT's cheeks unobstructed with any remnant of a masculine facade having evaporated.

I started to cry myself. The story was both horrific and beautiful.

"Brandon?"

"Yeah?"

"I felt peace after I said it. There I was, bleeding like a stuck pig all over my new carpet. I knew I was going to die but I was okay. I can't explain it. After I said that, the kids just up and left. It was like I became invisible to them or something. He saved me, Brandon. He saved me."

I lowered my head. "Thank you Father. Thank you for rescuing his soul, and for saving him."

"Amen."

"I'm gonna make this up to you for any lost income you have at your place," I said.

He both winced and chuckled through his tear-streaked face. "I got plenty in the bank from my days up north. The storage business helped keep me sane."

"Well, promise to call me if you need anything okay?"

"There's something you could do?"

"What's that?"

"I'm getting discharged tomorrow and I'm a bit nervous going back to work. As you know, I'm no MMA fighter and could use a firearm to keep on hand. Come to find out face-slapping isn't a form of self-defense which is about all I got."

"When you get settled I'll take you to the local farm supply store and we'll get you a gun."

"A farm supply store to buy a gun? I love this place."

"For the short term, I'll take care of getting you security. I promise you won't be bothered again."

"Thanks dude. And Brandon—"

"Yeah?"

"Watch your six."

"Roger that."

On the way out, I stopped in front of Bud's room again. The door was shut. I knocked, and after no response I reluctantly opened it. An elderly man was on the far side bed asleep and the bed that Bud had been in was empty. A wave of relief washed over me. I did my part and attempted to see him. I assumed he'd been discharged. As I turned to leave I walked into an orderly pushing a bed with Bud in it. My stomach dropped.

Bud perked up when he saw me. It was clear it took him a second to recognize me without my beard. "Brandon, I'm so glad to see you."

I held the door open so the orderly could usher Bud inside. "Hi Bud."

"Can you stay for a minute?"

"For a minute," I said, standing next to the door in case I needed an exit.

The orderly helped Bud roll into his room bed. Bud grunted clearly in pain. He waited for the orderly to leave before he said, "I owe you, Dale, and the entire church an apology. I've begged Sarah for forgiveness and need to make the rounds."

"Did you make the rounds to the woman's family who died?"

Bud went silent. I was shocked to see him start to cry. He'd always been a tough guy cowboy type. If he was faking, then he was quite convincing. I wanted to apologize for the comment, but chose not to.

"I—" his crying turned into near hysterics. "I'd do anything to change places with her. I'd do anything to have never done this to begin with. I've sinned against God, I've sinned against my wife, my friends, and the church."

"Sorry Bud, I shouldn't have said that. I just have a lot of baggage when it comes to drunk drivers and death."

His eyes opened in realization. "Your son! Oh Brandon, I forgot."

"I wish I could."

"I can't imagine how much you hate me right now."

"I'm fine," I said. "I care that you've repented, and I care about Sarah."

"I'm already going to see a counselor with Sarah and asked Dale to pair me up with a couple accountability partners. I don't know what else I can do. Tell me what else I can do, Brandon?"

"Sounds like you're starting to do all the right things. The proof will be in the pudding, Bud. It's gonna take people a while to trust you again, especially Sarah."

"I know. How did I ever become so blinded?"

"Sin nature," I said. "I gotta go."

"Will you come by the house after I'm out of here?"

I was general in my response. "I'll see you soon. Take care, Bud."

Out in the hospital parking lot a man with his back turned to me stared into the driver's side window of my truck. My hand instinctively dropped to the appendix holster. Part of me wanted this random person to be trouble. When he turned around I recognized agent Drake from Charlottesville. He was dressed in a navy blue suit and had on a grey fedora.

"Ah, there you are Mr. Hall."

"Agent Drake," I said, removing my hand from under my shirt. He clearly noticed where my hand had been, but didn't say anything. "Don't you clean up nice."

"The wife does say I look handsome in this suit."

He seemed worry free. The antithesis of what I thought a government agent would be like. "What brings you here?"

He looked over at a guy sitting in a blacked-out suburban and raised an open palm to signify he needed five minutes. "You were next on my list of people to talk to." Drake took out a pair of sunglasses and a handkerchief. He breathed on the lenses and started polishing.

"This about the info dump tying Schultz to Antifa?"

He pointed a thumb towards the hospital. "That's why I stopped by here earlier. I know you guys leaked that info, but your buddy didn't give me anything yet."

"He's a good guy who really had nothing to do with this," I said.

Drake finished polishing the sunglasses and put them on. "Based on the info you released to alternative media, you believe Drew Schilling fell for Rebeca Shaw who's an Antifa captain?"

"Yup."

"Walk me through the rest of it."

"Drew Schilling falls for a radicalized girl. Finds out she's using him, and is sleeping with other people, namely Gaspar Schultz. Schilling finds vids of Rebecca and Schultz in bed together on her computer and goes off the deep end threatening to expose her, and her financial backer. And the next thing you know, bingo-bango he's dead."

"What's her motive for using Drew in the first place?"

"If Schultz is funding the group then the motive isn't

money." Drake nodded as if he were a professor who already knew the answer to his own question. "It could only be one thing. To get to Senator Schilling and use his political influence to help sway the country towards open borders, one-world-government, and whatever other socialist utopia Schultz is pushing." Drake kept nodding but added a smile as if he were happy his student had come to the right conclusion. "I'm assuming this incident is a microcosm of Schultz's Svengali approach to DC, and there are other Senators he has sway over."

"Assuming that's all correct," Drake said, "do you think he got to Senator Schilling?"

I pursed my lips showing my neutrality on the subject. "At this point I don't think so, but then again my wife says I'm too trusting. You're thoughts?"

"I'm with you, but we are looking into it."

"Are you gonna arrest Schultz?"

"He technically hasn't done anything wrong," Drake said. "Antifa is not an official terrorist group and we don't have any proof Drew Schilling was murdered. Authorities were too quick to call it an accident, which allowed most of the evidence to disappear, and the rest to become tainted."

"So there's nothing you can do?"

"My optimism for seeing justice with this situation is low. That is, unless you have anything further to add?"

For some reason I couldn't look him in the eye. "Not really."

"Brandon, whatever's going through that brain of yours, you need to talk to me. Schultz is too big for you."

I looked back at the hospital and thought of JT.

"Best thing you can do to protect your friend," Drake said, "is give me anything else you have." I didn't respond. He handed me a card with a cell phone number and non-government email address. "I thought we were becoming friends."

Drake walked away flustered for the first time since I met him. I got in the truck and started it up. I looked down at the card in my hand. He was right, Schultz was beyond me, and I was off the case.

I rolled down the window. "Drake."

He was about to get into the SUV but turned around and walked back in my direction with a smooth saunter, as if he knew I'd give in. I walked out and met him halfway in the parking lot. I reached into my pocket and took out the flash drive JT had given me the other day.

"Here," I said.

"What's this?"

"No idea. I found it on Drew Schilling's computer. It was encrypted. JT broke into it, but found garbled code and what looked like transactions. He said it's useless without a cypher of some sort. It could be nothing."

He took the flash drive. "Or it could be everything. Thank you for trusting me."

We shook hands and I watched as Drake walked back to the waiting SUV. Before he stepped in he turned back and gave me a low thumbs up as if he didn't want any of his cohorts to see. There was nothing I could do with the flash drive. It was in good hands.

SEVENTEEN

For lunch I stopped at a small country store at the end of Main Street for a chicken pesto sandwich and an iced coffee. I sat in the cafe scrolling through a to-do list on my phone to make sure I didn't miss anything that needed to get done while in town. The drive out from Nathalie was a hike so the last thing I needed was to forget something before leaving South Boston. The phone blinked, with the familiar Johnny Cash ringtone following a moment later.

"Tollers, I'm hearing from you an awful lot lately."

"Brandon, I got a strange one for you?"

"Oh what now?"

"Where are you today?"

"In town, why?"

"There's an interstate prison transport going from Richmond to a facility in southern Florida."

"I heard the weather's nice in that part of Florida in the winter."

"Justin Damascus is part of the transport."

I hadn't heard that name spoken out loud since the

judge sentenced him to prison for killing Jonah. I looked down at what was left of my sandwich and suddenly felt that chicken pesto was no longer one of my favorite sandwiches.

"You there Brandon?"

"Yeah."

"He's being held over for two hours in Halifax prison today." Tollers paused before adding, "You once said that you needed to forgive the man face-to-face."

"I did," I reminded myself.

"This may be the only time in your life you get the chance. I can meet you there if you'd like?"

At some point I had left the restaurant and now found myself behind the wheel of my truck. "I don't know if I can do it, Tollers?"

"I'll be there."

A million excuses why I should not go ran through my mind. They were all garbage reasons. I was being a coward. "Give me ten minutes."

I started to call Annie but tossed the phone aside. She didn't need to see the man face-to-face in order to forgive him. For some reason I did though. The eight-minute drive to Halifax felt like seconds. I parked across from the courthouse in front of an antique store and sat in the truck. My heart was beating like crazy. I removed my appendix holster and moved to place the gun under the truck's bench seat, but I felt like I couldn't let go of it. I gripped the pistol's handle like it was a lifeline tethering me to a safety buoy at sea. I knew this buoy was my sin nature wanting to inflict harm on this man. I had to take a step of faith or I'd never let go of the anger.

"Don't leave me, Lord," I whispered, and let go of the gun, and got out of the truck.

The next few minutes were a blur of images, sounds,

smells, and feelings. There was a guard with heavy cologne who took my wallet, cell phone, flashlight, and pocket knife. Someone else frisked me. There was an X-ray machine to walk through. A hallway with a fluorescent light bulb flickering. A heavy door that was automatically opened by someone out of sight. After passing through another door I stood facing Tollers and Dale in a small room with candy vending machines.

Tollers was in his full Sheriff's outfit. "You allowed to be here while on duty?"

"Coffee break."

I shook Dale's hand. "He called you too?"

Dale pulled me into a hug. "I wanted to be here."

"Okay, so how do I do this?"

Tollers pointed to a black door. "Step through there and you'll sit in a booth with a phone facing a glass partition."

"Just like the movies huh?"

"Just like the movies."

Dale said a quick prayer asking God to give me strength. They both patted me on the back, a morbid reminder that they could go no farther with me on this journey. I took a breath and stepped to the door. A dull buzzer went off signifying someone unlocked it. I stepped through and the door automatically closed behind me. In front of me were three alcoves each with a wooden stool divided by MDF partitions for privacy. A thick glass wall ran down the middle of the counters separating the prisoner side from the civilian side.

A single prisoner in an orange suit sat opposite me in the middle glassed alcove. He was skinnier than I remembered and now wore a goatee. He was mid thirties, but looked like he was fifty. Justin Damascus reached for the phone on his side of the glass. I remember the tattoos on his arm. A naked lady, a swear word, and someone's name with a date. I sat down and picked up my phone.

Before I could speak he started talking with a thick southern accent I remember despising. "You know I was barely over the blood alcohol limit when I was arrested. Had the judge not labeled this a class five felony I might be out by now."

"You were well over the blood alcohol limit and this wasn't your first offense," I said, trying to keep my tone even. "I came here with the distant hope that I'd hear some contrition on your part rather than excuses."

"Are you kidding me? My life's been ruined."

"My son is dead!" I shouted, tears forming against my will. "My son is dead," I repeated in a softer tone.

I could see his mind racing as if he were a salesman facing a client who didn't want to purchase his product. "I regret what happened, but if I could get you, or your wife, to write a letter to the DA I think I could make a case to argue that I've changed enough to—"

"I forgive you," I whispered.

"What was that?"

"I came here to tell you that I forgive you," I repeated, and hung up the phone.

Justin Damascus stood on the other side of the glass giving me the finger and screaming what I knew were obscenities as spittle appeared on the glass. I took one last look at the man who killed my son. For a moment, I wondered if I were staring at a reflection in a mirror rather than through a piece glass. That same unrepentant murderer was inside all of us, but it was as if God had taken the grotesque sinful creature that was once inside me, ripped it out, and stuffed it onto the other side of a clear prison wall where it could never hurt me again.

A prison guard stepped from the shadows and threw

Justin to the ground. I left the room and fell to my knees in front of Dale and Tollers. I had no energy left even to stand. Both of them knelt down and let me cry for what felt like an hour. I no longer wanted to kill the man who killed my son, but the painful longing to hold my boy was still there. It would always be there.

Dale helped me over to a chair while Tollers got me a water from one of the vending machines. "Did I ever tell you guys how much I love you?"

"We love you too, buddy," Tollers said. "We're here for you."

Dale added. "You're gonna be healing from this for the rest of your life and we'll be with you every step."

"I can't have you guys—"

"You can't, and won't, do this alone."

A short while later we exited the building and it was as if I had just been released from prison. The sun seemed stronger and I picked up the scent of fresh cut flowers from an open door to a small organic market. My two friends followed as I wandered into the store. They hovered like I was going to pass out. I picked up a bouquet of flowers for Annie, and poured myself a cup of organic coffee from a self-serve counter.

"You okay, Brandon?"

"I'm good," I said. "Tollers?"

"I'm here?"

"There a prison minister where Justin is going?"

"I'm sure."

"Can you put in a request and ask him to pay a visit to Mr. Damascus once he gets there. I'd appreciate it."

"Consider it done."

Tollers and Dale each got a cup of coffee and joined me on a bench outside as the pedestrians went by on their daily business. I watched as both old and young passed, wondering what sorrows and burdens each of them carried? It seemed like only a few minutes passed before I was saying goodbye to Dale and Tollers. We hugged some more and cried together never once laughing at each other for the perceived masculine weakness. A weakness all believers knew was, in fact, strength.

Back in the truck I called Annie. She knew something was wrong by my tone. "You okay, sweetie?"

"I just called to say how much I love you."

"Love you too," she said. "What's wrong? I can tell something's wrong?"

"Relax. I was just calling to tell you that we're going to be okay."

Annie giggled. "Gee thanks. Something you're not telling me?"

"I sometimes forget the world isn't on my shoulders, and that God has our back."

"Amen. Are you sure you're okay?"

"I'm going to be fine. We're going to be fine."

"When you coming home?"

"I got one more stop while I'm in town."

Some day in the distant future I would tell her about my meeting with Justin Damascus.

* * *

IT WAS AROUND five p.m. when I pulled into a long dirt driveway in Scottsburg. It led to a five-acre lot with a dozen trailers spaced out in no particular order. Chickens ran across the dirt path in front of my truck. I pulled up to the one of last trailers. Colt sat on the front steps dressed in the same denim overalls he had on when I first met him in back in Virgilina. He still wore no shirt on underneath. The young guy he spoke with was also bearded with darker hair. I assumed he was one of Colt's brothers. I got out of the truck and the young man left Colt's side to wander past me without a word to inspect my F250.

"You got a 460 or 390 in this?" he said.

"390," I said.

He spit dip near my tire. "Edlebrock carb?"

"Yup."

He pursed his lips and nodded like I had passed some unannounced test.

Colt got up from the steps and walked over to shake my hand. He pointed to my beardless face with his other hand. "Mr Hall, so weird to see you without your man-card on your face."

"Please call me Brandon."

"Oh no, you're a real PI," he said in mock sarcasm. "I gotta treat you with respect."

The other man turned to me. "You're a Private Investigator? Ever shoot someone?"

"Moss, git inside. Momma wants a girl to help her peel those potatoes for dinner."

"Shut up."

"Go on now, son, before I tell Mr. Hall you still suck your thumb in bed at night."

"Shut up."

"That all you got? C'mon now."

Moss stormed into the trailer and slammed the screen door behind him. I heard him call for his momma and start complaining how Colt was picking on him again. I tried not to laugh.

Colt thumbed towards the trailer. "He does suck his thumb you know."

I laughed. "I'm sorry for the way we left things back at the garage."

"I apologize as well," he said. "Drew was like a brother to me and it's been hard to deal with the loss."

"I should have been more understanding."

"Forget it." He motioned for me to follow him. "C'mon, let me give you the tour."

We walked the dirt driveway and Colt pointed to each of the trailers we passed saying this was his uncle's, aunt's, or cousin's. His entire extended family lived on this land. He spoke with pride and seemed blissfully unaware of what the US culture thought about trailer parks, and those who lived in them. It was clear he loved his family as he waved to each of the relatives who were outside.

We stopped at the first trailer in the lot. "This is grannie's place," he said, walking up to a screen door and knocking. "She's a real pistol."

An elderly woman no taller than five feet, and all of ninety pounds, came to the door. She had thick glasses hanging off the end of her nose. "How's my baby," she said, coming out to kiss Colt on the upper arm, which was as high as she could reach. She slid her arm through his.

Colt pointed to me. "Grannie, this is Mr. Hall."

"My grandson giving you the tour of the compound?"

"Yes Ma'am."

"I'm sorry it's a mess," she said, turning to Colt. "We need to let Auntie Anette know if your friend is staying for dinner?"

"I'm good thank you," I said.

She pushed me aside and shouted. "Hey Anette, that smell's coming in my kitchen."

We turned to face the next trailer. Out front another elderly woman had just chopped the head off a chicken. The headless animal ran in circles for a few seconds before flopping on the ground. The woman wiped a butcher knife on a soiled apron before wiping her brow with the back of her hand.

"Anette?" Grannie shouted again.

"I heard ya." She pointed at me with the bloody knife. "That boy coming to dinner?"

Before I could say no again, Grannie shouted. "Yes he's coming to dinner."

Anette nodded and kicked the severed chicken head under a bush. She pulled up the body of the bird and started plucking feathers.

"Guess you're staying for dinner," Colt said.

Grannie tugged on Colt's arm. "Tell Anette to have Angus get another bird."

"Auntie Anette," Colt shouted, "Grannie says to tell Angus to get another bird for dinner."

Anette nodded and put her bloody hand up to the side of her mouth. "Angus, we need another bird for dinner."

A voice called back from somewhere behind her trailer. "Okay momma."

There was a trail of smoke coming from the direction of Angus' voice. I sniffed the air to pick up the scent of burning hickory and something else. I turned to Colt.

"Moonshine," he said. "Cousin Angus still holds to family traditions."

Four picnic tables were pushed together to make one single long line. Twenty people came out to eat under a string of dangling lights from surrounding oak trees. The food was better than any fancy restaurant in Halifax County. There was fresh salad, fresh meat, and fresh homemade bread. I sat in between Colt and his brothers enjoying the meal. Colt and Wesson picked on Moss who was the youngest brother and babied by all the elders. A couple of young children who kept getting up from the table were shouted at, and a few ended up with smacked bottoms.

After dinner I pulled Colt aside. "Aren't you even curious why I came out here?"

"I figured you'd tell me, but we needed to break bread first."

"You're an interesting guy."

"I'll take that as a compliment," Colt said. "So why you here?"

"What have you been doing for work since Drew's passing?"

"Not much," he said. "We do some auto work, but there's a lot of guys in Halifax County who can work on cars. And working on a race car is a prestigious job. It's doubtful me, and my brother's, will ever get on another team."

"I came to offer you some side work. You interested?"

"Does a bear poop in the woods?"

"I need someone to keep an eye on my buddy, and his business for a week or so."

"He a moonshiner? Because I gave up those ways—"

"Nothing like that. My buddy got jumped at work from some misguided Antifa kids. He ended up in the hospital and I want to make sure he's gonna be okay when he goes back to work."

"Sure thing. Me and the boys can handle any little college kid."

"I don't want to stir up any trouble. If anyone shows up to cause trouble, I'd rather you deter, and not engage."

"Punks have no idea about what their daddy's fought, and died, for. Kids think the Constitution's a piece of toilet paper. Don't even realize that every day we step on the fourth amendment with the surveillance cameras everywhere."

Two things ran through my mind. The first was how I pegged Colt as being a simpleton redneck, and the second was how I had to struggle to remember that the fourth amendment was about illegal search and seizure.

"When do we start?"

"How's tomorrow? Do you want to discuss rates?"

"As I said, we broke bread together. I know you now. I trust you now. Whatever you see fit to be fair is fine with me, and my brothers."

EIGHTEEN

THE NEXT MORNING I TOOK A FOUR-WHEELER OVER TO MY parent's cabin. They sat on the porch drinking coffee with a Bible open on a table between them. My dad was dressed in his hunting outfit with his rifle resting against the cabin beside them.

"Morning," I said.

"Want a cup of coffee?"

"I'm good."

"I'll get you a mug." Mom got up and went inside.

"Mom, I'm good—"

"Always said that woman dotes on you too much." Dad pointed to the sky. "Nothin like a clear morning in Southern Virginia. My joints tell me it's gonna be nice and warm. Wanna come for a few hours on the hunt?"

"I can't, but thanks."

Mom came out with a hot mug of coffee. She had made it just the way I liked it. "Want something to eat?"

"I'm good—"

"I'll get you something," She said, going back inside.

I threw up my hands and my father rolled his eyes.

"Something we need to discuss?" Dad said, clearly picking up on why I was there.

"Daddy, I need you to keep an extra eye peeled. This case I've been working on has turned sour."

"The Schilling boy?"

"Yeah. A friend of mine who was helping me on the case was almost murdered the other night."

"What happened?"

"I think I've stirred up a hornets nest. A hornet who happens to have deep pockets, and no morality. You and mom are camouflaged back here in the cabin, but just in case I want you to carry a gun with you for the next few days." He reached for his black powder rifle resting behind him. "No daddy, I mean a real gun."

"This is a real gun. Something your ancestors used to defend their homes, and provide food for their families."

"You know what I mean." I pulled out my Smith and Wesson from the appendix holster. "A gun that holds multiple rounds. You ever hear of something called a magazine?"

He waved his hand. "Phaw. Old tech was good enough for your ancestors, and's good enough for me."

I put my gun away. "You drive me nuts."

He smiled and took a sip of his coffee.

Mom came out with French toast covered in syrup and powdered sugar. "Here."

"Mom, I said I was fine."

"Told you woman," my dad said. "You spoiled this boy. It's amazing he still doesn't wet his bed."

I took a bite of the breakfast. The butter and maple syrup blended perfectly with the thick pieces of homemade cinnamon bread she used for the French toast.

"I'm gonna have to jog ten miles to burn this off," I said, my mouth full of food, "You're killing me mom."

Dad started polishing his rifle with a handkerchief. I tapped the butt of the rifle with my fork. "This conversation up for debate?"

"Nope," he said.

I took another bite of the French toast and turned to mom. "Your husband's one stubborn man."

She kissed his head. "Yes, he is."

"Don't know how you do it."

My dad took her hand and kissed it. I said a silent prayer for the dark cloud God had removed from over my dad.

On the drive back to the farmhouse I saw a brown mass in the main pasture. I dropped my sunglasses from my head onto my nose and gunned the throttle of the four-wheeler. The mass quickly morphed into the shape of a cow. The lump in her belly told me it was the last heifer. I jumped the split rail fence and ran over to the fallen animal. She was dead, but still warm to the touch.

"Oh no, no, no, no, no," I kept repeating, mad at myself for not checking on her sooner.

I ran my hand over her belly and outlined the protrusion. I took out my stockman pocket knife and ran my hand over her belly again. For the next few minutes I cut, tore, and pulled. When I finally got the calf out he was dead as well. I cradled the limp animal in my bloody hands. Another dead child.

When I got home Annie was at the kitchen table with her face in her hands like she had a migraine.

"Oh no, what's wrong?" I said.

Without looking up she pointed towards the stairs leading to the second floor. "I had an argument with Emily." She looked up at me and put her hand to her mouth when she saw my bloody clothes. "Brandon, what happened? Are you hurt?"

I looked down at my blood-stained shirt and jeans. "I'm fine. The last heifer died giving birth."

"The calf?"

I shook my head no.

She came over with a dish towel and wiped specs of blood from my face before kissing me. "I'm sorry."

I started to cry again and laughed at the same time. "I don't get it. I can't stop crying lately."

"We both know it's not the heifer," she said, giving me a hug.

After a quick shower and change of clothes I came back out into the kitchen. "Care to tell me what happened with you and Emily?"

"I told her she could go to your parent's house for the day, but it wasn't good enough. She wants to sleep over."

"And you still aren't ready to let go?" I said.

Annie tried to say something but got choked up. After a couple deep breaths she said, "I can't yet. I just can't. I keep thinking of Jonah and—"

From upstairs I could hear the faint weeping of Emily. I took both of my wife's hands in mine. "Annie, tell me who's in control."

"God," she said.

"You've reminded me before of Romans eight-twenty-eight."

She said, "He works for the good of those who love him, who are called according to his purpose."

"And your ten-year-old daughter is upstairs crying because we won't let her stay overnight at her grandparents' house, which is next door to us. You're being fearful."

Annie turned her gaze towards the stairs then back to me. "I can do this."

"You can do this," I reiterated.

I led her up the old narrow staircase. There were two

bedrooms on the second floor. The first had been Jonah's, but after his death neither of us could stand to pass by his room to reach Emily. Annie was adamant that we were to leave his room as is, so we tried keeping the door shut for a few months, but we still passed by it. In the end we swapped Jonah's room with Emily's placing her bedroom first.

I placed everything in Jonah's new bedroom the way it had been before he died. I knew it was unhealthy, but at that point Annie was bordering on a nervous breakdown. I repainted the bedroom to look like Jonah's, and even reassembled the crib the way it had been. Annie agreed that we would leave it this way for one more year and then turn it into a guest room.

Several nights I found her sleeping in the rocking chair she used to nurse Jonah. She usually held one of his blankets up to her nose. I could tell she was trying to inhale the remnant scent from the blanket that still held a minutia of Jonah's baby smell. I hoped she would hold up to her end of the deal when the time came for me to disassemble everything?

Emily's new room was painted a light shade of lavender. She had a full sized wrought iron bed with matelassé white bedding, a distressed white bookshelf and matching desk. Annie got her an oversized white lounge chair for window reading. When we knocked on the open door Emily was in the chair gazing out the large window at the front yard like a prisoner longing for freedom.

"Honey," Annie said.

"I don't want to talk to you," she said lifting a book up.

"Sweetie, just listen to what your mom has to say," I said.

Emily kept staring at her book but I knew she wasn't reading.

"I'm sorry," Annie said.

"For?" Emily snapped.

"For being over protective." Annie started crying. "I just can't imagine what I'd do if anything happened to you. I love you so much and—"

I pulled Annie in close as her crying turned to sobbing. Emily put her book down clearly frustrated that her mom's crying was an ace card she could no longer be mad at. She came over and joined in the group hug.

"I'm not a baby, mom."

"I know sweetie. Please forgive me."

"I do."

"Your mom and I discussed this and—" I turned to Annie who was the one who needed to say the words.

"And you can stay overnight at your grandparents," Annie finished.

"I can?" Emily hugged us tighter. "I promise I'll be home after breakfast in the morning."

"It's fine," I said. "Have fun."

Emily grabbed a rucksack and started filling it with books and her pajamas.

"Don't forget your toothbrush," Annie said.

"And clean underpants," I added, in an annoying parent voice.

* * *

AROUND FOUR O'CLOCK MY phone pinged while I did paperwork at the kitchen table. I opened a text to see a picture from Colt. His three brothers held two skinny white males tied up with cowboy ropes outside Cozy Cavern Self Storage. They had handkerchiefs around their mouths and the brothers stood around them like they were prize large mouth bass they had just caught. The next picture showed cop cars out front of the business and Colt getting yelled at.

I showed the picture of the hogtied kids to Annie. "These college kids are amateurs," I bragged.

"But they're full of anger, which makes them ten times as dangerous as normal criminals."

"I don't know. Most of these kids have lived privileged lives. They all got participation trophies and were told how special they were every day. It's hard time to take them seriously."

"Odd," Annie said, looking at her phone.

"What's up?"

"I'm trying to text your mom to check in on Emily, but I have no cell signal."

My cell signal went dead as well. I turned the phone off then back on. There was still no signal. "Odd? We both have no signal, but we have separate cell phone carriers." I picked up our hard line phone and it was dead as well. "What the heck?"

A hum started to emanate throughout the house. I wandered through the living room towards the front hallway.

Annie called back from the living room. "Maybe, we got hit with one of those EMP's your friend JT talks about?"

"Don't even joke," I said.

As I approached the front door the hum turned into the sound of a revving engine. I pulled the curtain aside from the small glass panel in the front door. A white van spun its wheels in the front yard. It was stuck, launching mud everywhere due to the leach field failure.

"What the—"

It took me a second to realize the driver was the kid from Charlottesville with the dreadlocks. He saw me in the window and grinned. The truck stopped revving. My mind raced like a slot machine. When it stopped, all the numbers lined up, and my military training kicked in.

"Who's tearing up our yard?" Annie said, coming up behind me.

I grabbed Annie and moved her back towards the living room. "Move."

"Brandon, what are you doing—"

Even with my back to the door I could see the flash of light pour into the living room from the front door window behind us. A second later the sound of an explosion rocked the house. Everything turned upside down. Wood, glass, heat, and smoke washed over us as I fell on top of Annie. She screamed and I tried not to scream when something stuck in the back of my leg.

NINETEEN

I KEPT ONE HAND OVER ANNIE'S HEAD AND HAD MY GUN out. There were seven in the clip leaving one in the chamber. It took a few moments for Annie's pleas to register through the buzzing in my ears. Unable to hear what she was saying I kept repeating that it was an IED and to stay down. I reached around and pulled out a splinter of wood about six inches long from my hamstring. The pressure and pain subsided allowing me to crawl back towards the hallway.

The entire front of the house was gone. It was as if some giant reached down and, in one swipe, took away the front porch and first floor exterior wall. The master bathroom attached to our bedroom was exposed spraying water into what was left of the smoldering hallway. Out on the lawn the van was a flaming shell. The young man, who only moments earlier, was laughing at me had blown himself into eternity.

I rushed back into the living room. "You okay?"

Annie was wiping her face and coughing. "Yeah. You?"

"Stay down" I said, crawling into our bedroom.

Out the window another white van tore into the driveway. The side door slid open and a bunch of people in masks stepped out holding rifles and handguns. I counted six and a driver, all of whom appeared young from their posture and size.

"Lord help us," I whispered.

Annie came up beside me and handed me her gun which was a .380 version of mine. The kids were starting towards the back door. I lifted the window and proceeded to unload the entire mag into the engine block of the van to let them know not to come inside. They scattered around the yard.

"Got another clip?" I said.

In the jeep glove compartment.

I tossed the gun aside and moved to the bedroom entrance with my Smith and Wesson aimed down what was left of my front hallway. I remembered my extra mag was in my truck as well. An amateur mistake. Unless the authorities showed up, or God intervened with a miracle, I'd have to hit almost a hundred percent of the attackers with each bullet. A near mathematical impossibility. They had rifles and could stay out of my handgun's range. Annie was calm, and looked as if she had been through this before. I was worried she'd snapped.

"You okay?"

She grinned as if she were only annoyed. "This is nothing compared to giving birth to a son, and then having to bury him."

A moment later she took off into the kitchen.

"Annie, get back here."

She grabbed Jonah's lever action rifle off the top of the refrigerator and a box of .22 ammo out of a drawer. She came back into the bedroom and started loading the rifle.

"Give me the rifle," I said.

Her stoic face was that of a mamma bear about to protect her cubs. "No" she said. "This is my home too."

"I love you."

A flurry of gunfire resounded outside. Bullets rained on what was left of the front of the house. Some of the bullets penetrated the remnant exterior front wall and the secondary wall of our bedroom flying over our heads.

I looked down at the gun in my hand then up to the eight foot high ceiling. "Lord, we need help."

A thundering boom outside stood apart from the other noises of modern gunfire. It was a familiar noise. The loud crack of a black powder rifle. I rushed on all fours from the hallway back over to the bedroom window.

Outside, my father was just tossing aside a rifle and taking cover behind the oak tree Emily's tree house was built in. He was still in his full leather hunting attire, with a powder horn and rucksack criss-crossed over his chest. In the corner of the muddy front lawn a guy lay wailing and clutching his stomach. His mask was off revealing a young man no older than twenty.

My father swung a second rifle from his shoulder into firing position. He cocked the hammer and aimed at another masked male who stood next to the van trying to unjam a modern AR rifle. My father fired, and a moment later the guy was thrown back into the van like he'd been hit by a truck. My dad moved forward and used the butt end of the rifle to knock a female holding an AR-15 onto her backside. He was fast, and looked like a frontier character from one of the childhood stories he once read to me.

"Pick up one of their rifles you stubborn old man," I said to myself.

As if he heard me, he paused over an AR lying on the ground and tossed his empty rifle down next to it. He pulled out a black powder pistol and continued towards the house. Someone from behind a wood pile stood and fired off from a revolver. They couldn't have been more than twenty feet from him but missed every shot as he zig zagged like a wild animal.

Annie handed the rifle over. I started unloading at two guys hiding behind my truck. At a minimum my gunfire would keep them at bay allowing my father time to get to the house. The two retreated from my truck back behind a wood pile.

My father unloaded the pistol at the person behind the far woodpile and stepped over another modern rifle. Instead, he stuffed the pistol into his belt and pulled the hunting knife and tomahawk. He continued to run in a crouched zig zag pattern into the front yard. The chubby bearded red head male from Charlottesville got out of the van's driver's seat holding a revolver.

My father rushed him. Before the red head guy could raise his gun my father put a shoulder into his chest knocking him into the van and onto the ground. The chubby man rolled over and raised the handgun. In one motion my dad used the tomahawk to finish him off. The back door to the van burst open and a male wearing a vest wrapped with explosives sprinted past my dad towards the house.

"Annie get behind the bed," I yelled, unloading rounds as fast as I could at the strapped man rushing the house. I grazed his leg but he kept hobbling towards the house.

In one motion my father threw his tomahawk end-over-end striking the man square in the back. The blow must have shorted the vest trigger mechanism and the man exploded with a thunderous noise launching my father back into the van where he rolled over and stopped moving next to the dead red-haired male.

I handed the rifle to Annie. "Reload and keep shooting."

"Where you going?"

"To get daddy."

Annie quoted Psalm 23 as I rushed towards the back door. I burst through the door reciting the verses to myself. "I will fear no evil, for you are with me; your rod and your staff they comfort me."

I ran around the side of the house. The two men behind the wood pile were sideways to me. I fired off three rounds from my gun splintering wood in front of them. They took off towards the road. I rounded the front yard and fired off a round at the other far wood pile that I knew someone was still behind it. Seconds later I had my father cradled in my arms. He looked up at me and smiled.

"You stubborn old man," I said. "What were you thinking?"

"That I'd die if something happened to my son."

"Daddy, you drive me nuts. Can you move?"

"Negative, I think I broke my ankle. I need you to get back inside."

"I'm not leaving you."

"If you love me you'll get back to safety," he said. "I won't be able to handle it if something happens to you."

"I'm staying here, daddy."

He started to cry. Not out of fear, but something had broken inside him and he held onto me like a newborn needing its mother. "I love you so much, Brandon." He looked skyward, "Lord, protect my boy."

"Love you too old man," I said, trying to remember how many rounds I had left in my gun. Someone fired off at us.

It hit the side of the van with a loud ping. It was the person from the far wood pile again. I dragged my dad around to the front of the van to give us cover. The firing continued. I rolled out from behind the truck and fired off four rounds from my gun knocking logs off the top of the pile forcing them to duck down. The gun clicked empty. I looked around trying to find a weapon. There were a few rifles on the ground but not within reach. I prepared to run for one of them. A bullet exploded the mud in front of my first step and I was forced back next to my dad. Without a word, he handed me his hunting knife and started to reload his black powder pistol. I held the knife with the blade tucked down towards my forearm. Annie opened fire from the bedroom window but had no angle.

"What's the plan?" My father asked.

"Pray," I said.

"I think the Lord's forgotten me," he said pouring powder into the gun barrel.

"Nonsense," I said. "You were an answer to my prayer a minute ago."

More bullets hit the side of the van. This time above our heads. I turned and saw the two guys I'd chased away down the driveway coming back to face us. We were exposed to them. Annie fired off two rounds keeping them back. I had to get to a rifle. My father leaned over and fired off the single shot from his pistol forcing the two men back down the driveway.

A shadow stepped out from the side of the truck. I turned as the figure took off a mask. It was the brunette from the Antifa rally, Rebecca Shaw. She held .357 revolver in her petite hand. A snarl covered her gorgeous face.

"You're stubborn man to kill. If I'd believed in God I'd say he's watching over you."

Behind her the sky was dark as if it were about to rain.

She lifted the revolver and pulled the trigger. It clicked empty. She laughed and pulled the trigger again with a click. It was a deliberate move to torture me. Before I could move with the knife in my hand she pulled a smaller revolver up from her left hand and fired it over my head into the van. The sound brought the buzzing back to my ears.

"You know," she said, blowing on the end of the gun barrel like some cheesy B grade western outlaw. "The night of the race I begged Drew to take me back just so I could be there."

"So you could plant the explosive," I said.

"I could've had anyone in my group plant it. I wanted to be there to see him die. You know, I thought I heard him scream once from the car when the explosion went off," she giggled, leveling the gun to face me. "I only wish he could have suffered a little longer."

"You're a sick young lady," my father said.

"You wanna see sick" she said. "Your boy is gonna get a bullet in the head and I'm gonna make sure you live long enough to watch it."

From the road the beautiful colors of blue and red flashed to life against the dark canopy of trees and sky. A moment later the sound of sirens joined in. The two guys in the driveway ran onto the street to face the incoming black SUV's with rifles raised.

"There's one road in and out of this property, Rebecca," I said.

She didn't seem phased. "At least I'll complete my mission."

My dad pleaded for her to stop which only seemed to feed her happiness. She cocked the hammer on the revolver and I shut my eyes. I reminded myself that I was saved in Christ, and that I would see Jonah in a few moments. The familiar sound of gunfire went off. I waited for the pain that I thought would follow, but instead I heard Rebecca scream. She dropped both guns and clutched her left arm. Blood pouring out of her shoulder. A moment later I realized the familiar sound of gunfire came from Jonah's rifle. Rebecca started crying and dropped to her knees revealing Annie standing behind her holding Jonah's rifle. She kicked both the handguns away from Rebecca.

"Momma always said never send a man to do a woman's job," Annie said.

Annie handed me the rifle. The moment I touched the rifle a shiver of warmth run up my arm. It was at that moment I realized the rifle I had once purchased to give to my son had saved both me and my dad. In death, my son played a part in saving his dad and grandpa.

On the street the two kids opened fire at the oncoming SUV's. One of the trucks swerved to a stop but the other continued on and struck both of the young men knocking them to either side of the vehicle. The SUV stopped and six agents between the two vehicles sprinted out and disarmed the bodies.

Rebecca was still crying and started to crawl away. Annie walked over and put her boot on the girl's back. Rebecca screamed in either pain, frustration, or both. She wagged her face back and forth like a child whose rattle had been taken away. Whether on purpose, or by accident, she slammed her face in the filthy mud of the leach field.

"Quiet young lady," Annie said.

Two of the agents rushed into the yard with guns drawn. I pulled Annie behind me to stand in front of both her and my dad in case one of the agents thought we were the bad guys. I handed the rifle back to Annie and held my hands up. To my surprise my friend from Charlottesville approached with a kevlar vest on and gun drawn.

"You okay Mr. Hall?" Drake said.

"Yeah," me and my father answered at the same time.

"You can lower the rifle now Mrs. Hall."

Annie lowered the rifle. A moment later she dropped to her knees next to me and started crying.

"You did good baby," I said, kneeling down to hold her. "You did real good."

More sirens and lights lit up the dark sky like fireworks. EMT's red lights joined in. One of the agents tried to take the gun from Annie but she ignored him.

"They're all fine," Drake said. "Go into the house and sweep the yard."

The agent complied and Drake kneeled down to join us in the mud as an EMT tech worked on my dad's leg. The other EMT's spread out to triage the bodies around the yard. A mist started to fall and within moments it turned to rain.

"Finally," I said, looking skyward.

The EMT tech winced. "I think you got an issue with your septic leach field, sir."

"Thank God," I said.

"Huh?"

I pointed to the shell of the other van. "Had the leach field not failed that van would have driven right up to our front door and killed both me and my wife. Instead it only took out the front portion of the house."

"Romans eight twenty-eight," Annie said.

"He works for good."

As if to reaffirm her statement something drew my line of sight up to the second floor where Emily's room was. "Look," I said to Annie.

Emily's bedroom window had been shot out and the

outside wall around it was littered with bullet holes. This was exactly where her reading chair was positioned. Had Annie not trusted God and let Emily go to my parents, then my daughter would have been in her room and more than likely killed.

"Romans eight twenty-eight," I repeated back to her.

EPILOGUE

I WISH I COULD SAY EVERYONE LIVED HAPPILY EVER AFTER, but there were too many who didn't live. From Bubba's son Jordan, to Drew Schilling, to the misled youths who followed a political system that told them anarchy and violence were the answer.

A week after the shootout what media outlets covered the story on Antifa had moved on, but we were left with half a home. Contractors were put on hold as my insurance company refused to payout for terrorist bombing damage.

My cell phone rang as I readjusted a tarp over a gaping hole in the house.

"Brandon Hall speaking?"

"Mr. Hall."

"Agent Drake, you're calling to tell me the government wants to help rebuild my house?"

"Insurance giving you a hard time?

"Well, IED's aren't covered under my policy."

"I can make a couple phone calls—"

"Thanks but it will work itself out," I said, half wanting to take him up on the offer. "What can I do for you?"

"I wanted to let you know that I found out what Drew Schilling was killed over.

"I thought we both knew why he was killed over. Those pics and Schultz funding Antifa—"

"Schultz is a sociopathic narcissist. I knew there had to be something motivating Drew Schillings murder beyond nude pics tying Schultz to this young girl and Antifa."

"Like what?"

"We all thought the clash in August of 2017 in Charlottesville was between Antifa and the Klan right?"

"It was."

"That's what Schultz and the mainstream media would have you believe, but the flash drive you gave me said otherwise.

"You broke the code?"

"Yup,"

"And?"

"Schultz was funding both groups."

The only thing I could say was, "Why?"

"Mr. Hall, the devil doesn't care about fascism, socialism, marxism, or racism, or black lives, or white lives, or blue lives. He likes chaos, war, and death. If he can whip up one group against another to cause trouble he doesn't care. It all serves the same end."

"Not much in this world surprises me Drake, but you just rocked my world."

"Schultz doesn't realize that he also serves a god. He doesn't realize that in his quest for a one world government, open borders, and anarchy that he's going to be devoured."

I sat down on a piece of foundation and looked out over the devastation in my front yard. "This high level stuff is too much for me. How do you operate in this swamp on a daily basis and keep your sanity?"

"Joy comes from the Lord, not this world," Drake said. "Needless to say I've seen a lot of burnout in my line of work."

"I'm glad there are people like you in the world who do what you do. I just want to go back to my boring life on the farm."

"I don't blame you," he said. "I spoke with the Sheriff's department and they're going to beef up patrols around there for the next few weeks. I think the high profile shootout has actually made you safer. I'd still watch your six for the time being.

An old F350 pulling a dirty fifth wheel RV turned from the road onto my driveway. "I think I'm good," I said. "Talk soon okay?"

"Be safe, Mr. Hall. Remember, you're my new friend and I don't want to lose you."

Colt pulled up and spit dip out the driver's window. "Where you want us parked, boss?"

I pointed out back towards the barn. "Out there. I think I'm being overly cautious, but having some people I trust onsite for a few days can't hurt."

Next to Colt his brother Moss held up a shotgun. "We gotcha back, Mr. Hall."

Colt turned to his brother. "Sit down son, before you shoot your eye out. I'd be riding solo if momma didn't say I had to take you."

"Shut up," Moss said.

"You shut up," Colt responded, putting the truck in drive. Before pulling away he winked to let me know he was toying with his little brother.

No sooner had Colt pulled around back than a familiar limo pulled into the driveway. Senator Schilling stepped out dressed in khakis and a highly starched white button down shirt. I walked down to meet him.

"Senator, what brings you here?"

He looked at the devastation to the main house and property. "Brandon, I'm beyond sorry for what happened."

"I lost a house. You lost a boy," I said. "I can live with my end."

"Thanks for saying that. I just want you to know that I've taken up the fight to bring Schultz down. Your shootout brought to light the evils of this man. The media and government can no longer look the other way."

"What about the safety of your family?"

"I wish I could say you woke me up and I found the courage, but the fact is Schultz is on the run. Now's the time to strike. It's tactical move rather than bravery."

"Regardless, you're doing the right thing."

"Thanks to your work."

"So what brings you out here, Senator?"

"To offer you a job."

"Huh?"

"I've hired my own security firm to watch my family. I don't suppose I could hire you to head up the group? I'd pay you top dollar?"

"Thanks but my home is here." I pointed to the house. "Or what's left of it."

"I figured you'd say that, but thought I'd at least try."

There was a crash out back followed by shouting. The Senator stiffened as if he were nervous.

"That would be my security firm setting up shop. Not as polished as yours I'm sure."

The Senator started walking towards the front of the house. "I've reviewed the final bill you sent in to my assistant and I'm going to increase the payment."

"Sir, I can't take a handout—"

"I'm not giving you money." He looked at his watch then towards the road. "Bout time," he said pointing to four brand new pickup trucks stacked with lumber coming down the road like a line of military Humvees. Without turning from the trucks he said, "I made my fortune in construction and my brother still runs the family business." He waved the trucks into the driveway.

"Senator, I can't—"

"There's no way I'm taking no for an answer," he said. "I owe you more than you can imagine." He turned and looked me in the eye. A genuine smile on his face for the first time since I met him. "The question is do you want the house back the way it was, or do you need any adjustments. A second story deck? A longer porch?"

I started to choke up. Not about money or the gift, but just how faithful God was. He met my every need so long as I trusted in him. I managed to get out the words, "The way it was will be fine, sir."

A man about my age came up and shook the Senator's hand. "What's the word, sir?"

The Senator thumbed my way. "Whatever this man needs, you do. Stay as long as needed. Did you file the paperwork for the permit?"

"Yes sir. We can start staging and demo as needed until the permit's approved."

"Atta boy, Lex." He put out his hand. "Brandon, if you ever need me don't hesitate to call. And if you ever make it to DC please come see me."

"I try to stay away from that place."

He smiled. "Ironically, so do I."

A LOOK AT THE DISMAL SWAMP: A BRANDON HALL MYSTERY

John Theo Jr. delivers a fast-paced mystery pulled from current news headlines.

Life has drifted back to a quiet routine on the Hall's Farm in Southern Virginia. New memories are being made, which help to cover past tragedies. However, full-time farmer, and part-time private investigator, Brandon Hall is soon drawn into a new case. This time it's personal when the daughter of a close friend is abducted at a convention in Richmond, Virginia.

The trail leads Brandon into the depths of Virginia's Great Dismal Swamp as well as the swamp of Washington, D.C. politics. There, he must face down an unimaginable evil in a world he never knew existed.

Follow this unlikely Southern hero on another mystery where he must rely on faith, family, and friends.

**As with all of John Theo's novels, The Dismal Swamp is devoid of foul language, and gratuitous sex scenes, but does contain the subjects of human trafficking and child abduction.*

OUT NOW

ABOUT THE AUTHOR

John Theo Jr. received a bachelor's degree in psychology from Salem State University, and an M.F.A. in Creative Writing from Pine Manor College in Chestnut Hill, Massachusetts. For almost two decades his diverse writing portfolio included roles as a movie critic, a magazine freelance writer, and a college professor where he taught screenwriting.

John grew up in the suburbs north of Boston where much of his youth was spent buried under stacks of comic books. He latched onto any story involving far off places and fantastical characters. Years later he realized the novels and movies that impacted him on the deepest level were ones with a spiritual component. In hindsight, he realized that his youthful obsession with these stories was, in fact, a longing for the Divine.

Today, John Theo Jr. writes novels from a Christian perspective. Like the stories of his youth, John enjoys tales with an otherworldly component to them as well as a good measure of action, adventure, and romance.

Beyond Real

Surviving 9/11 … And How It Changed The Way I Think

by Richard Post

For

My wife and best friend,

My daughters, my angels,

My family.

I have tried to recreate events, locales and conversations from my memories of them. In order to maintain their anonymity in some instances I have changed the names of individuals and places, I may have changed some identifying characteristics and details such as physical properties, occupations and places of residence.

Table of Contents

Prologue

My sister jokes that I have nine lives … like a "cat." She jokes, not because we think any of this is funny, but because the alternative, to give in to the deadly seriousness of the issue, frankly is a little too much to deal with.

I'd like to say that the insanity, the sickness, the sheer and perverted atrocity of terror is something that wc know cxists, but more for the news channel head-lines than for anything that comes too close. I'd like to say that ... I just can't.

It started when I crossed the mid-point of my 30's, at a time when I enjoyed life as much as anyone could. I had a beautiful wife, my first child, a terrific house, job, cars, bank accounts … mostly earned, but some of it just the blessing of being born into the freedom and opportunity of the great United States of America.

It's funny, not ha ha funny, more weird funny, how certain things just seem to spring from nowhere; like when the scourge of HIV and Aids hit this country … from something unheard of to the cover of *Newsweek* and *Time* magazines, almost overnight. That's how I think about terror.

It just didn't seem to be around when I was growing up.

I mean, we all heard of war. Heck, my dad was a soldier, surviving the combat of World War II, amidst the jungle rot and foxholes in the Philippines. I even remember seeing his old photos of soldiers in the jungles of the Pacific Islands. I used to try on my dad's old soldier uniform. Fortunately for both him and his kids, we were soldier age during a time where our country was generally at peace … no draft, no mandatory enlistment. Vietnam and my teen-age years simultaneously came to a close. I entered early adulthood reading about war, never experiencing it.

Then, from the infinite strife and conflict of the Middle East came terror. It was something that seemed more absurd, somewhat more disgusting than how I thought of war … something that goes beyond and well over the line of sanity, even in comparison to the horrible reality of collateral damage, the unintentional killing of innocent civilians, during all of our world's wars.

No, terror is very intentional, in fact it's intentional collateral damage … the murder of innocent individuals, -- often women and children --, human beings who have very little to do with

the policy of it all. Somehow, I liken it to the shit you hear about mafia groups who don't follow the mafia code, which is generally to leave families out of the conflict.

Terror is like a gangster who has a problem with someone, so he tortures and kills the guy's wife and children. You know, stuff that even criminals would find despicable.

Another surreal thing about terror is that it happens on a surprise basis. In fact, for these sick bastards, that's part of the plan. Instill fear in innocent people, so whole populations live with one eye over their shoulder. Have everybody's first inclination in a stadium, a movie, a restaurant, wherever, to look and memorize the path to the emergency exit door.

Finally, so that we can wrap this whole despicable concept together, a terrorist wants to die, many times intentionally blowing himself up so others die along with him. There is no "let's-plan-the-escape-route" stuff, just intent to kill as many people as possible before (or while) he pushes the button. Oh yeah, sorry, one more thing … terrorists claim that their good-and-all-powerful God wants them to do this.

The seemingly zillion-year conflict between Israel and the its Arab rivals, mostly

third-world types of the Middle East, was now seeping into our country.

Then, without warning, it started to get personal.

My sister-in-law, (my wife's sister and godmother of my then 2-year-old daughter) worked in the World Trade Center (WTC) in 1993. I had just crossed my mid-30's. My wife was, is and always will be very close to her sister. It was not uncommon for my better half to often meet her sister in the city.

On Feb. 26, 1993, the WTC North Tower was bombed just a couple of weeks after my wife and little girl had visited their loved one in her offices in the WTC. It was the first time that a thought of the unthinkable made its way into my brain. It was inconceivable to even think that my family could have been included in that day's horrible ending … six dead, more than 1,000 injured.

The whole event seemed senseless, demented, mind-boggling and without cause. But we now had a name for it. They called it "*terrorism.*" At the time, it was defined by me very simply … an evil, most-fucked up thing to do, by the most evil, fucked-up of individuals.

After the event, time moved on and, as they say, life got in the way. My family grew with another gorgeous female (I now had three) and mind waves eventually eased, focusing each and every day on good things, beautiful things … within a beautiful family. That's not to say there weren't challenges, even a few of the serious kind, but they were dealt with and, generally, I lived the saying on my favorite green, beat-up hat: *Life is good.*

Until September 11, 2001.

I won't get into 9/11 here, it's all in this book, a truly gripping experience, the understatement of all understatements … and, unfortunately, as close and personal as it gets, without actually my becoming part of the statistics.

The difference this time, though, minds (at least mine) would not ease. I was affected for life, in the worst of ways. My belief in goodness, in safety, in my career, in a world of sunshine for my wife and daughters, was inwardly shaken. To most, I carried on fine. To some, I might even be called strong. I started and ending each day with the only thing that now really mattered … my love for my family and my prayers for their safety .

I think, even if 9/11 represented my last bout with terror, it would be bad enough. Unthinkably, terror seems to have my scent, because it seems to be following me.

It was April 14, 2013, our bags were packed and my youngest daughter and I were getting ready to leave for Boston. My wife and I had the unenviable task of dropping her off at college in Massachusetts. There, she would spend the next three days with her new classmates, all scheduled to arrive for good that September.

Freshmen orientation they were calling it … another in the long line of parent things to which I would have to adjust. Along with my wife, we would take the several-hour car ride to Boston, meet a few of the kids who were to become her classmates, get a big hug, and drip a few hidden tears reserved only for dads and their daughters. From there, it was off to some hotel in Boston both waiting for the three days to pass and experiencing the first effects of what some call *emptynestfulness*.

But there's more. Given my past, I couldn't help in the weeks preceding our trip and her permanent departure in September, to worry about my little girl and, God forbid, the possibility, now in 2013, of terror. It was, after all, fairly easy to hear of terror events occurring

overseas. Our country was still involved in wars, both in Afghanistan and Iraq, both conflicts now engaged for over 10 years. As used by so many now in my country, the conflicts were labeled the *war on terror*.

I refuse to simply accept that my past has made me paranoid. The facts would simply not support any charge of paranoia or psychosis.

In 2013 alone, according to START, (the National Consortium for the Study of Terrorism and Responses to Terrorism), there were 9,707 terror attacks worldwide, resulting in 17,800 deaths and more than 32,500 maiming injuries. Additionally, during that same year, the year my little girl was leaving for college, there were over 2,990 people kidnapped through terrorism and taken hostage in some form or another. Although I had little control over any of this, I was really nervous about depositing my little angel several hours away. Damn, she was only 18 years young.

Turns out, we didn't leave for Boston, as expected.

On April 15, 2013, two terrorists, two clearly misguided dudes, decided that rather than enjoy the blessings and excitement of being young, they would instead detonate bombs in the crowds at the Boston Marathon. The stats: 3

people dead, 264 others maimed and injured. To add to the mayhem, one of the sickos was still on the loose. I started thinking maybe this was me. Why the hell does this insanity keep following us? My daughter, already anxious prior to the now every minute terror news stories, looked my way for answers. Like I had done on so many other occasions, I mustered a little assurance her way, doing my best to conceal the once again returning 9/11 feelings of disgust, concern, fear, and a whole bunch of anger. What were we going to do?

Well, we did what everybody does, what everybody is forced to do. We kept-on-keepin'-on and despite a now mostly private life of daily stress over the potential of it all, my daughter, now 21, is about to enter her final year of college in Boston. She is thriving and frankly loves it. I hide my anxiety pretty well these days.

Until very, very recently!

Almost 15 years after my 9/11 survival, I have come back to the beginning, as my family has been reminded that we are no better off than the unreal chaos of that Tuesday in 2001.

On Nov. 13, 2015, the world watched as so many were murdered in Paris, the second terror event there in months. The stats: 129

mostly young people dead, over 415 injured, 80 critically. Another mass murder event of innocent people, this time against mostly kids just eating, singing and enjoying life in Paris. It's so pathetically and ridiculous absurd that we continue to put up with this, in what has become incredibly, and unbelievably, routine.

But this time it was different. My daughter was in Paris!

Only a few minutes from that night's terror, she was there on a few-day trip, taking a break from studying overseas in Seville, Spain, as part of her American university's Study-Abroad-Program. I sat shaking, thankful that she survived, but heart pounding stressful that she was locked down in her Paris neighborhood hotel.

During dinner that evening at a local Paris cafe, she heard sirens, too long and too many to ignore. She and her friend quickly left the restaurant and ran back to her hotel where she learned what was happening and immediately called home to let us know she was safe. I quickly turned on the TV to find every channel reporting that Paris was under attack … suicide bombers at a sports stadium, hostages at a theater being killed mercilessly one by one, machine

guns opening fire at a mall and a Paris restaurant. Thank God it was not the Paris restaurant where my almost grown-up daughter was eating.

My heart raced back to 2001, but this time it was worse. It wasn't me who was seeking survival, it was my daughter, my little girl … and I was an ocean away.

She was six years old during 9/11's chaos. In 2001, her youth (and her mom) provided a shield from full comprehension of that day's peril. Upon her daddy's hug, some 16 hours after leaving for work that day, I carried her upstairs and tucked her into bed. I kissed her and she faded to sleep, unknowing that it would take many years of maturity to begin to grasp the gravity of what I -- of what our country -- went through that day.

Until her return home from Europe, dozens of times a day, I connected with her, to check on her safety, amid stories of French and Belgium army terror attack raids, to kill and capture other radicals who had participated in the Paris terror event. France's leadership spouted a decree of war on the decadents who murdered their country's innocent citizens.

One week before the attack in Paris, I had gone to John F. Kennedy Airport in New York to

pick up my wife and my oldest daughter, both returning from their travels to Europe to see our studious loved one. On the ride home, we counted the number of days until my next airport trip, when my daughter would return, her period of study over.

We spoke of Christmas and how we looked forward to having our family together again. My oldest daughter spoke of her recent trip to San Diego with her friend. We debated the often-spoken-about decisions regarding our plans to relocate someday. We all agreed we might like to try life away from the tri-state area, a region that has represented our home for all of our lives.

One week later, I sat sickened for the safety of my daughter. I recalled over and over our discussions, several months ago, when my enthusiastic college student first brought up the idea of going to Europe for her fall semester. I recalled the private discussions with my wife, about the fears that I had, that now were becoming reality.

We all agreed at the time, pushed by our daughter's youthful exuberance, that we must live our lives unafraid to experience the opportunities that present themselves. While privately fearful, as the day of her departing flight drew closer, I conjured up assurance, telling her that her chosen

experience would be wonderful and one which she would remember forever.

Now innocent people, with no responsibility for leadership's politics, many so young and often displaying our society's most accepting postures for our world's different views and diversities … were dead, murdered by decadents who are so demented that they truly believe they are justified in the name of their God, unknowing that no God of goodness could ever support such despicable actions.

All this barbaric chaos, as America's leadership seems confused on how to deal with terror, now inconceivably almost 15 years after I witnessed first-hand the senseless and still unbelievable murder of my friends and associates.

ISIS is contained, no longer presenting the threat it once did. Those were the words of our leader only hours before the Paris terror, and we all watched as our divided nation remained paralyzed from a leadership unwilling and incapable to rally us as the world's greatest nation. We are born of strength and power, but have become so pathetically sympathetic to everyone's cause but that of our own nation, and our own nation's children.

There was an unspoken lesson during the Paris attacks, one that unfortunately and temporarily impacted my daughter's exit from the chaos. France's first order of action was to shut down its borders. Ironically, this came about as we watched Syrian refugees, with the very real possibility that they include ISIS terrorists; plan their arrival in the USA. Their entrance to our country, a policy being pushed by our commander-in-chief, seemed to ignore that one of the Paris attackers was a Syrian refugee who made his way to France. All of this while our President came up lame in his explanation and his ridiculously naive ISIS containment comments to our nation.

Our President called the Paris attacks a *setback,* a fucking setback, so callously insensitive to the loved ones of those just murdered. Clearly to the families of those butchered, Nov. 13th was a devastation from which one could never recover. A setback? Words can't describe the stupidity of this statement.

Bent on doing whatever it took to bring my daughter home and ultimately succeeding, I again move forward with a hangover of terror. Over time, I will privately assess this event's impact on my daughter, someone who left for

Europe as a loving, contributing, intelligent, funny and caring young person.

Along with my best friend and partner, we will continue to live, doing our best to keep our family together and safe. But what do you do? Where can you go? Back to college? To work? Out to dinner? To a club? To a ballgame? On a subway, or a plane?

When can we move forward without worrying each and every time our children take advantage of the things that life has to offer? Or like my daughter, or me, do you just have to be lucky when the guns open fire and the bombs explode?

If 15 years have taught us anything, it is that these atrocities on mankind, from those who appear inhuman, are far from over. I am more lost on this subject today than even 15 years ago when I watched my friends die and the towers crumble.

Introduction

I consider myself a patriot. I love my country. Having narrowly escaped death from the 94th floor of the World Trade Center, Tower II, on September 11, 2001, I was the guy who would be chanting USA, USA, USA, at local shows and concerts in late 2001. I was the guy driving around with American flags attached to each side of my car, proudly waving in the wind.

Unfortunately, I now see an American society and its values spiraling toward irrelevance, even destruction. The terrorists have us right where they want us, confused, distracted and overloaded.

Our once clear and simple values, those that our ancestors fought and died for, are fading in the rearview mirror. Our diversity of people and views, once our greatest strength and the confirmation of our freedom, now threaten to paralyze us, robbing us of the required unity to face and conquer the most serious of challenges.

And I think that most Americans realize this.

Fading fast is the pride to join a melting pot, a country where we all, through our heritage,

came from somewhere else, but we spooned out as Americans; a nation united with common beliefs and values. We didn't let go of our differences; we just didn't demand the right to make them more important than being an American. You think that's an exaggeration? The reports out of the media this past winter was the call to do away with the term *Christmas*. Too offensive, they said, for too many of our new citizens. Good grief, even Christmas is under attack!

Terrorism has changed the world. September 11, 2001, has changed me. It has changed the way I think, in ways that go far beyond the insanity of terror.

What will become of our country when all those who remember a time of common sense, values, morals and appropriateness are gone? Who will speak on behalf of that way of life when there is none left who remember it? When the memory of American values resides only in our graveyards, who will be left to fight for those values?

If we do not wise up, if we do not in some form revert to the strength and the values of those before us, we may be sacrificing our nation, disgracefully, soiling those values for which our forefathers fought and died.

Disturbing I know, but someone has to say this, and someone has to hear this. Maybe solutions start with a simple thought akin to, "shame on us for letting it get this way."

Our country needs better leaders to crystalize who we are, what we are about, and for what we are fighting. Otherwise, we will become weak enough and lost enough that the insanity of terror and its agenda will overtake this once great nation, rendering us as another once powerful empire left only to the pages of history textbooks.

For this book, I hope that zoning in on the present causes some to open their eyes. I hope that zoning out on my past causes some to think about the wonder of their past. I hope that telling my 9/11 story rips through the heartstrings of some, causing them to remember the lessons which have faded and dulled over time, yet are crucial to combatting the present danger and challenges that face us.

With only gratitude for our forefathers and the many before us; from the heart-felt respect that comes only from something truly earned, I write for no self-gain. While I will go through the effort to publish this book, I don't expect it will make money, but if it does, I had intended (in the book's first draft) to donate any and all proceeds to America's Wounded Warriors Project, for

those men and women are among the few real heroes left in this world. They continue to fight and risk their lives for us, for our freedom and for our safety. Then, a new story hit the airwaves; one that described the executives who run the Wounded Warriors Foundation stealing much of the country's donations to fund huge parties and retreats at lavish hotels and resorts. The details described them blowing millions of the nation's donations, inconceivably and selfishly partying on the funds earmarked for our wounded and maimed soldiers. If this story doesn't make you sick and depressingly depict the state of affairs in this country, nothing does!

We have so allowed our American values to gray where defining the problems has become as confusing and complicated as crafting the solutions.

And I think every soldier knows this.

Life moves forward for everyone, each of us experiencing our own intellectual metamorphosis. Sharing only the certainty that each year adds a digit to our age, people move in different directions. For us who remember a different world, those of us with a different frame of reference, we make our way adapting to society's new ways and new priorities.

We try not to let the myriad of distractions place us too far away from what is truly important. At times, we attempt to relate the ways of a simpler, more rewarding world to our children, but current times and current ways are the only world they know.

We find ourselves thinking about a time that was safer and when communication with others was less complicated and less frequent, not watered down by the constant and trivial noise of social media, where every thought and every picture is posted for all to see. But so often we just sound like a broken record, someone who is living in the past and incapable of change. Eventually, we just shut up.

We accept ways from our children that never would have been accepted in our time by our parents, knowing that drawing a line in the sand only isolates them from almost all others. My fear, however, is that we make them softer, not tougher, unfortunately in a world where toughness may ultimately determine survival. Mostly, we accept that we can do very little to change this.

I wonder if I would have grown the same and feel the same as I do now, if September 11, 2001 did not happen. I also wonder if my dad might have had similar thoughts as he grew older and perhaps was just better and stronger in his

ability to be private about them. I wonder if I were not continually taken back with thoughts of 9/11, would I have a brighter outlook on life. I think I would. I think that my hopes for my children's future would be brighter, certainly less concerned about fears of atrocities initiated by their own human kind.

It's difficult, mentally, to make the leap from my life as a young person to now. Even from the first 25 years or so of adulthood, I think so much differently now. I mean, moving from a mindset of optimism, that I belonged to the best of all possible worlds, to feelings of angst and cynicism can take some doing.

For over 44 years, (44 years and 334 days to be exact), I had as good an outlook as any guy. Taking, nurturing and developing what God had given me, I was living the American dream.

First enjoying thoroughly the pleasures of youth, carefree and happy, I bounced through life's lessons without much fanfare, but with exuberance for many things and most people. In fact, I was so content as a youngster I milked that time as long as anyone could without bringing those "when-are-you-gonna- grow-up?" comments from the world's establishment.

I was swept into adulthood with optimism and a real kick in my step. Often thinking that

nothing was out of reach, I defied most odds, building an enviable career from nothing in the most famous city in the world.

Reaching big-shot status, I was enjoying a life filled with challenges, travel, friends and excitement. My persona was strong and fit, maintaining a presence that seemed attractive to most. I was young and proud, firmly believing all good things were possible. Thinking back, it was truly the time of my life.

With confidence in tow, I demonstrated first the gumption to pursue, then the wherewithal to convince our planet's most gorgeous woman to marry me. She was everything for which a guy could hope. Successful in her own right, she was down-to-earth, funny and family-oriented. Wherever we went, I was accompanied by my best friend and always the prettiest lady in the room. For reasons seemingly clear to our circle of friends and family, we each considered ourselves the lucky one.

After a few years of enjoying the fruits of marital bliss, we were gifted with the first and then the second of our creations. I was so happy and so exceptionally blessed. Our life included a loving extended family, friends from all circles, interests that made each day exciting and energy that looked forward to early wake-up calls and often late evenings. A firm believer in character

and privileges that were earned, I had a shortage of neither.

Then, through one event, a few short hours destined to be highlighted in the world's history pages for the rest of eternity, things changed forever. Years of certainty instantly were replaced with trepidation. With family providing, through today, their entire support, I have suffered mostly privately. I have always attempted not to bum out my daughters or rob them of any of youth's gleefulness. Lately such attempts seem to take more effort and more focus. I guess for those who have reason to look closely, the changes in me might seem obvious. I don't really know. Outwardly, I have managed to continue a life filled with mostly success, but on the inside I find myself looking backwards far too often, continuing to privately pursue recovery.

I have internally battled to insist (of myself) to pursue and come to grips with the true nature of today's world. In the past, and as the years have gone by, I so often tried to convince myself that it was a natural tendency to see things differently as one ages, or that my change in thinking was warranted, recognizing that the world, in fact, was changing.

Maybe all of that is true, but what also rings true is that one's transformation in this life has much to do with his/her experience and in my

case the single day on September 11, 2001, that represents the beginning of my mental metamorphosis.

Chapter 1

America the Beautiful

Looking back for me can be quite therapeutic.

I started in the 50's coming from a family without much education, money or worldly presence. Dad was a civil servant, working several jobs to make ends meet. He was a Bronx kid with overflowing character and a shortage of expectations, never embodying the thinking that one's ambition to do great things was worth much … more falling into the category that the best things in life were simple, left to the good Lord and not tied to money, which was good because he never really had any.

Mom was a throwback, a Brooklyn gal who found her pleasure in a tidy house, Sunday macaroni and her kids' report cards. She had her driver's license since she was 18, but I never saw her drive. Not once. There was no need. That was dad's job and, besides, where the hell was she going to go? Ambition? Well, that was something for the next generation, for those who were young, maybe something to ask of her kids. They were both good people, both church-going, both finding comfort in things like the Holy

Name Society, the PTA, the annual block party and, oh yeah, in each other.

My childhood was a different era, a happy time, people were young, and mom and dad were young, younger even than what I am now. I recall it differently than today's time, even for today's young people. I remember them as simpler times. We didn't have much, didn't really need much. I had a glove, a bat, a few balls, even a bike. Friday night, my dad used to bring home Chinese food, not the feasts that my kids are used to, just chow mein and white rice, and on a splurge day, an egg roll. We used to call it 'chinx.' Now that word represents a politically incorrect term, even bigoted, but we meant no harm.

I never heard my dad speak ill of anyone; it's just what we called it. No big deal. In fact, I don't remember knowing any Chinese people as a kid. I'm sure they might have been around, or maybe we just didn't notice since people were a lot less sensitive then. Everybody had to come from somewhere but what seemed to matter was we were all here now, each doing what was required, lots more help and support of and by neighbors; block parties and stoops and dogs, all in the same boat, all moving in the same direction.

My mother's Cousin Vinny, (really, that was his name) worked at the dumps for the

Sanitation Department. Stores used to throw out six packs of beer cans if they were mangled or dented in transport. He used to bring over the damaged goods and sit with my dad in our Rodney Dangerfield backyard, usually with my mom, Nick and Lucy and some of the neighbors. There was coffee, crumb cake, maybe even Good Humor ice cream for the kids if we were good and it was payday. We had lots of laughs, lots of kids, cousins, neighbors, teammates, all kinds.

I remember I was an altar boy. You had to train to be one. No girls. We were friends with the priests. They were good guys. They came to the house often and cared about our family. B and I used to get to the room on the side of the altar early when we were serving mass. We used to sneak sips of wine before the priest got there. It was disgusting, but we did it anyway, trying not to laugh and lead on when Father M walked in. We convinced ourselves it wasn't a sin and we could still receive communion without going to confession. You got the feeling back then Father M would have understood. Not condoned it, mind you, but understood.

In fact, church was a big deal back then. We never missed mass on Sundays. After mass, we all stood in front of the church, neighborhood people and kids, feeling like we were part of something. We talked, planned and just were

there because that's where we were supposed to be.

Maybe on the way home, we would stop and get some buns so dad, mom, grandma and grandpa could have some with their after-mass coffee, or for others who might stop by. There were always people stopping by. People would be in our tiny kitchen or in the tiny living room when the games would come on TV or in our tiny backyard sitting around, inventing games. No one was ever bored. No cell phones, little to no money, just family, friends and neighbors.

Forget it, God forbid (as mom might say as she would bite her fist refusing to acknowledge any such potential) if something bad happened. Like grandma was sick or one of dad's friends got laid-off. The support was off the charts; genuine concern and real help, food, babysitting, car rides or handholding. You got the feeling nobody left and secretly made comments or two-faced remarks. Today, shit, that's all people do.

Back then; if you needed a priest or a doctor, he was at your house before you knew it. I remember each lawn (usually the shape of a square about 8 feet by 8 feet,) had some version of either a Blessed Mother statue or God with his right hand up (giving a blessing) statue. There

was no graffiti, no chance of malicious behavior. It was God for Pete's sake, and his mother.

As we got older, we started to notice the difference between the neighborhood boys from the neighborhood girls. Man, that was fun, and the thing about it was there were so many kids, so many possibilities. What a great time.

I don't remember schoolwork all that much. We certainly weren't overloaded like the kids are today with homework, tests and projects. I always got good grades, (mom saved all my report cards and gave them to me when I got older, along with my 8th grade autograph book.) I have had a pretty successful career so I'm sure I got a decent education; I just don't remember it playing the dominant role that it does now.

As we got a little older, I branched out a little more. I had many friends, loved sports, girls and, of course, my cousin. Although she was in every sense a girl, we did everything together. We had fun at the shore, at her house or mine and later in the cars. Half of the girls that I dated (yes, we actually dated back then,) were her friends and half her boyfriends were my friends. What a set-up. Not a care in the world.

Our parents were best friends and so were we. I think of that Honeymooners episode where Ed Norton is describing some good times to

Ralph. I could vision it like yesterday when he says. "Just fun, good clean fun!" That's what it was for us. And somehow, money was never part of the equation. Man, have times changed.

Sometimes, when we were kids, we would actually go on vacation. We would rent a huge house with a dozen rooms on some lake a few hours away; all of our families squeezed in and enjoyed the water, the town, each other. My dad used to tell me we could have had that house right on the lake. The owner offered it to us for $4,000. It's probably worth 300 times that now. We didn't get it because combined our families couldn't afford it. I can't even imagine how inexpensive it was to rent back then. Let's just say that I have paid twice the total cost to buy it for renting a shore house now … for a week! Also, maybe back then, we just didn't need it and at that time you reserved your money only for the things you needed. Besides, back then it was cool to be home. I can't think of anyone back then who would be saying, "We need a break" or "We need to get out of here." People were of faith, people were content with what they had and, while everyone worked to survive, money just didn't have the priority it does now.

So I grew up as a Catholic school kid, getting whacked on the knuckles by the solid wood ruler of Sister Getawaywithanything and

later pushed around by the confused Brothers at St. Tuition High School. My parents found a way to get me into college enrolling me as a tuition remission kid, as mom spread her wings in the college's bursar's office. Told to major in something that would give me employment someday, I chose business and graduated with a high GPA, finding myself making a whopping $13,000 a year post-graduation at some bank in New York City. Back in those days, one found a job through a recruiter, often one that started in a few months.

I used the time between college and being "on the job" wisely as I hitchhiked across the country with a good buddy, through mountains and deserts finding as much adventure as any kid could through the rose-colored glasses of Coors beer cans and Acapulco Gold cigarettes. Those were the days where friends were way too important and all our answers were found in the new wave of junkie musicians' song lyrics. But, somehow, I found my way. In fact, I worked my way up with the perseverance of the great athlete that I thought I was, all the way to big Wall Street money, nice houses, cars and a myriad of fine toys and possessions.

I married the most beautiful girl I had ever seen and I think even today, some 25 years later, we would both admit we didn't have a clue what

we were doing. Yet, still today, I love her with all my heart although there are times one could argue we still don't have a clue. All the time, I loved sports and coaching, fun, drinking and food, not always in that order.

In 1991, however, all things changed forever. My first daughter was born and then my second in 1995. Kids change a man; at least they changed me. Overnight, I would never again come first. They were everything to me. Still are. For years I lived with three women, coining the phrase "hat trick" on those special days where all three would cry within a 24-hour period. I like to think that I have taken good care of my wife and daughters but the truth is they really have taken care of me. During the process, I have come to have great respect for loyalty, love, and family and only with kids did I even begin to understand the lessons from my now thought of as pretty bright parents.

Man, life was good and I was good in it. America was the land of the free and the home of the brave and we were all believers.

That doesn't mean that I didn't do stupid things. There were times that I could lead the league in errors and screw-ups, but I tried. I really fucking tried.

Chapter 2

Smooth Sailing

Really, how much does any guy know at age 27? At the time, I thought quite a lot.

I started my career at 21 with three quick stints working at Wall Street banks, each approximately two years in length. I had quickly used my newly gained employment savvy to elevate my salary three times as quickly as those company loyalists, remaining at one company and settling for an annually approved salary adjustment. I wasn't getting adjustments, I was getting raises, big bumps, the benefit to someone who was willing to jump across the street to another firm and take a whopping 15 to 20 percent pay hike, while my Wall Street buddies were settling for the five to eight percent adjustments, and that was for the top loyalist guys only.

Of course, back in those days, the 80's, there were plenty of jobs to be had. It was not uncommon to get a blind call from a recruiter who had gotten your name off some list, privy only to employment agent types. Talk about a killing, back then recruiters were making a bundle, earning quite the percentage of a new hire's starting salary. Payable from the employing

firm, these large amounts were both budgeted for and, in those days, routinely accepted.

Someone early on, in college, had explained to me the power of mathematical compounding and I've never forgotten it. In fact, I've played it since day one. As evidenced on a simple Excel spreadsheet, the effect, over time, of salary percentage increases (raises) had everything to do with a quick base salary build up. In other words, as quickly as you can, arrive at a point where a raise (whatever percent) is calculated on a meaty base amount, thus giving the recipient a meaningful kick up in take-home pay and lifestyle.

By the same token, leave, also as quickly as you can, the point where a raise (whatever percent) is calculated on a shit base salary resulting in, well, a shit raise with little to no kick up and certainly no elevation in lifestyle. The guy taught me that when you were hired by a firm, they would never dare offer you less than you were making, thus salary increases and their powerful compounding effect were forever. What a great country!

I've since passed this concept along to my daughters, now making their mark in this world. Smart kids they are, as they clearly get it. They also have figured out that the concept of compounding also applies to saving, that if one

opens a retirement account early enough, they become the people (making earlier contributions than those who wait) who enter retirement with millions. Ahhh, compounding, interest on interest, among the most precious of all of Wall Street's secrets.

I had some good teachers back in those days.

My parents taught me the intangibles, without which everything else was meaningless; stuff like working hard, honesty, and the most important lesson I've ever learned ... to use my brain. Thinking can be a very valuable tool. Even though it's free, one might be surprised how many people don't use it, those who never seem to get around to thinking things through.

The times in my life where I've come up, say, less than optimum, are those where I didn't heed that sage advice. In fact even now when my young adult girls shoot me a text, such as "*arrived safely in Atlantic City*" or something as simple as "*going to dinner with friends*," I always take the time to respond with three things. First, I say "*have fun*," (damn it, they're good kids who have earned and deserve some fun) second, "*love you*" letting them know beyond all else I am here for them and always have their backs and third, "*please use your brain.*" Thanks, mom. Thanks, dad. You were the best of the best.

Beyond the intangibles, I always found a way to solicit those things from those in the know, those essential to the trade. I remember one of my Wall Street mentors really coming down on me after my first home purchase because I had agreed to let the mortgaging bank collect from me then pay both my homeowner's insurance premiums and real estate taxes.

He explained the scam that it really was, having the bank hold, in most cases, excess escrow amounts for which they, not I, received interest. I learned the hard way on that one. I also found out quickly that mortgage companies rarely hold your mortgage, rather opting to pool multiple mortgages and then sell them. Upon the sale to another creditor, and under the arrangement whereby your initial lender collects and pays your insurance and taxes, the transfer of instructions for these payments routinely gets screwed up. Unbeknownst to me, upon the sale of my first mortgage, my insurance and tax payment instructions failed to be transferred properly to the new lender. After receiving notice that my homeowners insurance had been cancelled due to the new lender's failure to make the premium payment, I never agreed to those terms again. Turns out, it's actually law, a consumer's right, that if a borrower puts down 20 percent or more on the purchase of a home, he can tell the mortgage company or bank to go shove it when it

is suggested that they make it easy on you by collecting additional monthly escrow to pay your insurance and taxes. In every house I've purchased since, I made sure I put down at least 20 percent and received the bills directly from my homeowners insurance company and my township for taxes. One might be surprised at the savings in their monthly mortgage payment when heeding such advice.

I also learned through my mentors that at some point resumes are best built when disclosing an ability to eventually stay the course. Companies get tired of training individuals only to see them take their newly developed talents elsewhere. At some point, one has to prove that a company's investment in you is worth it to them. As a youngster, a company might understand the moving around between jobs routine, but at some point job-hopping turns into a resume negative.

At 27, three jobs in, my fourth would have to be one that evidenced some ability to stay the course, displaying some serious one-company employment longevity, you know, stuff of which pensions are made. This decision was important and, like most things in my life, I had to use my brain.

As fate would have it, I was gifted with the perfect excuse to move to company No. 4, where I would stay until I truly made a name for myself.

Turns out, company No. 3 decided to move its operations to Long Island, N.Y. Clearly, no Wall Street executive would expect a New Jersey resident to commute that far. I placed a call to a recruiter who was more than willing to help me locate a company that fit my objectives like a glovc. Bingo, this was way too easy!

I opted for a British firm. The offer assured me of another 19 percent increase and the promise of upward mobility if I was good. Being good was all part of the equation and there was no doubt that I wouldn't disappoint.

I was 27, making my way in a world foreign to family and my mostly blue-collar friends. I was single, as good looking as I would ever be in this world, and with endless stamina and enthusiasm for success. I've always felt, and said, that my most exciting time on this planet was when I was 27 to 29. Not necessarily my happiest, since I will reserve that for the beginnings of my family, but 27 to 29 represented my prime, clearly a memorable time in each American male's story.

I had freedom, some money to enjoy it and the confidence and guile to do and try almost anything. My personality made up for those every-man flaws to which I was not immune. I found it easy to get along, make new friends, and juggle a number of girlfriends without

committing to any, all those things one might expect from someone in the prime of his life. I was really happy and it wasn't hard to see that. And, of course, I was making pretty darn good money, and it was beginning to show.

My first day on a job that I would give my heart and soul to for 14 years presented me with an interesting decision, the first of many that I would make over the next several years. Upon entering the office on Day One, it was early, before one's cerebral bell went off to start the day. I was nervous, as anyone would be who was forced again to navigate through new surroundings until comfort replaced unfamiliarity. There were two groups standing around chatting. I could hear neither. The group to the left was my age, young men and women on a path for greatness but clearly knowing their current boundaries. The group on the right was older, containing more supervisor types and even some older men, manager material. The more comfortable choice was left. I decided to go right, feebly attempting small talk and accepting the handshakes that either group would have provided to a newcomer.

The message had been sent. I had enough friends, enough drinking buddies and enough women on my radar. I was there to get ahead,

make money and eventually take my place at the throne.

If not immediately, certainly by the end of the week, everyone knew I was there to be serious. One even wondered out loud, I recall, whether I was ever going to loosen up and take my suit jacket off. I paid it no mind as I had all I needed socially out of the office. For now, I was hell bent on making an impression on those who whirled the power to elevate one. This was my fourth job and while only 27, I had already been to more than my share of happy hours.

I was learning the company's ropes quickly, using my strengths and my brain to make quick and positive impressions. Three things were becoming crystal clear to anyone who was paying attention. First, I could absorb new concepts quickly and comprehensively, a strength that I had often promoted during interviews. I don't know why but I could always seem to catch on quickly, often using my ability to see implications that doing this impacted or affected that, an attribute that was a must-have to get ahead. Second, I could always write well and quickly. So much of Wall Street has to do with written communication, memos, reports, procedures, etc. Business writing, clearly a unique form of writing, came naturally.

Most big shots never had the time or the patience to search for the point. In business, it was common for executives to read something halfway through, get the point and stop, moving on to the next thing. No one had to ever guess or search for my point. It was usually well described in paragraph one. Third, I wasn't intimidated by multiple assignments, coining the resume phrase that *I welcomed large elements of responsibility and their associated accountability.* Never, ever seem taxed, overloaded with multiple tasks and assignments. In fact, being multi-functional, accomplishing multiple things both simultaneously and qualitatively might very well be the primary ingredient for Wall Street success.

Soon the title of Senior moved to AT (Assistant Treasurer), a term invented by the industry to describe an up-and-coming player. Upon promotion, in addition to a nice bump in pay, I was selected to participate in a three-year management degree program, paid for by the company and being offered by a Big10 university out west. For the better part of the next three summers, I earned my degree while simultaneously enjoying my single status at the University of Wisconsin at Madison, the land of many lakes and many good times.

I became friends with many interesting professionals from around the country, often

sharing in our collective but somewhat unprofessional antics during late night parties and adventures. I developed close relationships with two equally eager maniacs, one from North Dakota, and the other from Alaska. Each summer for three years, I shed my business suit for shorts and a T-shirt, earned a degree and created memories, some still hard to believe to this day. At graduation, I flew my parents out for the ceremony and, other than their honeymoon in Florida; it was the farthest they had ever been from home. They had a ball and, needless to say, were proud of their creation.

As time moved on, the accreditations were rolling in, earned through both test work and additional course work. My resume was clearly beginning to look impressive, management-type impressive. My boss, a larger-than-life Jewish chap and the head of the department, was treating me very well, understanding that all good Wall Street perks were reserved for those who could consistently accomplish one single objective, making him look good.

With only a few years at the firm, my traveling started in earnest. There were times where I would spend weekdays at our office in Miami, putting in systems that serviced high-net-worth Latino businessmen, fly home for the weekend and then back to Florida on Monday

morning. This did not suck! I was single, working daily in an office filled with young and pretty woman of South American heritage, followed by 25-minute commutes back to the Fontainebleau Hotel in Miami Beach in that week's Lincoln Town car rental. I would enjoy some nightlife that only resort areas might provide and then head back to the office in the morning. Really, life was being way too good to me.

As the times would have it back then, I was about to open yet another ridiculously exciting chapter in my life. Needless to say, my confidence was now bordering on off-the-chart levels.

When working in New York City, my commute from central Jersey was long and routine. I would drive over the bridge that connected New Jersey to Staten Island, head down to the farthest point on the borough's north shore and park in my reserved area within the Staten Island Ferry parking lot. From door to ferry, I could expect at least an hour of driving time. Given my office was located just over the water in downtown Manhattan, I would grab a coffee and take in the sights of the harbor, often getting ahead on that day's work assignments during the 30-minute boat ride. I stored open assignments neatly in my hardcover, stand-up briefcase, which safeguarded these materials

while also serving as my portable ferryboat coffee table.

No one truly enjoyed commuting but as they went, there were worse ones than this. Once docked, I merely crossed a few downtown city streets before arriving at my office. Such a set up was convenient both coming and going as boats left every 15 minutes during rush hour and I could get to the boarding ramps literally within five minutes of leaving the office.

All too often, I wound up taking the boat home with my department's second in charge. At the time, (stay tuned) I got along with this guy but honestly taking the boat with him served no more than to extend an already long workday. On Wall Street, sometimes one had to do what was necessary and, at the time, this was one of them. At times, I really needed to be alone, to once again step out of my very comfortable comfort zone.

Occasionally, as Deputy Dog and I would force small talk, charting through the harbor on our way to our collective, and, thank God, separate cars, I would see this one young lady among the boat's hundreds of passengers. To say that she rocked my world was an understatement, often even ruining my night, as when her vision was fresh. I could not stop thinking of her. She was as beautiful as anything I had ever witnessed,

and more than that, she was the definition of what appealed specifically to me. She had the most beautiful face that I had ever seen. Her physical features head-to-toe were mesmerizing to me, clearly at this point creating something in my mind that would be extremely difficult to deal with.

At the time I was thinking, even with my ever-growing and impressive stature in life, she was probably out of my league. It was immaterial whether that was true or not, only relevant was the fact that I thought of her like that. Shit, if I was alone, I might have trouble staying calm enough to make any sense when trying to talk to her. With one of my bosses next to me, making a move was impossible. His small talk often centered around questions about me and another young lady I was off-and-on dating, a girl he had the pleasure of meeting at a company affair.

I would have to give this a lot of thought. After all, what were the chances that someone so beautiful could be available anyway? It was driving me crazy. What happened next convinced me that I had to act.

It was downstairs on the boat one lazy afternoon. I was leaving the office early to start the weekend because I had a party to attend to that evening. I needed to get to my apartment in Jersey and get ready, as I was meeting a girl who

had asked me to go with her. I remember actually looking forward to this as she was attractive, fun and clearly interested.

Shockingly, as I never would have expected at this time of day, there only a few rows away, appeared the girl of my dreams, alone and looking radiant. I had played this woman up so much in my head that she could have just vomited in the decrepit ferryboat ladies room and I still would have thought her present beauty was unmatched. Not only did she magically appear, but also it was an early boat, many open seats all around, including the one next to her. Best of all, Deputy Dog was still locked in his Manhattan office, giving me free pathway to do or say anything.

I blew it, big time! I froze, paralyzed to my seat, incapable of mustering up the courage to do what I so wanted to, so needed to, if for nothing more than to begin the healing process once her final rejections were in.

I just sat there, first watching her incredible beauty being wasted in silence, then watching her rise, as the boat grew closer to the shore, then finally disappearing off the ramp in a direction opposite my parked car. I was sick, I was disgusted, I was pissed at myself, never calling it anything other than what it was; a classic non-act of a coward.

I drove home, stopped quickly at my apartment, went to the bar down the street and didn't move off my chosen stool for several hours. I didn't call my date, a truly classless act; I didn't go to the party; I didn't do anything, just sat there like a big, fat jerk. Before finally rising to head home, I made myself a promise. If and when I ever see this woman again, I solemnly swear I will, under any and all circumstances, move my pathetic fat ass to her and speak. Words must come out of my mouth. Dumb-ass!

It was winter, sometime in early February, and very cold. I boarded the boat, early evening and it was dark. The boat had a limited number of outdoor seats, front and back. At this time of year, only the brave sat outside during their harbor run, as the winds could turn a hot cup of coffee into an icy treat real quick-like. Two steps on to what would be the back of the boat, there she sat, outside, bundled in a body-length coat, reading a paperback. Great, I thought, not only would I find it difficult enough to fulfill my very serious self-promise, but I would have to fight weather's elements to boot. I was not deterred!

Approaching her, making as feeble an attempt at conversation as one could, I introduced myself, deciding that honesty was the only shot I had. At first, clearly put off, she had the look of any young woman who was trying to decipher if

her new and annoying space-taker was anyone she should fear, perhaps one of the often seen crazies on the ferry.

As the boat chugged up the harbor, it actually started to go well, I thought anyway. Not getting too personal or inquisitive about her world, I poured out who I was, noting that my intentions were only of the good kind. As the boat neared shore, I asked if I could possibly give her a lift home. Yeah, right! That wasn't going to happen. Ditto for her forking over her personal phone number, after all our relationship was less than one half-hour old. Finally, I struck pay dirt! She would, at my request, give me her work number if I wanted that desperately to call her. Of course, leaving the boat, it did come to mind that she might have blurted out seven random numbers just to rid herself of the moment. As it turned out, she actually gave me her work number.

We proceeded to go on three not-so-noteworthy dates, during which I tried way too hard to impress. The third date ended in disaster as I blatantly violated the *use-your-brain* advice that had become my mantra. Sitting at a bar, sipping a nightcap, after an uneventful dinner at another location, I completely overreacted to what I, thinking back, should have anticipated. Some guy, now armed with a full rack of beer

muscles, attempted to hit on her, showing the other-guy disrespect that only comes late at night in drinking establishments. Defending her not so offended dignity, I wound up embarrassing both her and myself, perhaps even causing discomfort to those close enough to hear my antics. The evening ended with her slamming my car door, mutual fuck you's and a lonely car ride back to Jersey replaying over and over a classic act of stupidity.

A few months went by, no word from either romantic, although I must admit, I thought of her constantly. Life went on. I even dated a few times, feeling closer and closer to normal, and chalking up another one of life's lessons learned the hard way.

It was almost three months later, the weather now springtime bearable, and I was readying myself to leave the office. Something made me pick up the phone and try her office. She answered, quickly rejecting my offer to get together that evening, noting she had a date. Once again, without thinking, I blurted out, "break it and call me back, I'll be here for another 10 minutes," and then I hung up the phone. The sheer nerve of such a statement threatened to end this fantasy forever, a thought only popping into my head after I had abruptly ended the call.

In less than five minutes she called back, called me a few expletives and demanded to know where I wanted to meet her.

We proceeded to see each other every day for over six months, culminating in our marriage two nights before New Year's Eve, less than one full year after meeting for the first time. This year, we will celebrate our 27th wedding anniversary, having raised two wonderful angels and shared everything that life offers. I am more in love with her today then even that one now-comical day when I blew it, paralyzed and too afraid to even talk to her. Amazing!

Three quarters through my 14 years at the firm, our company was purchased by one of the largest banks in Japan. Quickly, the culture of our company changed as existing management members scrambled for positioning. Looking to hold onto a good thing, our department head quickly promoted me first to AVP (Assistant Vice President) then to Vice President. Those with longer tenure now envied my new title and position in the firm. I was in my late 30's, married, a father, making lots of money and equipped with a wonderful outlook on life. I was so lucky and so happy.

In a reshuffling of management, my boss, who I had come to both like very much and respect, was reassigned to head the back-office

for one of the firm’s larger revenue units. You guessed it, Deputy Dog was put in charge of our department and I was the new deputy, second in charge.

Personally, I had nothing against this guy, a tall, thick man of German heritage. We had long since established a decent working relationship; it was more that we were so different in style and approach. Bluntly and crudely stated, I saw him often as a bully, never really bothering to be very genuine with anyone unless he could see a personal benefit from it. He also, in my view, was one of the most frugal men I had ever met. He was married, lived in a big Jersey home with no kids. He didn’t mind saying that he wasn’t all that fond of kids, kind of didn’t believe in them; somehow to me, even seeming disappointed that he was once one. He often complained about real estate taxes in New Jersey, where a significant portion went to the township’s school system. So unfair, he continually argued that an anti-kid type like him had to kick in for schools.

I once saw him throw a tantrum, clearly classic YouTube material now, because he couldn’t find a quarter. We had been at an uptown meeting and were taking a subway back downtown. Upon nearing the token booth, he flipped out; as a stood motionless as a witness to

his meltdown. Apparently, he had a routine whereby he would buy coffee each morning and get a quarter as change. While he had followed that routine that morning, the quarter was now no longer in his left pocket, where he religiously always placed it. My offer to give him a quarter to help with his token buy was met with a disparaging tirade about how I didn't understand. The quarter was not the point, as he noted that it would be difficult to stay calm until the precious piece of silver was located. No shit, the guy appeared at times to be damaged goods. Most took extra care to stay clear of him. Wonderful, I was now his direct report.

Time went on, my life couldn't have been better, as the years at the firm seemed to fly by. Japanese management seemed to get along with our now firmly implanted department head, sharing a too-often propensity for frugality. It was now the 90's, I was in my 40's and Wall Street didn't have the once enjoyed financial cushion it did in the 80's when all lived large, fat and happy. Firms were looking for ways to cut back, now so much more accountable to the ruling bottom line. Our company was no exception.

The Japanese honchos decided to hire a consulting firm to guide a company-wide project where those assigned would look to cut expenses

to the unheard of tune of 40 percent, while maximizing every bit of efficiency and creativity to grow the bottom line. Clearly, anyone who was someone was nervous.

The project included an interesting twist. The management committee assigned to recommend ideas, as creative as could be thought of, was to be made up of the second in charges throughout the organization. The thinking was those one step under the top in each department perhaps had a better feel or insight as to what could be accomplished. The top guys had long since distanced themselves from the detail of it all. The second in-charge guys were closer to the action, many of them more apt at the rapidly advancing technology within the firm; most of them working their asses off, hoping to one day take their rightful place at the department's throne.

This mandate drove the various department heads crazy, all now privately looking to sway decisions their way, privately looking to control the recommendations of those deputy's directly assigned. Cuts of 40 percent were daunting, to say the least. One would have to have the creativity of a damn Michelangelo, and then some, to accomplish such a feat without cutting heads. The deputies knew it and so did the department heads. Tension filled every

department, none more so than mine. My boss was going out of his mind, clearly, in my view, from a starting point closer than most.

While no one on Wall Street would have ever wished for such an environment, truth is this project was something that suited my skills well. I decided that I would approach it using the empty-box strategy. This meant I would consider only positions and work flows, not people; create savings and efficiencies by redesigning the way things were done without looking to place people in the new creations. I would leave that up to firm-wide management.

With the exception of my boss' attempts at throwing up a roadblock, I quickly became the poster child for this project. The mega-shots who would make final decisions were so impressed with my initial redesign offerings that they first presented them to Japanese management as support for the positive results being achieved through this exercise and then to all the other deputies as examples of what they should be striving for in developing their recommendations. The only one who seemed to be frowning was my boss.

As department head, he had to be careful. On one hand, he was looking to control me; on the other, he knew that technically that was against this project's rules. He was walking a fine

line. He didn't want to be viewed as a detriment to management's mandate yet, as with a baby who instinctively puts anything it can grab in its mouth, he just couldn't help himself.

He asked me, private-like, if I could run all future recommendations by him before submitting them to my project report. Explaining that he could give me the advice that could only come from someone of his stature (yeah, right!) both the company and I would gain. I knew where this was headed but I also realized that someday this exercise would end and that the chances of me moving back completely under his reign were good. I agreed to his request.

My next recommendation was significant and, well, brilliant. Not only would it result in huge savings but it also could be accomplished without the need to fire anyone. Simply, it involved combining two top paying positions, one of which was open and in the process of recruitment. The synergy between the two tasks fit perfectly, and while challenging for a single person, these were challenging times.

One could argue that after it was implemented operations would actually be more effective. The cost savings were indisputable. I knew those running the project would consider it a grand slam. It did contain one little issue. The recommendation made sense only if the

combined position included the transfer of a top technician out of our department and into another. Transferred from another department into ours did not make sense and the new workflow would be highly ineffective. As agreed, I first communicated my intended proposal to my boss.

Did you ever see someone who has taken something unpleasant for a while and has finally been pushed over the edge? The prospect of losing a key report was too much for him to handle. His reaction, all these years later, still is as vivid and fresh as something that happened yesterday.

Without speaking, he finished listening to my calm description of the recommendation and why it made sense, turned bright red, got up, stormed out and slammed the door behind him. All that was left was me, now seriously contemplating the possibility of a physical confrontation, but still sitting stoic-like in a chair, IN HIS OFFICE. I got up, opened the door and walked through to find him gone, leaving only a *shit-has-hit-the-fan* expression on his secretary's face, cowering at her desk directly outside his office.

Knowing he wasn't stupid enough to go and display his 2-year-old-like reaction to anyone of significance, I thought he just went off somewhere to compose himself. It being toward

the end of the day anyway, I decided to go grab a few things from my office and leave, praying I wouldn't bump into him on the way out. I would seriously have to think about this tonight.

I decided two things. The first was that I would document the finishing touches on my recommendation and hand it in. Fuck him and his insecure psychosis. The second was that I needed to protect myself so that evening I took a drive to the closest electronics store and purchased a pocket tape recorder, knowing that if I needed to I would have to communicate his less-than-professional behavior. While we all live in a world where lawsuits have become the norm, I don't subscribe to that thinking. Rather, I simply wanted to protect myself from a guy that was now capable of almost anything, most of which put me in peril.

The next day, in early, I was summoned to my boss' office. Thinking that maybe he understood that he was putting himself in harm's way, he was to offer an apology and request that we simply move on. I was wrong. Prior to leaving my office, I clicked the tape machine to on, placed it in the inside pocket of my jacket and made my way down the hallway to his office. Nervous, I used my short walk to make sure that the recorder was, in fact, as quiet in the on

position as when I had tested it last evening. It was.

I poked my head in, and said, “You wanted to see me?” and was calmly asked to again have a seat in one of the chairs placed in front of his desk. He quietly got up and closed his office door. Oh, shit! Calmly and with a rehearsed tone, he told me that he had thought long and hard last night regarding my soon-to-be-submitted recommendation. He continued that he hadn’t changed his opinion that it was a terrible idea, one that would leave great impact on our department.

I couldn’t help thinking that what he really meant was that it would impact his empire. Then he said something that confirmed my decision to record this conversation. “If you, knowing how I feel, continue in your intentions to submit it, I will bury you!” Trying to lighten the moment but really interested in his answer, I responded with one word, in the form of a question, “Literally?”

Not amused at my response, he proceeded to tell me that he would do everything in his power to see that my progress in this company would halt and that I would be stuck facing a dead end as long as we both were employed at this firm. “Is that it?” I asked. I watched as he pompously nodded yes and I got up and left his office. Instead of heading back to my office, I headed for

the elevator, out of the building and over to the far end of Battery Park, a few short blocks away. I picked out a secluded spot in the park; made sure no one was within earshot, rewound the tape, listened to it and thought, nice quality. It was as clear as if he was standing next to me in the park, repeating his bully threats. I am so many years removed from that meeting, but I still have that tape. It's been resting in the same spot in my home for almost two decades. Recently, I replaced the batteries in my now old-fashioned pocket recorder. His threats can still be heard.

Needless to say, and always going back to my parents' lesson to use my brain, I laid low for the rest of the day, leaving promptly at 5 on the dot. After some discussion with my best friend at home, I decided four things. The first was that I wasn't a whore. I would not turn this into profit although I understood well that most thrust into such a predicament would have disagreed because this was as open and shut a case as labor attorneys' could fathom.

I would not look back at this decision, knowing that if I did, I would eventually come to the same conclusion. It wasn't who I am. Second, I would not screw my boss to the wall over this; an option I knew was easily accomplished. Third, life was too short for this shit. I would begin to act on something that I had been thinking about

anyway. I would put my name out there as a candidate for positions as a department head within other firms.

I had spent over 13 years at my current company, more than enough to confirm my ability to stay the course. Leaving a company that was looking to chop expenses almost in half wasn't the dumbest thing anyway and one that frankly was being considered by most big and mid-shots with which I worked. Lastly, I would submit my recommendation first thing in the morning to the project's leader, which I did.

As I had expected, my recommendation received rave reviews. In the coming months, it was the item that everyone pointed to when they needed an example to describe the project to anyone new or uninformed. The person who would move from our department to another instantly became my best friend, recognizing this as being his ticket away from a department where most could cut the daily tension with a knife. My boss, as with all bullies, backed down, left only to put forth his coldest shoulder toward me, helpless to back his threats with any real action.

At the 13½-year mark of my employment with this firm, I received a phone call inviting me to apply to an asset management firm, as division head of one the company's important support units. The salary of the position would put me at

another level and the responsibility was significant. In addition to New York, I would be responsible for conducting business at various domestic and overseas subsidiaries.

The firm had been around since 1960, was always growing and although not nearly the largest; it had established a nice niche in the investment management world of Wall Street. The new director's office and his department were located on the 90th floor of the World Trade Center, Tower II, with the company conducting its business on floors 90 through 97. Without much reservation, I decided to go for it.

When applying for such an influential position on Wall Street, the interview process is unlike that of lesser jobs. One had to meet and discuss his qualifications with several individuals, often over lunch or dinner, and display not only a competence to fulfill the job's responsibilities but also a personality that was perceived as a good fit within the employing firm. Because on Wall Street everyone had a busy schedule, the process could take a few months. A candidate needed patience to allow the meetings of the mind that such an interview process would require, knowing full well that after investing much time, energy and thought, including some serious homework prior to each meeting, you might not get the job. Mathematics is a factual

thing in this world. If you are one of 10 applying, well, you do the math.

After a number of meetings at the Trade Center, various lunches and dinners around the city, all followed with professional thank you notes to each person taking the time to meet me, I received a call from the company's Director of Human Resources. I was asked if I could break away from my current job and come in to receive my offer and fill out the necessary forms. I had gotten the job! Besides being elated with the opportunity and relieved that my efforts had paid off, I personally looked forward to handing my boss my letter of resignation. I was not immune to such selfish and personal pleasures. No true executive on Wall Street is.

Chapter 3

A Job in the Sky

It took me a few days on the new job to know that I had made the right decision. Not intimidated with the prospects of being held responsible for anything under my domain, I was pleased with the quality of the staff members that worked for and with me. Being a support unit -- and an important one -- I quickly developed a plan to earn the cooperation and respect within the company, aspects required to both enjoy nature's need for belonging, along with securing one's entrenchment within a Wall Street company's powers that be.

Every in-charge, if honest, will tell you that his administrative assistant, prior to the days of political correctness when they were referred to as secretaries, always lead the way when assessing those most valuable. Like the lovable and efficient Radar O'Reilly on the old *MASH* sitcom, these individuals represent the glue to an office.

A manager type will go to great lengths to ensure that his assistant is happy and content, leaving little to no chance that the assistant would ever voluntarily leave. If they did leave, a canyon-sized void would instantly rear its head in

the efficient running of the office and, more importantly, in the efficiency of the in-charge.

For the most part, a good assistant spends the greater portion of each day making his/her boss look good, keeping him or her on time and understanding what's important and what is not. The best ones are also totally trustworthy and honest, often even telling the boss what is crucial whether they want to hear it or not. They are the in-charge's confidant and always have their back.

In my new position, I had inherited the best of the best. JV was all of the above and more. Early on, after earning her college degree, she had an honest discussion with herself, deciding that other things in her life held a great deal of priority, thus she would sacrifice the clawing-up-the-ladder routine and be satisfied as an executive assistant. Basically, she maintained an intelligence level rare in those maintaining these positions. An absolute wiz around a computer, she never had to be told anything twice and, as time went on, our conversations often defied who was the boss and who the assistant.

When told of my intention to earn cooperation and support from the other executives around the firm, she entered my office the next day, handed me a piece of paper and said, "I will remind you each Tuesday that it's time to prepare for tomorrow." Confused at her

lack of explanation, she told me that the paper just handed over neatly listed my Wednesday lunch dates with each executive in the firm.

Over the next three months, my first three months on the job, Wednesdays could be used to forge the relationships that would be necessary to win the support and cooperation I desired. A portion of Tuesday could be used to do some homework to research tomorrow's lunch partner so as to always present an informative and interesting lunch discussion. She was a smart, smart lady, quite astute on how the game was played!

I was equally impressed with my staff of professionals. They were composed of men and woman with solid backgrounds and experience. Along with their credentials, they showed consistent signs that each of them understood it would be in their best interests to make me happy. Conversely, I let them understand that I was intimately familiar with what was important to them.

I operated mostly on a bottom-line basis, meaning that as long as they were professional, always conscious of the impression put forth by our group to the rest of the firm, and that I could count on performances that were complete and of quality, they could expect an end to the multitude of rules that often do more to hurt than help a

group. I explained that honesty and loyalty, from both them to me and from me to them, should be on display every second of every day. I would be in their corner genuinely and consistently. I suggested that any apprehension that may inherently exist with a newcomer walking in as the in-charge was unnecessary.

After a few weeks, I loved coming to work and, more importantly, the concerns that the firm had with our department prior to my arrival was rapidly being replaced with comments of approval and support. Over the next four years, I raised the performance level of my position (and my division) to new heights. My evaluations from the Board and executive management were as positive and complimentary as imaginable.

My salary adjustments and annual bonuses reflected how well I was thought of and my requests to secure excellent raises and bonuses for those working for me were never denied. I was a senior vice president with an impeccable reputation and, as a group, my department was rocking and rolling on a heck of a ride.

During that time, while I never particularly enjoyed leaving my very young daughters, traveling as a division head was exhilarating and productive. I forged great relationships at our offices in London, Switzerland and around the states. When my new associates visited New

York, I often spent quality time with them both in and out of the office.

I understood the mechanics of World Street, the scratch-each-other's-back of it all, careful never to cross the unwritten boundaries that frankly could take a man out in minutes. From where I came from, my existence was the sheer definition of the American dream.

The cast of executive characters, now my peers, was priceless examples of the *haves* in this world. Most were from backgrounds of serious money, most were the jet-setting types and all lived in worlds unbeknown to me growing up in civil- servant, blue-collar USA.

There was HL, current CEO, who once at a meeting of top mega-shots, asked that the chatter and panic that was accompanying the firm's conversion to a new and critical computer system cease immediately. He suggested that all would be wise to read my report on the project, as it was the only sensible take on this important conversion. One did not often receive such praise from HL and for a few weeks I was the target of quite a bit of riding from my fellow executives.

HL was a sailor, and I often enjoyed being in a meeting with him that was interrupted by the head chef of his boat, where this weekend's menu could be agreed. He had no reservations of hiding

his love of the high seas, once voting on who should be the new head of technology, among several impressive outside candidates, stating that he would have to opt for "the sailor," the savvy candidate that listed sailing as an important activity on his resume.

There was GJ, a star within investment management and a leading member of several critical committees. Once, over lunch during a business visit to Delaware, GJ explained the criticality and necessity to send one's offspring off to boarding school right out of grammar school. One needed to recognize, he explained, that the process of exceptionalism must begin as early as possible. GJ was a sweet guy with very, very expensive suits and winter outerwear.

There was MM, complete with his hideaway in the Dominican Republic, who routinely traveled to Scotland, as he had a fondness for its golf courses and elevated living styles. CM once indicated to me that if our relationship continued to progress, he quite possibly might distribute the honor to "socialize" with him, clearly a privilege that had to be earned over time and effort.

There was TA, serving on numerous boards of varying companies, an art lover and often quite convincing in her example to serve the general good of the world. TA, of high intellect

and one of the boys, despite her female gender, often gave the impression that our conversations were taking place amidst her numerous other, unrelated, but equally important thoughts, occurring simultaneous to our discussion.

There was TS, as down to earth as any aristocrat could be, daily displaying an ability to relate on equal grounds with both mega-shots and janitors alike.

My favorite perhaps was YB, a man who blew away all competition, complete with degrees from seemingly half of our nation's Ivy League institutions. YB was the classic example of the term *chosen one,* earning penthouse status, both personally and in business, at a very, very tender age.

And of course there was HS, who always gave me the impression that he had left his once high school world of insecurity and nerdiness, graduating to levels of stock ownership and confidence envied even by those of wealth and fame.

All these Wall Street kingpins possessed only the most elevated of intellect, guile and bravado. They strutted the upper floors of the tallest building in the world as if they were truly the made heads of one of the world's most powerful families.

My days were filled with important stuff, navigating through, and belonging to, Wall Street's maze of strategic meetings, reports, business trips and social invitations. My opinion was routinely requested and my place secured within the world of high finance and blue blood elitism. Each evening, upon my return to our suburban paradise, I enjoyed my partner, my kids and numerous and interesting friends. Sitting on my large stone deck, overlooking manicured landscaping and the ripples of my crystal clear pool water and sipping a well-made cocktail, I often let my outdoor sound system entertain us through the night.

I was in love with my life, feeling it would continue forever. Man, was I wrong.

Chapter 4

Beyond Real

It changed everything. The only word that describes that day is surreal. I think people use that word too often. Anyway, in this case it applies perfectly; having the disorienting, hallucinatory quality of a dream, unreal or perhaps better said beyond real.

Tuesdays on Wall Street were nondescript, really the least defined day of the workweek. Those in the trade know Mondays well. They follow the queasiness of your Sunday night stomach, the anticipation of another five days to prove your worth, to get things done; your quest to, in five days, start another Friday night ride home, secure that your past week's performance earned you a two-day good time and the right to enter the office on Monday, make some more money to pay tuitions, eat out, deal with rising prices and, you know…keep on keepin' on.

Now Wednesdays, they were OK. In fact, especially if it was nice out, you might even consider stepping out at night, with the wife or the boys or with the kids, firmly believing that fatigue (or hangover) was best dealt with when only two days remained. Heck, on Wall Street one could get through anything on Thursday and

Friday. And on Thursday and Friday, well, one actually could enjoy work, the mind repeating a thought of "hey, this is not so bad."

Like those old eight-hour drives to gloomy Rochester to see my college cronies back in the 70s, those last two hours could be done blindfolded. Sort of the way I work out … a half hour on the treadmill always seemed easier at the 15-minute, one-second mark when time goes from counting up to counting down. But Tuesdays, man they were brutal; not quite enough time gone by to declare the week productive and too far from Friday freedom to kid yourself with any real sense of excitement. Except, this Tuesday would be different. Surreal different.

September is an odd weather month in the Northeast. Personally, I have always felt the Northeast weather to be way overrated. It seems like I sit around a lot waiting for the perfect weather day, which so rarely ever comes. You know the type, not the ones where people say it's nice out only to be blasted with a whitish sky, the Northeast excuse for sunny. No, I'm talking about the old Knick uniform-blue taking over the sky, no clouds, little to no humidity, cool in the morning and blossoming into a warm and no-excuse-not-to-appreciate-things day. Like those days in Santa Barbara when I was young and carefree. Sunny, full of joyful carelessness and

the only decision was what time to order the first cocktail.

Frankly, I don't remember those days all that well anymore. They somehow have faded into thoughts of Jack Tripper rollerblading down the California boardwalk in the opening of the old show "Three's Company." I don't think I have ever rollerbladed in my life, so it's strange that I remember those times that way. I guess it's just time fading memories more into a blurry feeling, a real happy, good feeling, like when my new friend at the golf course (Ronnie) talks about the Dodgers and Ebbetts Field. Tears-in-his-eyes happy, but perplexed as to why it can't be like that anymore. Man, those were the days.

Anyway, that Tuesday, New York weather hit Lotto, a perfect morning with all the characteristics of how the country often speaks about San Diego on most days. Little did anyone know that on that perfect Tuesday, all that's wrong with the world would manifest itself to surreal status.

I was a big-shot, an SVP, the head of a whole division in a company that sold people on giving them either their hard earned or (in most cases) their undeserving inherited millions, two million minimum, in the promise that they would turn it into more. Yup, daddy's in charge sweetheart. Nice talk around the family BBQs.

Sometimes I question if that was really me or am I thinking of someone else? Yeah, it was me, although it was the work me, not exactly the real me.

Growing up, when your age reached a beyond teenage level and people (always people) began shifting conversations from what your plans were to what you did, I always think back to my good friend Alan (*Aldo Cella*, we used to call him.) He somehow always used to beat me to the answer when someone asked what I did. He used to say, "He's an actor, and one of the finest this world has known."

He knew the deal. No matter what my title or the size of my paycheck, he knew the real me, a cigarette-smoking, scotch-drinking athlete. I know, I know they don't go together, but for me they did. I was a guy with only blue-collar friends mocking most things, on a quest for another good time, daily leaping like Superman onto Wall Street earning the respect of millionaire peers of boarding-school prominence.

Not bad people, but certainly not like me, or for that matter, my dad, a great man, who used to invite his friends over to the house for canned beer and Yankee games because he didn't have the few bits required to pay for those cold drafts down at the local bar. He's passed now, only living through his kids' character. When I think

back, I am convinced he was in fact great, if only because his friends (while clearly understanding the difference between an air conditioned bar with laughs and good times versus a hot living room, a shitty TV and six kids) … usually said yes to his offer. Unlike my dad, I was quite the actor.

I was in early that day, as I was on most days. I had decided to bypass my usual Staten Island Ferry route and drive to Jersey City, first getting ripped off by the lucky guy who had inherited some open land from his long deceased grandparents, now using it to charge $22 a pop for the privilege of parking your car. From there, one could enjoy the pleasure of being sardined on the Path Train, where you could gradually develop disgust for all perfume or after-shave fragrances.

My normal commute would unleash my $285 a month Staten Island Ferry parking pass, hopping on the 6 a.m. boat headed for downtown Manhattan and arrive in the office before the clock struck 7. The fact that I changed my routine that morning, in hindsight, was only the beginning of a day that would change my life forever. At the time, I just needed a break from the waterway people mover.

The Staten Island Ferry was like most good things around New York, things that could

draw the girls and me to it with the excitement and membership into something promising or memorable or drive me away looking urgently to rid oneself of the stink of it all. At times, you could gaze out over the harbor, the sunlight producing a blanket of sparkling stars resting on the carpet of waves and breaks of the greenish ocean water.

Your temporary feeling of peace and appreciation of the beauty created by nature's clashes often was interrupted by, well, something let's say of a lesser beauty. Perhaps like a homeless guy crossing the path of your sunlit view, greasy haired, dirty with shoe tongues (no laces) pointing up, out and away from their intended place, exposing a murky film of month-long crud on each of the man's insteps.

New York City, the Big Apple! Wealth, fortune, fame … somehow overlooking the see-it-everywhere poverty, filth and desperation. NYC was clearly pretty cool for the haves, more rat-like and danger lurking for the have-nots. Anyway, that morning my 8,000th something ferry ride (no joke), would have to wait, as the Path got me to my 90th floor corner office, WTC Tower II, about an hour to spare before my big-shot management meeting in the board room on the 94th floor.

Before 7, my wife no doubt still sleeping, kids secure in their suburban Jersey mansion, I stepped into my big-shot office, the one that looked down over the Hudson into New Jersey, also looking down, by the way, on passing helicopters or small military planes seemingly using the river north or south as some sort of video game guide or path to their final destination.

As youngsters, my girls, at the time 10 and 6-year-old angels from heaven, always marveled at how high in the sky they were when visiting daddy on the rare occasions that the workplace would recognize the realness of its members. I will never forget the big-shot phrase often used to capture the sheer loftiness and pompous nature of Company Wall Street and Mr. W.S. Executive ... *"On Wall Street, you can talk about your kids, just not that much."*

Everybody there got it. Families, kids in particular, were more verbs than nouns … something you did on occasion, an action … of course until you sent them off at 12 or 13 to boarding school, a small price for the little brat to pay considering his pending inheritance. Shit, someone had to educate him, or even her; on how much better they were than most others.

I placed my keys and sunglasses on the corner L of my desk, a place I had reserved for

them for years, took out my big shot meeting packet, which I had prepared the day before and thought good thoughts, mostly about Vicki, my secretary, walking in and making me coffee … the way I liked it, damn it … the way I deserved it.

At 8 a.m., Vicki's coffee now devoured, I left the comfort of corner office 90, took the elevator to 94 and took my place at the throne, one of five big shots about to discuss important management stuff. Joining me were DC, the firm's Chief Corporate Counsel and a nice lady who will be remembered mostly for taking the time to befriend me when I joined the firm as a young, not so sure big-shot. I worked closely with legal in those days and DC was the real deal, a woman of intelligence few possessed, the toughness to take on any chauvinist not giving her due respect, but always a lady. She was my friend, and a genuine one at that.

There was GA, the Head of Human Resources, a competent and youthful woman of much experience who used to "sneak out" early and make me promise that I wouldn't mention that she had to go to help her two little ones with their homework and studying for tomorrow's big tests. She was another woman who took no shit but if you met her at the kids' PTA meeting, you would never guess her place on the Wall Street

throne. GA always had time for anyone who needed help. She was as respected as anyone in our firm.

There was MB, the head of Custody, a big chap with an equally big sense of humor who had a way of talking to the mega-shots like he belonged and could not be intimidated.

There was HS, the head of Fixed Income, who, at the tender age of late 30s had grown a fortune in salary and company stock; a guy who was way too young to be that confident. He reminded me of a guy who spent weekends sailing and eating caviar.

And then there was me, the SVP in charge of his own division; a position that even the Grand High Exalted Ruler and mega-shot No. 1 had to listen to when he spoke.

The meeting commenced without incident. Even this room's inhabitants of superior guile and intellect could not predict or imagine the surreal chaos … only a few short minutes away.

The boardroom was an internal room, meaning no windows. Picture a huge square piece of property, one that would take a good few minutes to walk the circumference. That was each floor of the trade center. Now picture a smaller square strategically placed within the larger

square, closed completely, only accessed or exited by single, heavy hard wood doors at either end, unless you entered or left through a small, almost unnoticeable swinging door tactfully placed at a far corner of the room.

This door led to a small kitchen where servants could prepare food offerings to the big shots as they were deciding on the fate of many. I loved when they brought out food. It always was something unusual and delicious, like salmon or crepes, served on fine china with bright, white, cloth napkins and beverage, complete with iced water served in crystal glasses.

One learned to navigate through this process … when to raise a fork, sip a glass, bite and chew. Heaven forbid, one was up and delayed a response or answer to finish the processing of a mouthful. If it wasn't seamless, then you probably didn't belong. This was the boardroom, each setting a leather chair lying claim to the table portion directly in front of it, each accessing its own private electrical outlet and Internet port. It was big stuff for big shots.

BOOM! The kind one hears at the end of fireworks lighting up the sky. Loud, jump loud. The boardroom table -- a huge, heavy-wood centerpiece, with twenty seats around, SHOOK. Something just happened. Something big and bad just happened in our real estate in the sky.

Meeting stopped. Eyes frightened and serious shot wide-eyed stares first at each other, then at the walls and doors as if somehow they would provide answers.

Being the first to force self-mobility from our combined state of frozen-ness, I got up and turned right. (It is strange the things one remembers some 15 years later. I won't say every day, but many times I find myself remembering turning right.) If I had turned left and opened the exit door on the left, I would not have seen the panic, the flames, the smoke and no doubt would not have had the same urgency, fear and overwhelming purpose to leave. It was only that first scene upon opening exit door right that kicked my ass into action.

More than once during that insane morning, I turned right and in combination, it is the reason I still exist. It is the reason that I can still love my wife, the reason I got to see my angels grow up into the talented, gorgeous young ladies, the reason I can play with our dogs, won five straight championships, swim, laugh, cry, golf, bake in the sun, drive, eat and enjoy watching baseball. It is the reason for everything. I turned right … more than once.

Situated at my leather big-shot seat approximately half way between exit door left and exit door right, I stood and turned right. I

scurried to the door, bent the handle and pushed. As the door opened, I realized for the first time that the Boom did not originate in our building. At the time, this represented small relief but nonetheless a factor in my opportunity to continue to live and 15 years later strike these laptop keys.

Turning right and opening the right door exit placed me in sight of Tower I. My focus initially stayed in our building, as I witnessed co-workers frantically negotiating through the maze of workstations that permeated the areas outside the boardroom, to the main carpeted runway leading to the elevator and stairs.

Quite honestly, their urgency, their expressions and mostly their panic, served to scare me, as I have never been scared before. My eyes shifted up, over their heads, over the tops of half wall workstations to the window panels that had so defined the once beautiful views from the upper Trade Center floors. What I saw turned any hope for calm judgment and sound decision-making into instant reaction fueled by a surreal setting and a rush of adrenaline, which clearly took over my being. Flames shot from building one toward our building as if from the throat of a fire-breathing dragon. Black smoke billowed out from the building, interrupted only by the flames that cut through the black hell. I turned, saw my

four big-shot companions waiting for my report and blurted the only thing that came to mind … "WE NEED TO LEAVE, NOW!"

Some years later, at the request of one of my angels, daddy signed us up for karate lessons. She being 8 or 9, me being five times that, we regularly drove up Route 22 to the lesson, angel mixing with a small group of her own age and me one on one with a master. Shortly after starting them, like the piano lessons, oboe lessons, rec basketball (if you're a parent, you get the idea) discontinued the lessons but in my short stay I learned a few things.

First, small wood planks actually exist that are so weak even the most timid 8--year-old can karate chop through them, much to the delight of mom and dad, mostly dad. And second, martial arts teaches you vision through self-control and calmness. When your assailant is flailing away looking to take your head off, a trained martial arts guy steps back, and through a focused calm has the ability to slow things down (no panic), visualizes in almost slow motion, sees his opening and strikes with nasty intentions.

I always envisioned great military leaders in the heat of battle maintaining an ability to slow things visually, stay calm and make sound decisions. A guy once told me the way he stayed alive in the brutal jungles of Vietnam was to stick

with his commander who had an uncanny ability to calmly lead and direct amidst the most ferocious of warfare. He also told me that Vietnam taught him another valuable lesson … that a man can live a long time on simply a diet of coffee and cigarettes; a good thing to know. That morning, only the very few thought like a black belt. Most, including myself, displayed the unenviable trait of sheer panic.

Bolting the boardroom followed closely by my four now not so big-shot peers, I headed for the elevator only to be stopped by others declaring emphatically that the transfer shaft had been shut down. In the WTC, one could only go from ground to floor 78, and then transfer to another bank of elevator shafts to go higher.

Deterred for only a split second, we all headed for the stairwell on floor 94. Upon entering, it seemed calm and civil, but as we quickly started our way down, the stairs became increasingly crowded as each floor's passage to the stairwell became a wave of entering bodies; tough ones, short ones, old ones, white ones, Asian ones, black ones, females and males all made their way into the well-lit exit down.

The WTC stairs were not what many might envision. Rather than a stairway where quick turns spawned the next set of stairs down, these were built whereby one proceeded down

five flights, walked down a narrow hallway to the next five flights down; repeat the narrow hallway walk (the opposite direction) to the next five flights down. Do that a few times and one becomes disoriented to their exact location. I remember thinking, (at the time it felt like brain wave screaming) ... “Where the hell are the floor numbers? Didn’t anyone paint the damn numbers next to the stairway entrance/egress door? Am I on eighty? Sixty? Where the hell am I?”

At this point the stairwell was now crowded, filled with all types, nobody talking, everybody rushing … but civil and professional. Even quick strong guys who, if faced with an empty stairwell could almost fly down the stairs, now were being patient to those who could not. All I could think of was the street, the one where I sneaked a smoke from time to time, the one where on a sunny day you could grab a dog with sauerkraut and onions with a cold diet Coke and breathe real air for a while before returning for the afternoon workload. Please let me get to the street.

As for my meeting associates, none were within eyeshot. GA had disappeared from my vision somewhere early on in our move toward exit; DC had (it was rumored later) stopped off on floor 90 to retrieve her pocketbook, MB and HS were nowhere to be seen. For now, the stairs

were a mix of workers from many companies, all with the same, single goal. Get out of the sky, get out of the building, keep breathing, and stay alive.

What happened next is something that I have thought about thousands of times since that surreal morning. Like the right turn I made when jumping from my leather chair in the boardroom, I was faced with a similar crossroad, only this time there was a few seconds to give it some thought.

The crowd descending in front of me seemed to have two options; stay close to the wall left and continue down or veer right and enter an open, wider space. Because going right meant flattening your movement onto level corridor and left clearly welcomed a continued angle down, most were staying left. I decided, despite the unknown pathway, to veer right.

I have thought many times, even now, why I chose right. I had never been in the stairwell before. It was clearly the riskier choice. Was it because I am right-handed, or because going with the herd was easier than crossing over the stairwell? Was it divine intervention because I have kids or because I coach kids? Or was it because on this surreal morning, one just had to be lucky? Whatever it was, the decision saved my life.

For those within four or five flights above or below me, staying left meant the inconceivable as within a few minutes the second plane would slice through the building, through the stairwell and spread fuel and explosion in all directions. People died. Good people, old people, young, married, fathers, mothers, sons and daughters deserving none of this chaos were dead! Those bastards, those evil fucking bastards.

For me and the others near me, our path proceeded through a small concrete room, through a doorway and out … miraculously to an elevator hallway … floor 78, the top of the transfer shaft with working elevators going DOWN!!!

WTC elevators were also not what most people think. They were mini rooms, fitting 4 to 5 times that of a typical elevator, doors on each side, entering and exiting in one direction though opposite doors. Going down 78 floors took merely seconds as the people box free falls only to slow quickly as it reaches its instructed destination.

I managed to squeeze on an over-packed elevator, so crowded that my heal tips slightly protruded outside the line of the bottom door panel. As the doors attempted to close, they went into auto open mode as they caromed off each of my shoulders.

"GET IN OR GET OUT" was heard from some male voice from the opposite side of the elevator. So with my forearm, my RIGHT forearm, I shoved the person directly in front of me and created the six inches I needed to fully enter the elevator. The doors closed inches behind me. It started moving the only way it could … down. Thank you, Jesus, I was moving down.

A lady angled to my left was shaken and silently weeping. A young man, clearly used to having the answers spoke up ... "It was a plane! A plane hit tower one." For most, I presume, and certainly for me, this was a revelation. Until that time, I assumed a bomb had detonated in tower one. For a very brief second, I was relieved.

Was that terrible of me? Even knowing the devastation and tragic results that the first explosion must have caused, I was temporarily relieved. It was an accident, an accident that hit the other tower. My God, I thought, we are safe. As the elevator door opened to the impressive WTC lobby, I was met by chaos, people running, scrambling in all directions. Quickly my sense of relief was gone. I was back to adrenaline mode. It was a free-for-all, no directions, and no one seemingly in charge.

Later I learned of instructions to my tower to stay put, do not evacuate. Safety forces did not want two towers evacuating at the same time. The

thinking was my tower was safe and would be emptied when those in Tower I were out and clear. I never heard that announcement. Honestly, I remain skeptical that it was ever given. I have convinced myself over the years, that even if I had heard it, I would have ignored it. My instinct would have always been to get out, to get the hell out of the sky and ask questions later.

Faced with more decisions, now standing by the turnstile, the one in which I had entered and exited each day for several years, I looked left. Liberty Street was clearly not an option. It was filled with confusion and peril. I jumped through the turnstile, turned RIGHT and headed for the underground mall. Now sprinting, I zigzagged through a maze of people headed in every direction. Serpentine, serpentine, still with no instructions, no direction, no supervision, only panic. Finally, I saw the light above the upcoming stairs and escalator to the revolving doors out to the Broadway side of the Trade Center. The escalator would be for another day, as I took several leaps, three steps at a time. Winded and now fatigued from the journey, I reached for the door. Halfway through, about to breathe outdoor air and get my bearings, my senses were shocked with a deafening BOOM No. 2 coming from directly above me. I ducked quickly, as if avoiding contact; not realizing the impact was thousands of feet above me.

I sprinted across the double section streets of Broadway until I was met by the storefront of Century 21. Feeling it time to look, I turned back and saw the inconceivable again, a repeat of the disaster that I had witnessed from the boardroom… black smoke and fire screaming from the top of the Trade Center, this time from my building.

My view paralyzed any further immediate movement. I just stared upward, in shock and not fully cognizant of what was happening. My statue-like pose was interrupted as I sensed and saw through the corner of my vision, an object coming toward me quickly, very quickly. Only in time to see slightly before impact, someone running very fast, head turned completely staring back and up at the surreal scene tens of flights up.

The person hit me, never seeing or caring about anything in their path, consumed with getting away. I played football for years, but never took a hit like this. I went flying several feet, landing on Manhattan's pavement and with an adrenaline rush like never felt before; I popped up immediately, feeling no pain.

The human Mack Truck was gone, long gone without a word. Since that sidebar hit, I think often about it, always relating it to the Alexis Arguello/Aaron Pryor fight so many years ago. This was during a point of my life where I

actually cared who won a boxing match, a prizefight as my dad used to say. Arguello (my guy) was a lanky lightweight with a right cross which, if solidly landed, could break your neck. I once saw him turn the lights out on Kevin Rooney, Mike Tyson's old trainer, with a right cross that had all at ringside concerned with Rooney's ability to get up; I mean ever get up.

In the Pryor fight, I sat in utter amazement that time after time when Pryor received flush right-hand crosses, he never budged, never wavered. I am now convinced that Pryor worked himself into a state of adrenaline where he could not be hurt. The pain and its effect would have to wait. I was Aaron Pryor in that second of collision, bouncing up, off the pavement, refusing to give any credence to just being run over. That shit, that pain, would have to wait.

I turned and sprinted east toward the East Side Drive, hoping and praying to get away from the madness. When I arrived at the FDR Drive, I saw a familiar face, a co-worker GS. He hugged me, let me go quickly and, staring at my legs, asked if I was all right. Only then, did I realize I was hurt. My pants, only hours ago half of my nice, big shot olive green suit was ripped from thigh to shin. Blood had soaked the rip and was now streaming down resting on my shoe-top.

Manhattan’s pavement had taken its toll on my leg, but a small price to pay because, on this morning, so many others never made it to the street. Sitting on a half wall, we watched as hundreds moved quickly, others standing in groups trying to work cell phones that were not responding. We decided to go south to the ferry and take heed of ourselves in Battery Park.

The park contained thousands as we walked its perimeter, first resting on a two-story ramp, then thinking the wiser, deciding no height was the best height. We finally settled against the water’s edged iron fence, about to witness and experience the next leg in what had increasingly become too long of a nightmare.

As soon as we entered the park, information began to spread rapidly. It was planes; it was deliberate; …it was terrorists. Additionally, word spread that the Pentagon had been hit and a plane, which had been hijacked, had crashed in Pennsylvania. For so many of us, it was our first experience with war. My thoughts moved from escape to my family, my wife, my daughters, and my parents. Amazing how all other things seemed meaningless. I thought of my family and the only desire I had left ... to get back home.

Two things, previously taken for granted without much thought day in and day out, now

became painfully obvious roadblocks during this emergency. The first was that communicating was not possible during an emergency. Cell phones did not work when overloaded with usage and call attempts. Pay phones, still around in 2001, contained massive lines; desperate people looking to contact desperate loved ones.

Weeks later, I was told a story by one of my company-employed friends who was approaching the Lincoln Tunnel when the planes flew into the buildings. With traffic stopped, all now standing outside their cars stunned with the sights of the visible towers roaring with flames and smoke, he was without a cell phone. He approached a man unknown and offered him a hundred dollar bill if the man was kind enough to let him use his cell phone. It was that kind of urgency!

The second roadblock was that Manhattan was an island and in an emergency, very difficult to leave. Many had taken to walking to one of the bridges, hoping to walk across and gain public transportation or car rides once free of the Rotten Apple.

As GS and I stood on the edge of the park where walkway meets water, MK, a female co-worker displaying deep-breath relief to meet up with familiar faces, joined us. The three of us stood silent and listened to groups around us tell

their story of escape. Even today, anyone who was there on this frightful morning has a story, each gripping, each capable of mesmerizing listeners.

It was that kind of event, both powerful and lasting. Standing in the park, sweat, blood, fatigue and emotion all spilling into one fucked-up mess, we had no idea of the lasting impact of this day nor what was only seconds away.

I bummed a cigarette, not giving a single thought to my briefcase, car keys and who knows what else that remained in my office, somewhere in the firestorm of Tower II. Finally able to calm down, I began to think, for the first time, about the people I was with on 94 and other co-workers who shared office space in the sky.

I felt sick, and at one point began looking around for a place to throw up. My leg was raw with the deep blood-drawing scrape, courtesy of someone I knew I would never see again. Time had caused the blood to dry up and down my leg. For the first time, I noticed that I was limping. Bastards, I thought, as I faked a smile to MK, letting her know things would be OK … until the ground under our feet started shaking.

I had never experienced an earthquake. I was convinced I was about to. Thinking my adrenaline tank had been emptied, a reserve never

before needed kicked in. People closer to the park's grass fields began to scream that the tower was falling. "It's the tower, it's falling!!!" Thoughts of a toppled, massive building falling through the park brought panic to the faces of my two companions and me. Facing the center of the park, thousands began running toward the water, toward us. Now flash thinking stampede, I envisioned the next step would be to jump into the water. Someone yelled the boat is open, more than once. I grabbed MK's hand, GS grabbed mine and we raced south to the park's exit amidst screaming, crying people with a now gray wave of something quickly approaching the park north to south. People were running under the terminal and toward the boat, unmanned but open. It was the new boat, the one with three levels. We ran and followed, as fast as any three could while holding hands.

Again, for what seemed like the hundredth time that morning, we were running for our lives. Mixed with the fear that only comes from imminent danger, I began to see (and feel) anger within myself and from others, like screaming enough already … we have had enough. Only there was no enemy to scream at, to retaliate against; only innocent people caught in another bizarre and contemptible moment.

The three of us sprinted onto the boat, staying on the lowest level. Why? I have no idea. Upon scurrying to the backs of those that preceded us, about to the midpoint of the boat (back to front), we were instantly pinned in our spots by a sea of people running directly behind us onto the boat.

Now, literally stuck in the middle of the boat, lower level, only a few feet above water level, I thought … this is not good. We were now at the mercy of another fate, no longer able to move, control our direction or get the hell out. Not exactly the world's biggest optimist on a good day, at this point, I conceded to just waiting for the next bad thing to happen. I felt beaten. If not for the seriousness of the moment, I could have broken into the Allman Brothers classic, *Tied to the Whipping Post* … just plain shit whipped from the morning's unbelievable moments.

The boat became engulfed in what appeared to be fog. Not realizing it was bad air from the falling tower, it seemed just the next obstacle to this very bad morning. People started to panic, some crying, some screaming, some shaking, some on hands and knees in search of the boat's hidden life preservers. Civility was replaced with panic, anger and fear.

Confusion and crying filled the air from hundreds now stuck on the boat. A guy jumped onto the seat next to him, giving him a few more feet of height and began screaming "SHUT THE FUCK UP, SHUT THE FUCK UP, SHUT THE FUCK UP!" As ridiculous as that sounded, it shocked people closer to sanity and actually helped the once riotous scene. One by one, people began to be quiet as if they were listening for instructions or just now realizing that their behavior was not helping.

Unexpectedly, the boat's engine started, a sound I had heard hundreds of times right before takeoff. Slowly one could feel the boat move slowly out of the dock, although seeing out the windows was impossible due to the dust and large telephone like poles that blocked the view from the boat's lower level.

Instantly, the boat stalled, engine stopping. Again, the masses began to panic, scream and carry on. In seconds the engine re-started, seeming to calm the all-but-spent crowd. Unable to move, I dropped to one knee; sweat dripping down my face, my body giving in to the unchangeable surroundings. Saying a prayer and almost passing out from the past few hours, I was brought back to the moment by MK who was standing over my knelt body and eagerly tapping my shoulder, my right shoulder. I rose looked in

the direction of her finger point and saw the most incredible sight ever witnessed, one that is etched in my brain for all time.

The boat had outrun the massive cloud of death and was now streaming up the harbor in what had to be the most beautiful combination of sea and sky that I had ever witnessed in my 20 some odd years of taking this ocean people mover. A perfect weather day, a San Diego day.

To the left of my line of vision was an older ferry going in the opposite direction toward New York City, a sight that I had seen hundreds and hundreds of times before. Except, this was different. The crossing boat was a map of blue uniforms cramming every nook and corner available. Cops, the police were storming downtown Manhattan. For the first time in hours and what seemed much longer, I smiled and hugged KM, now, her head down, holding back tears of joy.

As we approached the Staten Island side of the harbor, I could see thousands of spectators, families, loved ones waiting anxiously for the boat to dock in the hopes that it contained their dad, their mom, their son, their daughter. The boat docked. I walked off with my companions, undaunted that car keys were lost forever and my means home was now stuck in some Jersey City parking lot.

I crossed Richmond Terrace, paying no mind to the two block long line at the street's only pay phone and entered a deli that I never before had visited. I bought the biggest water bottle that they sold and a pack of cigarettes. We decided to walk up Victory Boulevard toward my parent's home. It was but a short 8 or 9 miles away.

On that evil morning, some 3000 innocent people died, 87 of which worked in my company … friends and associates. Among the dead were three of the five management members with me in Tower II's boardroom on floor 94 when the first plane hit Tower I, with only HS and myself surviving. I have not seen HS in many years. The last communication we had was some months after that tragic morning, sitting on a bench outside one of the company's back-up sites in Short Hills, NJ. At that time, he indicated that he was cashing out, taking his savings and retiring, despite his young age. Off, he said, to focus on coaching his young son's soccer team. I expect that at some point he returned to do what he did so well. I also hope to someday see him again, although I doubt I ever will.

I think differently now ... much stronger views on the war against terror … sure that the

moral fiber within our society is decaying ... equally sure that world peace, while still worth pursuing, is farther from our grasp than ever before …convinced and depressed that America must negotiate all things from a position of strength and dominating power, for reasoning with those whose core principles include the destruction of the west is impossible …a cynical view on the genuineness of world and local leaders … a smaller circle, limited mostly to my wife and daughters to soak up my love … home more, out less … more enamored with and interested in a Viet Nam or World War II veteran than a sports or entertainment star … a disdain for the greedy, selfish agenda of most people and institutions …more of an observer and less of a fan of sports teams and spoiled athletes … .more inclined to enjoy a round of golf … a person still of faith, but no longer following the hypocritical Catholic church … less *of an ability to sleep the entire night through … and convinced that on that shitty morning where evil and misguided human beings wrecked the lives of so many, I was lucky, nothing more, nothing deeper than that.*

Unfortunately, it was the beginning of a change in me. Perhaps it was an unconscious transformation brought on by emotional trauma, something best assessed by a professional. Sometimes I think maybe it just served to age my thought process quicker than what is normal, you know, the negative old-man syndrome. But on most days, I think it just robbed me of my pre-9/11 abilities to be carefree, turning me far too introspective, not crazy mind you, just the ultimate realist with too sharp a vision for my own or anyone else's good.

Chapter 5

The Aftermath of My Escape

Victory Boulevard starts from St. George in Staten Island. It runs right to the water's edge, ending across from the ferry slips made of hundreds of telephone poles tarred together to corral incoming people movers. The Staten Island Ferry terminal was usually reserved for people moving quickly to board the next boat to Manhattan or after day's end to get deposited back on to Staten Island, find their way to their cars or scurry to the bus or train slip, making their way back home.

If it wasn't rush hour, boats left less frequently, turning the terminal into more of a waiting area. Gathered on both sides of the turnstiles, people filled their wait with conversation or by spending a few bits at newsstands, coffee stops or at the terminal's local McDonalds.

Since those days, the terminal's wait has turned to nine out of ten people standing silently, feet stuck in one spot … staring at their phones. Marketed as a condition of social advancement, phone staring really represents the beginning of the decay of genuine communication in this world, serving really only to bulge the pocketbooks of inappropriateness. Clearly, that is a story for another day.

While the views from the boat were front and center in every new "I Love New York" commercial, the terminal often felt greasy and dirty. It represented a repository for the homeless looking to stay warm and dry, or for that day's truants, skipping class in favor of some apple-wine or a marijuana cigarette.

In early November as Election Day grew near, the terminal was a favorite rush-hour stop for local politicians to shake some hands and pretend they gave a shit about you. They looked so out of place, entourage in tow, with boxes filled with flyers promising a cure for all of life's evils. After Election Day, they conspicuously disappeared until their need to again be re-elected.

The area in and around the terminal always felt pretty safe when the crowds were moving to and from, less safe during off-hours

when one had to walk to the car or bus after working overtime or having a few pops at some Manhattan brewery.

On this day, downtown St. George was filled with a crowd of humanity in search of any information about their loved ones. So many were there -- wives, husbands, dads, friends, moms, sons and daughters -- all hoping for the best and fearing the worst. I spent many a moment imagining the torture those left behind experience during the unknown period when loved ones are in real peril. This day's peril was as serious as it gets; death-like real and information to help calm the worst of our fears was impossible to come by.

I heard this feeling best described by a veteran once who spoke of his family's torment when he was shipped out into harm's way. During war, he said, it's not only the soldiers who travel to the brink of human atrocity, their loved ones go with them, not in body but in full spirit, experiencing the same fear, emptiness and internal torture. In the movie Cinderella Man, when an aging James Braddock leaves to fight for the championship against the much younger, stronger and dangerously fisted Max Baer, his wife remains home. Hyperventilating with the fear for her husband's safety, she shares with him each blow, the pain, the sweat and every bit of the

inherent danger. One could only begin to magnify a thousand-fold such a feeling to those military families wrought with anguish as their loved ones look to escape death each day while fulfilling their missions.

So selfless, courageous and telling was the letter to her family, sent by American Kayla Mueller, the modern day Good Samaritan, first held hostage then killed in the insanity of terror. In it, she wrote that any pain and suffering that she had experienced through her ordeal could not begin to equal her sorrow in understanding the internal torture being experienced by her family, indicating her unworthiness for forgiveness.

Such was the feeling in St. George that day, as breathing normal was replaced with deep breaths and punch-in-the-stomach nausea only reserved for the most serious of times.

Our exit from the ferryboat was like stepping off a lifeboat, finally onto solid ground, feeling that chaos and death was now in the rear-view mirror. I walked first through, then away from the crowd, stopping only briefly to secure much-needed hydration and cigarettes. I don't remember paying for these items only rather the caring face of the attendant at the Richmond Terrace deli. I wonder if the people in that store remember the look on my face.

We decided to walk up Victory Boulevard, an initially steep hill of a road a few miles long, until it leveled at the corner of Jewett Avenue; the tip of Silver Lake Park. With each step, MK and I recanted that morning's beyond real nightmare. The strong and glorious sunshine from that warm, blue-sky September day slowly began to thaw the shock and fatigue that had gripped my body, refusing seemingly for hours, to let go. My mind sprinted from my wife, my daughters and my parents to the whereabouts of my four friends in the boardroom and then to many others who shared seven floors in the sky and each day with me for the past several years.

I thought about the drills that had become commonplace at the World Trade Center, where we would line up in the 90th floor hallway and hear speeches from the floor's volunteer safety wardens. I remember thinking how insignificant any training had on the exit of those fortunate enough to get down in the hours before.

I remember that my leg hurt and that I found myself chain smoking in a ridiculous and stupid attempt to breathe normally. I remember thinking only in that moment, oblivious to what would become the daily reminders of this horror for months and then years to come.

At the top of the park, someone yelled at us from a truck. I don't remember who was driving the truck, but I think it was a red truck and that I was nauseous and dizzy. My memory blacks out from that moment until I recall stepping out of the truck in front of my parent's home. I am OK with a segment gone from my memory. I know I shouldn't be and perhaps with some simple communication, I could fill in the missing details. I simply don't want to remember. I don't even want to understand why I don't want to remember this part of my story. Perhaps, alone with my thoughts or even writing my thoughts are one thing; communication with others about this day is another.

Now almost 15 years later, rarely have I ever talked about this day. Once I was asked to speak to a group of kids on an anniversary of 9/11. I agreed, not wholeheartedly, but agreed nevertheless. Afterwards, I felt empty and I remember hoping that I would never have to do that again. I think it's an important story, a gripping and an interesting one both for those who were there and those who were not. In light of the continuing war on terror, still brutal and insane, still finding each day's headlines, I think it remains a critical story. I'm just not comfortable with any part of it. I don't know why and I don't care why. It's a part of me that I refuse to overthink or have analyzed.

I remember walking up my parents' front steps, a house only 40 or so feet wide with a 10-by-10 front lawn continually guarded by the Blessed Mother statue propped up against the house. The wood door to the TV room was wide open. A glass storm door was the only thing separating me from the endless hugs and tears of my parents.

All present had spent the last several hours, I was told, standing in front of the TV, first watching over and over the flames and black hell pouring from the Trade Center's towers and then, almost inconceivably watching my building crumble into that suffocating concrete dust storm.

Recently and many years later, alone in my bedroom, with my oldest daughter upstairs and my wife on her way home, I cried like a baby as I watched the last scene from the movie Captain Phillips with Tom Hanks. Watching the now-rescued, in-shock, hyperventilating captain as he sat on the nurse's table struggling to speak reminded me of my dad when he first saw me entering the house.

With hand on wall to balance himself, I recall his shock, his elation, at that moment too much emotion to be controlled within a single human being's body. The power of family and of

a father's love overtook a man who was a war veteran himself, having served first on Navy ships and then in combat zones in the Philippines during World War II. I remember seeing old pictures of my dad with his battalion and hearing his stories about how he and so many others were stricken with jungle rot from wet clothing and mud, thankful that each day ended with life not death.

It's funny how little things like a scene in a movie take you back to stored feelings and memories. Conjured by the acting of Hanks, the memory of my dad's reaction on this day, of his overwhelming love for his son and unfortunately of his recent passing was too much for me at that moment. It strikes to an emotion that I could not control.

Now with a landline only a step to the kitchen away, I called home telling my wife I was safe and hearing the voices of my little girls. Upon hearing the news and then beginning to follow it like the other millions of Americans, my wife had rushed to my daughters' school and brought them to the safety of home and out of earshot from stories about the World Trade Center.

My girls, in the first and fourth grade at the time, were young enough to be shielded from

the enormity of the day's events. As years have gone by, I've come to realize that the impact of this day on their lives was more profound that I thought. Like their dad, they are not inclined to speak much about 9/11.

Interestingly, I have come to know the depth of their thoughts through writings and essays by each of them as they grew and became increasingly capable of sharing their thoughts. My readings of their material often end in my private tears, as I remain thankful for my survival, the gift to be here for them and the recollection of the day that changed everything in my life.

The bridges connecting New Jersey to Staten Island were closed, I guess until the authorities could get a handle on what was safe and what wasn't. Truth is, nobody knew. So the next several hours were spent in my parents' living room watching the horrific aftermath on television.

I remember the projected number of those reported missing or unaccounted for was rising but truly only guesses at that point. Reporters looking to connect dots for their story's sake told of the limited facts, available at that time, along with their own and others' theories, to form stories for the public to understand. It was during this time that the related events of the plane crash

of a hijacked aircraft and the explosion at the Pentagon hit home. Our country was being attacked with coordinated and premeditated bombings, using aircrafts as weaponry. I remember realizing that so many people were dead and that it was quite possible that I knew hundreds of them.

Our now collective stares were straight-ahead toward the TV, with the exception of mom who was now in the kitchen preparing food as a medicinal remedy. Two visitors interrupted our stupors. The first was my cousin who, other than my three best friends at home, along with my sister, is one of the few left in this world who truly cares for me without much agenda.

She had grabbed her boss, a notable Staten Island doctor, threatening to quit if he didn't immediately comply with the demand to drive her to my parents' house. After heartfelt hugs and a few tears, they were off again, secure in the knowledge that I was alive.

A few minutes later, my cousin's husband, who clearly had been trained well in the demands of loyalty and obligation, left his Staten Island construction site and entered the TV room armed with a brown paper bag tucked neatly under his arm. A good friend always, and a faithful I-got-your-back guy, he proceeded to unleash a fine

bottle of scotch, clearly at the moment more appetizing than my mom's food. With a numbness now intact that only Johnny Walker and the surreal events of the day could produce, I was ready to venture home, making my way, designated driver secured, to the just opened Outerbridge Crossing.

My arrival home was met with some tasteful hugs as my life's true partner and I reserved our love display for private time, making conscientious efforts not to frighten our creations. My girls squeezed their dad sensing everything was back to normal and soon were ushered to the comforts of our mansion's wing for kids, the beginning for them of a good night's sleep.

The tuck-in and kiss goodnight was as meaningful a moment as any parent could experience. The rest is a blur, the cleanup, the shower, the leg bandaging, the phone calls, all of it, just a dreamy prelude to again staring at the TV, now sprawled on my back trying to make some sense of it.

At six a.m., the peace that only comes from being truly unconscious was interrupted by a phone call from Geneva, Switzerland. It was my company's Vice Chairman of the Board of Directors. After communicating his pleasure that I was alive and safe, he regrettably informed me

that so many of our associates were not. He asked if I could be at our recovery site in Secaucus, New Jersey, in 30 minutes. I nodded yes like he could see me, hung up the phone and looked for my wife's car keys.

When one is presented with tragedy, clearly of this magnitude, there are really only two choices. The first is to allow it to overcome you, where you are paralyzed in that moment. Defeated, you give in and submit to the inconceivable devastation of tragedy, all the while perhaps cognizant that this road probably doesn't represent the most heroic.

Inwardly, you feel the need to crawl up in a dark space, hoping that you awake from the nightmare. You become trapped in emotional wreckage accompanied by physical pain and, until it subsides, moving forward is not really an option.

Some of my associates became like this and it was a most difficult time for them, and for those who cared for them and had to witness it. The best one could hope for in this state was to mix in some vision of future ability to move on. Often it reminded me of the song lyrics from America back in the 80's when they sang, "Well I tried to make it Sunday, but I got so damn

depressed that I set my sights on Monday and I got myself undressed." Physically, today wasn't going to happen. Leave me alone and maybe you'll see me tomorrow.

The second choice was for those cerebrally capable of moving forward, mindless and operating more on instinct than anything else. Sure, those who could proceed like this often dealt with the pain reminiscent of bent-over contractions several times a day, but mostly they were zombies reacting to each moment without much thought or consciousness.

The magnitude of 9/11's tragedy prevented any real or meaningful production from anyone who had experienced it. I was in this category, spurred on by the three faces of innocence and beauty, my three girls, I put forth my best attempts to move forward with an empty head, dealing with the often felt jolts of reality as privately as I could.

I tried real hard to apply a "clear head" approach to the days following 9/11. Interestingly, the words "clear head" were my dad's harshest toward anyone on this earth. Saying someone had a clear head was sort of like saying, "not much between the ears" or "not the sharpest tool in the shed," nicely questioning someone's depth of thought you might say. But,

"clear head" also implied that one went through life oblivious to the real and serious things around them. What might have a real impact or effect on a normal person would have little or no effect on someone with a clear head.

Try to envision someone waking up, switching the TV on and being welcomed with the horrific news, hmmm let's say, that China has attacked the USA's west coast with long-range missiles. Instead of reacting to such an event with an appropriate level of rage and concern, someone with a clear head might focus on the little box at the bottom right of the TV screen which showed the current temperature outside and instantly start thinking about today's wardrobe. That's clear head.

Somehow I picture it in cartoon imagery, like a talking animal character strolling down a country road looking at an old fashioned map, say ... looking for Darla's house. As he is walking, he is oblivious to the roadsides being washed away with catastrophic mudslide like erosion on both sides of his feet, still simply focused on his map and seeing Ms. Darla. Clear head.

The connotation is that they are the happy-go-lucky individuals who, at times, draw envy from the realist who live bothered and affected by life's everyday tragedies and misfortunes. I've

even heard some actually bring religion and God into this discussion, like somehow God made people like this to protect or safeguard them from cerebral torture.

Ironically, my dad left this earth with a clear head, stricken with severe dementia over his last few years. During that time, I was thankful for his state of mind for I believed it spared him the everyday reality of a decaying physical state through old age and disease.

I did my best to move through September 2001, with a clear head for the alternative was to crawl up like a ball and temporarily shut out the world, a world that needed me at the time.

As I move through what represents my almost 60th year on this planet, I often try to fade in and out of clear head, having learned to apply it when my surroundings are somewhat falling short of George Baily's Bedford Falls.

The world, my world, is filled with almost daily stories of inconceivable atrocities by my fellow man. All of us are deluged with daily tales of terrorist horror, beheadings, burning humans alive, suicide bombings, murder, inconceivably acts of senseless violence at different locations around the globe.

I've witnessed our Pope brokering relations between my country and one that imparts torture and deprivation on its own people, in between his apologies for the atrocities that have so defined his despicable clergy.

We've dealt with cops in my hometown being ambushed and shot in the head over skin color. I read stories of weekly racial violence, in my country now more divided and antagonistic than ever before. I learned of drunks killing people by driving into crowds and street fights between citizens against and (ready for this?) in support of a Boston terrorist bomber. All of these hard-to-believe facts are recent and all of this amidst a backdrop of continued lame and pathetic rhetoric by a so misguided media and our so-called state and national leaders.

Clear-head living has become the norm for the vast majority of people in our world, part of the reason that we are all capable of moving forward, acceptant of the human atrocities that have become the routine for each day's headlines. Unfortunately, clear-head living is also part of the reason that little changes and the atrocities are allowed to continue.

Chapter 6

Forward March

Comforted only by my wife's full tank of gas, I turned her pretty white BMW right (what else!) leaving my finely manicured circular driveway. I was headed to a building that I was told was within eyeshot of Giants Stadium. Incapable of organizing or reconciling yesterday's events, I was simply and blindly complying with the Forward March command received in the alarm clock phone call from Switzerland. Little did I realize that I would never be the same again.

The turnpike was rather quiet that morning as I cleared my head with guzzles of dark, strong coffee. Mostly I thought about a phone call that I had received from GA's husband the night before. Even in my dazed state, I heard him say that he had not heard from her and was reaching out to me because someone had told him that she

was in the management meeting on floor 94; my meeting with four others.

I had confirmed to him that she was in fact in the meeting but had disappeared from my sight soon after our frenzied exit from the boardroom. I rooted hard at that moment that she was OK, as I could hear panic in his voice. I liked her very much. She was one of the few individuals at my company who was willing and comfortable to let you know that she was a mother and wife first, a HR executive after that.

The one thing that was always evident about GA was her love for her kids. Showing one's human side on Wall Street was not always easy at the top of the ladder, more reserved for underlings and those less paid. Heck, I'm sure even the mega-shots loved their kids but it was sought of like being out with the boys and constantly talking about your wife or girlfriend … it just didn't fit right.

GA always maintained a screw-that-kind-of-thinking attitude. From the pictures of her family front-and-center on her desk to the take-it-seriously approach to her kids schoolwork, she made the gravitational pull between job and family look easy. Frankly, she was more like me than most at the job. I think about that call often,

only hoping that her husband and her children are doing well.

As I drew closer to my destination, I thought about HS, MB and DC also in yesterday's early morning meeting. I didn't know if I would see them at the recovery site, but I was hopeful. As I advanced up the turnpike, I became very nervous, not knowing what to expect when I arrived. It was sort of like hearing there's an accident and you're rushing to the scene not knowing how bad it is. It was another torture-like moment. I remember having tears in my eyes, getting pissed off, shaking my head rather violently, pleading with myself to snap out of it.

I remember trying to think about work and what would be critical now that everything was destroyed. One of the first things you learn on Wall Street, especially in my role as division head, is the meaning of the word fiduciary. It is both the clearly written and fully understood code of financial institutions. It drives all regulatory entities, imparting a serious code of honor among those who either are tasked with assessing compliance to the code or those who are asked to live by it.

Simply put, fiduciary responsibility means that if others have entrusted their money to your firm directly and indirectly to you as an employee

of that firm, you must take the highest form of prudence in caring for it, completely in-line with the owners' directives. Non-compliance to fiduciary responsibility results in only real bad things for both firms and their employees.

Simple, unintentional infractions can result in poor regulatory ratings, eliminating a company's privilege to accept new business or monetary fines. The more material (and God-forbid) intentional infractions result in far more serious stuff, including shutting down a company and personal liability and criminal implications to those involved.

In the aftermath of destruction as this act of war clearly represented, both of records and personnel, the challenges and difficulties to put the company back together, calming the thousands of depositors and investors, would not be hard to find. Our company, at the time, was controlling somewhere in the range of 60 billion dollars in client-owned assets, relatively a moderate level compared to the much larger firms. Worldwide, our company employed not much more than 500 employees, the majority of them assigned to floors 90 through 97 in the once tallest building in the world.

Another very relative concept at play in the bombing's aftermath was system and record recovery. As standard, firms within most

industries but none more important than within financial institutions, were required to have back-up systems in place. These were duplicate systems controlling all aspects of a company's data, including the critical records of accounts, both the firm's and their clients.

These back-up systems were to be routinely tested to ensure that they worked and could be relied upon if needed. They were routinely assessed as part of both internal audits and regulatory examinations. All assessed them as integral to the continuity of a firm and critical. People took disaster recovery real seriously on Wall Street. As such, back-up processes continue to advance as technology advances.

I can remember first starting out in the early 80's when back-up systems were routinely updated weekly. This meant that should systems at a firm's primary location go down, recovery to a fully updated back-up system required re-entering of transactions not already backed up, limited in this case to no more than a week's worth.

As time moved on and technology advanced, daily back-ups became the norm reducing any exposure to transactions not already backed-up to intraday periods only. For example, if all data was backed up at the end of each day,

usually overnight, and the primary system went down today at 10 a.m., then the transactions that needed to be captured and loaded to the back-up system were those from the beginning of today through 10 a.m.

Now, and again through the advancement of technology, most back-up systems "mirror" that of the live, primary system. This means that the back-up system, through technology, is updated simultaneously as transactions occur on the primary system. In theory, should a primary system go down, a company could immediately turn the switch and begin using its back-up system as it mirrors that on the firm's primary system.

When my family's bank account grew to proportions equal to my big-shot status on Wall Street, my wife and I, really just my wife, for I had little say in the matter, chose a particularly unique mansion in New Jersey's horse-farm country to call our home. This custom structure came with more angles and designs than most others, so upon purchase I had insisted on receiving the blueprints of the house as part of the transaction.

As with most important documents, I stored them safely in one of the file cabinets in my downstairs man-cave, a finely finished

basement of entertainment pleasures. One day, prior to 9/11, I was sitting with one of my young daughters downstairs going through the cabinet, when she got a glimpse of the rolled-up blueprints. Upon asking me what they were, I explained that they were the pictures of how our house was built so if anything ever happened, we could build another one just like it.

She looked up and said, "but daddy, if something happened to our house wouldn't it happen to the pictures, too, because the pictures are in the house?" Feeling really fucking stupid, I hugged her and, in short order, moved the blueprints out of our house to a different location.

Oh yeah, and back-up systems are always maintained at locations far from a firm's primary systems!

One learns a lot about themselves, and about life, through tragic events. However serious or devastating a condition, mostly one must face that inevitable Robert Frost three-word masterpiece, "Life goes on." Other than through death, I have never seen life stop for anyone.

As I sit here, some 15 years later, it remains the lesson I most privately think about, a constant connection (and reminder) to that horrific Tuesday morning. September 11, 2001,

transformed me from someone always moving forward, spending far too little thought and energy on past events, often missing and oblivious to life's lessons to one now far too introspective and analytical, perhaps spending way too much energy hitting the replay button.

What Robert Frost and 9/11 confirmed for me, as World War II must have confirmed for my dad, is that life (like our earth) is an unstoppable spin. It has haunted me for many years, as I see it everywhere.

Robin Williams died in 2015; killed himself. At today's young age of early 60's, a man who seemingly had been to the top of the mountain didn't have anything left for which to live. On the morning after his death, and on one of the popular Internet web sites, appeared a story of the immediate impact that this event had on one of our nation's famous late night talk show hosts.

He was said to be a personal friend of Williams and someone who clearly shared his propensity for comical buffoonery. While I do not question the sincerity or the genuineness of the talk show host's feelings nor of his grief and despair, I was jolted with the other stalk reality of this event.

As I often do around midnight or so, I awaken, sprawled on our living room couch, ready for my routine to turn off the TV, stumble across the room in darkness into our adjourning master bedroom. I carefully tiptoe around the bed as not to step on our man's best friend and climb into bed and snuggle with my wife. Hopefully, I can then doze back into sleep, readying my aging body for the rigors of tomorrow.

The day following Williams' death, something broke this mundane routine. Pointing the clicker at the TV, cable box, receiver, sub woofer, and so on, I stopped short of pressing the off button. There on the TV screen was the aforementioned talk show host doing tonight's show. He was laughing with some unrecognizable guest, whacking it up with his myriad of verbal and physical attempts to make us laugh; the uncontrollable and unstoppable spin. Damn, I thought, is this the same guy that only 24 hours earlier was so devastated?

I blame no one for this, not the talk show host, his guest, the producers ... really no one. It's just the way it is. It's impossible to stop the world's spin, keep going, move on (and over time) become hardened to life's many moments. By the way, this certainty is not reserved for bad things only. It also applies to the world's most wonderful pleasures as well.

I remember my once good friend TJ, back in the early 90's, caught up in the New York Rangers playoff run, looking to break the 50-year drought without a championship. Living it, breathing it, consumed by every line change, fore-check, great save and SCOORE!!! (You get the idea), he was rewarded with his team's first chance to hoist the Stanley Cup in over five decades.

Entering work on the morning after the title game, I expected a TJ lit with pride, accomplishment and maybe even kicking down doors because his arms would be filled with Dunkin' Donut boxes, a celebration for us NYC office slobs readying ourselves for the big parade down the Canyon of Heroes. Not so. In fact, I was met with quite the opposite.

TJ, in early, was slumped over his desk, rather silent and clearly not experiencing the expected euphoria from last night's decree of THE RANGERS WIN THE CUP!!! THE RANGERS WIN THE CUP!!! THE RANGERS WIN THE CUP!!! Somewhat concerned, I approached with caution and uttered quietly "Are you OK?"

With the sage of an intellectual monk, seated on a hard floor, legs crossed, spending years pondering the meaning of life, TJ explained

that minutes after his triumph, he was hit with the reality that it was over. All that was left was his uncontrollable mandate to keep spinning, spinning in his tiring commute, his less than adequate take home pay, his cranky wife and his shit-head of a boss. Unlike Robin Williams, he would not end it there. He would keep spinning.

Sure, some things can stop you in your path for longer periods than others, but be rest assured of one thing ... at some point, like it or not, you will be swept back into the spin and move on.

Think of it like the roulette wheel; the little white ball will land, some around the table will rejoice, be rewarded with piles of happy chips, while others will shoulder slump as Ms. Pretend I. Care sweeps away your chips to the house's coffer. The table's only certainty is that the white ball representing each of us, and someday our offspring and theirs and theirs and theirs, will spin again, forced to move on from each and every one of life's magical moments, tragic ass kicking's and everything in between.

Of course, none of this means that we should stop our pursuits, strive every day, laugh, cry, sprint, think, fight, love, whine or feel. Nor does it mean that we won't achieve, take, fail, give, fuck up or accomplish. After all, that's what we do. All of us.

Chapter 7

Rebuild

When I got to the recovery site, I was met with warm greetings from many. The large rooms were less refined than those within the Trade Center. Each room was filled with many tables, some computers, piles of paper and reports and a surprising work-man-like attitude from the several people already busy planning and focused on the task at hand.

I learned quickly that of the five people at yesterday's meeting, only two were accounted for, myself and SH. Nobody dared used the word dead. It was too fresh a disaster to even contemplate publicly that many of our friends and associates were gone forever. The term used was missing. Like the thousands of families who would soon be faced with the inevitable, it was too soon to give up hope. The atmosphere in the quarters that would represent the work place for

the next several weeks was as professional as could be mustered up by the many caring, but clearly hurting, individuals.

It was to be a full hats-off approach to recover the business. That meant that other than trying to correctly utilize someone's inherent skills developed through specific on-the-job experience, one's previous position and responsibilities, (i.e. the previous hat that they wore) was now meaningless. A recovery template was being created, identifying required positions, empty boxes so to speak, that would be filled in with names once survival lists could be finalized.

Additional manpower was to be provided by the firm's new parent, an investment and mutual funds company that had purchased our firm back in April of that year. Talk spread that plans to integrate the two organizations, a complicated task of combining varying strategic philosophies, systems, products and personnel, originally considered a two-year endeavor, would now be accelerated on the calendar with target dates as aggressive as 2001 year-end.

Throughout the day, private conversations revealed several horror stories. Only rumors at that point, most are still mysteries to me, but perhaps eventually confirmed or rejected by individual families with the need to get questions

answered and bring some semblance of closure to the lives of their loved ones.

I was physically bent as someone relayed the likelihood that DC, a member of my meeting, had stopped off from her descent from floor 94, to her office on floor 90 to retrieve her pocketbook. Till this day, I do not know if this is true. I guess is really doesn't matter, does it? DC was one of those recorded as missing. She was the firm's Chief Corporate Counsel, our top lawyer, recently assuming the position through the retirement of DJ, a gentleman's gentleman who had accepted me with warm and welcoming genuineness upon my arrival at the firm.

Learning well from her mentor, DC had taken the time to assure me that she was my friend and her help was always available to me. I recall that her little daughter's drawings routinely were displayed within her impressive, but always inviting, office. When I was new to the firm, only beginning to prove that they had made the right hire, DC always had my back. Early on, she was concerned that I was OK with my year-end bonus. She grabbed me one January morning, saying she was taking me to lunch at Windows of the World, the WTC's top floor restaurant of fame and prominence.

I remember fondly her laughter, her charm and her always friend-like approach, concerned that I was happy and content within the company. When she asked about my daughters, I always felt that it was more than the typical Wall Street politeness. It is now 15 years later and I still think of her often, remembering her laughter and her way, always leaving her big-shot status at the door, only verifiable through the title on her nameplate. I hope her family is well.

The tragic tales were endless, as many family members of those missing had confirmed telephone conversations, on the company's landlines, with loved ones trapped on floors above the flames. The stories of final goodbyes, of the last opportunities to say I love you, … then of the heat, the desperation and the collapse of the building were heartbreaking and too much to bear.

When driving alone during the next several weeks, I found myself too often bursting into tears; emotionally wrecked, angry at the world and then at myself for letting my emotions overtake me. I would then arrive home or at work, now fully gathered and pretend I was strong and OK. Rare now, but my persona has changed forever, finding myself hiding the finger wipes of my dripping eyes from my wife or daughters as we watch some stupid tear-jerk

scene on TV. Often back then, I was consumed with the thoughts of floor 97.

Floor 97 was the workplace home to our technology personnel, many who were my friends and worked with closely. Technology positions were those special jobs within Wall Street where your responsibility fell somewhat outside the core of the business's inherent nature. You had to understand the product and the flow of investments but, like a trainer within a sport's team's locker room, nobody was asking you to pitch it, catch it or hit it. They couldn't do core guys' jobs but, at the same time, core guys couldn't do theirs. Both were valuable and everybody knew it.

As a result of, let's say, having your responsibility reside outside the lines of the playing field, technology positions often attracted a different breed of characters from the buttoned-up, Wall Street money-maker. The technology group was mostly made up of men and women with a refreshing, but often out-of-place attitude, an honesty and humor that often defied the political correctness found in most money managers.

At times, they could represent a Human Resource executive's biggest nightmare -- the Hawkeye Pierces of Wall Street. Make no

mistake about it though, if you were a top techie you had little competition and you knew it. Shit, those were the guys who could bring their damn dog to work if they wanted, entering the sacredness of executive office space with their hat on backwards and nobody would say a word.

There was no disdain for that, perhaps just envy. It didn't take much for a techie to let his hair down. So often the best of times on Wall Street, the laugh-till-your-stomach-hurt times were with the people from floor 97, the techies who never struggled to get it. On that evil Tuesday, floor 97 represented the one hardest hit and most affected by this insane attack.

Most at that morning's recovery site, at least those who were in the WTC's second tower and had escaped, were clearly still experiencing some level of shock. While we all drove to get there, I felt certain that if we had taken the time that morning to seek medical or professional help, we would have been advised to rest in quiet space, allowing the physical and emotional shock to subside. Instead, it was Forward March for all of us.

Additionally, the disaster was so fresh, that most could not negotiate to the thinking that it was over. Somehow, we were all still waiting to hear about the next explosion. I remember a good

friend, the then Assistant Comptroller, telling me that he had to now find a way to move off of Long Island. Learning yesterday's difficult and downright scary lessons in trying to navigate off Manhattan during an emergency, SL had convinced himself that on Long Island, he was trapped in the event of expected bombings.

GJ, another friend, indicated that he did 90 miles per hour over one of the bridges connecting to New Jersey, because he was convinced that the bridge represented a sure-bet target of the terrorists. That kind of aura permeated throughout the recovery site.

Day One of business recovery did contain some good news. A friend, a good personal friend, who had left the company only a short time earlier, offered to come back to help. He was accepted with open arms, much to my delight. GK was, and still is, the real deal. A commuting partner for a long time, we shared the same Jersey neighborhood. More than that, we shared the common thread of Wall Street, complete with its challenges, pains, jokes and wealth.

Our families remain friends till this day. He's a guy with a golden heart, and a dry wit that still makes me laugh out loud. Funny, while independently developing a friendship through work, I later came to understand that he ran in the same circles as my wife in much younger days.

They used to call him Tex, which now only causes him to shake his head like he doesn't want to remember those days. At the time of recovery, during the days directly following 9/11, it was a real big deal to have him back, both for the firm's sake and mine.

The other great news of the day was that each and every member of my department was safe. At the time, if I had learned that a companion in an adjacent desk was missing, I may have gone under. As it was, I was too often feeling disoriented and sick, continually trying to mask my current feelings of depression and uselessness.

If you want to get answers on Wall Street, you don't go to anyone describing himself or herself as a people person. For answers you go to someone in the trenches, the soldiers whose effort has more to do with either winning or losing the war than anyone else. You go to back-office operations.

Front office wining-and-dining types are the face of Wall Street. They are the ones who convince others to fork over their money. They are even the ones who instruct on the investments exchanged for that money. But back-office guys, well, they're the ones who make sure that every dollar stays with its rightful owner. They control account activity, processing both funds and

securities through a myriad of systems, interfaces and complexities.

They are the backbone to the entire financial system, mastering the infrastructure that controls the world's trillions. While the techies put together the systems, back-office people write the specs and devise the procedures and controls relating to the only three money things that really mean anything to us … adding to our money, withdrawing our money and on those days where we feel like doing neither, looking at our money.

It was not at all surprising that LJ, a tough-looking, thick brute of a guy, with a wealth of back-office experience and a Leprechaun luck to keep him safe on that Tuesday morning, had much to do with leading the firm's recovery effort. I liked LJ a lot. I always sensed that we had much in common.

Neither of us would ever be misconstrued as the touchy/feely type. Neither of us was known for taking any shit from a full-of-themselves big shot. We were both much more inclined to order a whiskey or scotch or a Budweiser while the money guys asked for the wine list. And we both had a propensity to swiftly, and if need be, callously cut to the chase and the bottom line.

Ironically, our personal discussions often took a much softer tone, as we shared the fact the each of our daughters was dancers. Often LJ and I joked about those days of dance recitals that one had to experience to truly understand. Endless car rides to practice, weeks in advance, finally culminating in a recital where your angel would perform in four or five of the more than 100 dance routines over an all-day or sometimes two-day event.

Only those involved truly understood driving to some remote theatre or gymnasium as angel, with mom's careful, helping hand, did pretty-up in the back seat. Only those involved truly understood having your angel, along with her 10 other dance buddies, complete her 90-second, two-step at 8:45 a.m. as your wife communicated that her next scheduled minute-and-a-half routine was at 11 a.m., followed by two more angel twirls generously spaced out in the afternoon, followed by another two-hour wait for tonight's big awards ceremony.

You had to be there to truly understand the feeling of leaving 14 hours after arrival, usually starving, but secure in knowing that angel's sequenced dance bag now contained four or five more two-by-six-inch gold, silver or bronze ribbons to add to her bedroom wallpaper. We

may have joked about it, but neither of us tough guys would have traded those days for the world.

After hours of trying my best to contribute to the planning and organization efforts, a mere 24 hours or so after both the shittiest and luckiest day of my life, I left with two clear directives. The first was that I was to lead the effort to establish the required new space and infrastructure from which our damaged company could operate. That meant organizing physical space, systems, communications and any other required aspect of operations for all departments.

Executives from both our company and from our new financial parent were already considering buildings representing viable options. I had little to no experience in such matters, which at the time was irrelevant. I was organized and competent. Not that I had a choice, but I accepted the charge without reservation. Second, the firm was beginning the process to develop a secured, informational web site for all employees to receive communication and instructions. First on its list of objectives was to record those confirmed as missing, a number that was growing by the hour, as communications continued with the families of our employees. Should I be asked to assist in any way, I was told to consider it a priority.

All I could think about for the second day in row was getting home and just as I started this first day of recovery, September 12, 2001, I nodded yes and searched my jacket for car keys.

I often wonder, some 15 years later, about the families who lost their loved ones on 9/11. I guess for most, the perpetual spin helped evolve new chapters and new relationships. Most received great deals of money from the numerous funds that were organized back then. Not much help perhaps initially, but still humanity's way of showing community care.

There were so many children, at the time only infants or perhaps then too young to remember much now. There were mothers and fathers, like mine, some who eventually passed but also those that remain and continue to dream each day about their lost creations. There were husbands and wives, forced to move on, forced to understand the finality of what happened on that Tuesday morning.

I wonder about them a lot. I wonder if life's way of imparting priority screw-up has helped them get through it all.

Just maybe, for those who had to deal with the unthinkable, it's a blessing that we take such effort and time in those things that mask and dysfunctionally re-order our priorities. Maybe the monk-like posture of figuring it all out contributed to the almost unspeakable ending for Robin Williams. Maybe there is something to the expression ... Don't over think it.

Yeah, maybe it's OK that a couple can fight for two weeks over the hair he left on the shower floor or the fact that she never buys the coffee brand that he likes. Maybe it's OK that my less-than-19-year-old niece cries because her make-up suitcase never made the plane to the Bahamas or that our kids continually change their major, oblivious to the financial impact on mom and dad.

Maybe it's fine that little eight-year-old Johnny is being lauded at the water cooler by proud, but seriously misguided dad because he made the paper for yesterday's CYO heroics. Maybe it's cool to rearrange the basement shelves for the fifth time this year or become friends with the Fed Ex guy because your wife hooked up your daughters on amazon.com.

It's probably OK that all the bushes in the back yard are dying from Fido pissing all over them eight times a day. We might even make a case that video games, divorce, being hooked on

Friends sitcoms, golf, getting excited over a stock split, the anemic Yankee batting order, going organic or even cursing the morning's traffic is all good.

These things take a lot of time. After all, priority screw-up is hard work, and might just be essential to getting through it all. It clearly beats dealing seriously, each and every day, with the realities.

Unfortunately however, that lack of focus, so healthy perhaps for our daily lives, in part, prevents the really serious stuff from getting resolved, moving forward to a safer world for our children.

Still, I wonder how someone who lost his or her soul mate on 9/11 thinks today. Do they think that anything has really changed for the better? Or do they feel an emptiness that their best friend died for nothing. I wonder if they feel like I do, moving more toward thoughts of eventual world chaos and even destruction than experiencing the warm anticipation of life's simple, innocent ways?

I think that life has become too complicated; too random for any of us to organize it in a way that allows a pathway to what we all must know is the better option for our children.

Seems so often, life (and our thoughts) moves without rhyme or reason, unorganized, frustrating the diverse level of control freak in all of us. We wake up hopeful for and maybe even expecting A, but life shifts our energies quickly to deal with B. It happens at home, at work and even at play.

Despite all the self-help trends, professing that we can control all that we do and all that we are, we quickly learn that, for most life seems out of our control. So little goes according to plan. Life goes on, jumping around, challenging those in it to navigate through good times and bad, through conditions that we can set our clocks by and so many others that we didn't see coming.

Most of us live life reaching our hand in a bucket of a 100-piece puzzle, picking out one at a time and trying to make it fit. We spend our time, mostly looking to arrange and organize conditions which are not orderly arranged but rather unorganized. Oh, there are things that, through our efforts, can be tilted one way or the other. We like to think this way about our health, our relationships, maybe even our paycheck, but in the end life moves forward mocking and disdainful to those who claim to have figured it out.

My almost 60 years has seen life fool so many, as hard to predict as the next lotto ball

number. Mostly, I think that our comfort, our happiness, our stress (or lack of it) depends on how we deal with each number, how much energy and how much of our focus is applied to today's number, letting go worrying about yesterday's and limiting the time and anticipation on tomorrow's.

Did you ever take a several-hour car ride by yourself? I mean one in which you decided not to turn on the radio, speak on the cell or press any button that conjures up sound of any kind. Just you ... and your thoughts, the myriad of unorganized things, from the past, in the now, even dreams or worries of the future, people, places, feelings and events, all that will pop into your head in rapid-fire succession.

To me, that car ride and those hundreds of not-in-any-order thoughts present the best parallel to today's life, to today's world, and maybe also to our combined inability to make things better. It's so much easier to leave the world's problems to others, shifting the responsibility and the blame to inadequate world leadership.

I wonder how my friends, the murdered 9/11 victims, would feel today. If they read our news-lines, surely they wouldn't think things are

better. How would they feel? No doubt, they would worry for their children and their spouse. Would they impart blame that their death wasn't a spearhead for a better world? Would they feel disservice that their deaths did not spark the common demand for decency in the world for those they left behind? Who the hell would they blame?

If like me, they would see that while contributions abound, religious leadership or the lack of any is clearly partially to blame. Maybe they would tell us that religious leaders have done nothing more than shirk their once-noble, tax exempt responsibilities to impart morality, respect for others and contributions to good.

Whether it be the religious-leader extremists who look to kill or maim all those not conforming to their own misguided religious beliefs, or pretentious religious leaders who define their success by the size of the territories they control, or preachers who line their pockets from their congregations or the out-of-touch, greedy Catholic church …. young people through the elderly are left to figure their own faith, leaderless and confused by the pounding of society's distractions. Gone in so many ways is the simplest of all creeds … "just treat others as you would want to be treated."

Maybe my friends would blame us. Maybe they would ask us to contemplate if it is our fault? Is the fact that we have become a nation that is so selfish, so partisan to our own agendas that we render even the most caring and intelligent among us, paralyzed to effect the changes so obviously and desperately needed?

Would they see that the diverse viewpoints of our nations' members have resulted in such canyon-like gaps that even the most factual of things now create a debate … one that prevents even baby steps forward?

Let us think about how insane our debates have become. Let us admit that even the most obvious facts have been blurred within postures of self-service and selfish agenda. Close your eyes for a second and picture *a gathering of our nation's diverse citizens, each and every type represented. Then picture yourself standing in the middle of them.*

Your job is to hold up large cards, each the color of the world's primary colors of red, yellow and blue. You have 30 minutes, more than enough time, to confirm with those present, the color of each card. Simple, obvious and non-debatable. Upon holding up the first card, say red, you request agreement from the crowd that the card is red. Quickly those against the color red cause a debate, questioning the card's true

color. Detractors, those opposed to red, raise issues of pigmentation, shading, secondary color mixing and so on.

Debate turns to arguments and your role, starting out as simple and obvious, now transforms itself into moderator and ultimately to referee. Soon the now-argumentative tone spins off-course and people are raising points outside the simple objective to confirm the primary color of the card. Before you know it, the 30-minute horn sounds, the first color has not been confirmed and you didn't even get to raise the remaining cards of yellow and blue, thus reeking failure on the once simple, factual confirmation objective.

Is it our fault that nothing changes for the better? Are we at least partially to blame? Have we rendered our leaders paralyzed to act because we as a people cannot agree even on the simplest of solutions, those things that are frankly nothing more than common sense?

Or maybe we are simply following the lead of our world's greedy and agenda-filled leaders on even the most elementary of matters. After all, didn't we so shamefully accept President Bill Clinton's response of, "It depends of what the meaning of the word "is" is," when asked if he was being truthful in his commentary to the Grand Jury when he stated that there IS

nothing going on between him and Monica Lewinsky. Good grief!

Maybe my friends would blame the media or our acceptance of it, and our demand for so little. Maybe they would wonder why we don't blink at horrific news reports, numb to even the most insane and catastrophic stories. Is it only me that cringes when reporters so matter-of-factly follow an atrocity with mindless blabber, like, "Today, a car bomb in wherever killed seven, including five local civilians and two children, with several more in critical condition. Also today, in Sea Bright, a community lemonade stand was clearly the cool place to be, for that story, let's go live to Sid Smith, standing by." Or, "Two more border control guards were shot and killed today as turmoil continued to engulf a southern Arizona town. On our local front, the weekend looks great weather-wise. Here's Mary Carnes with more."

I think my friends might question the sensibility that, in the days that followed a recent Super Bowl, our nation saw hundreds of replays of the big interception. Talk show phone lights were lit to the max, like the stations were giving away a crisp million to every 100th caller. Every TV and radio network repeated over and over and over again the question on EVERYONE's

mind: Did Coach Carroll blow the big game by (Oh, no!) calling a pass play?

Yet, we have to look deep into the DEEPLY misguided media to even find the details of yesterday's human atrocities. Not on the sponsors' radar, I guess.

Maybe my passed friends would see that our nation's priorities are not exactly paying the deserving homage to those whose life ended because they went to work that day. Maybe they would scream, "COME ON PEOPLE, WE CAN DO BETTER THAN THIS!" Maybe they would just cry.

Is it fair to blame technology, and so-called progress that has so contributed to changes in our society? Do you scratch your head wondering how those who killed our citizens on 9/11 are now putting stuff out on Twitter and putting videos out on the Internet; a venue in which they use to organize, recruit and finance TERROR.

Maybe those who died would think that if we cannot trace tweets, messages, emails and any other social media from a terrorist within seconds back to the specific phone or computer, its exact address, and its exact user then we should simply shut it all down until we can; that we didn't set up this tech stuff the right way and

that temporarily cutting off our smart phones or Twitter accounts (GASP!) would put a fire under the masses, forcing our leaders to take the harshest of measures to stop this insanity. Maybe my friends would wonder if it has to be someone's own dad or mom who is killed or butchered to feel this way.

Maybe those who died would be angry that their children are not living up to demands that require our young to be accountable and good citizens. Maybe if they were here they would remind their children of when they were young and their biggest fear was getting through the dad of their new sweetheart when he picked up the phone and said, "WHO'S THIS?"

Heaven forbid, they might relate the fear of having to knock on a door and stand in the kitchen and have conversation while your date finished her pretty-up before making her grand entrance. Maybe they would say that it was good to live in a world were one was forced to communicate, grow up and be accountable for everything one did. Maybe they would think that so much texting and tweeting stunts the growth of young people, doing nothing for the development and courage required ultimately in fighting and defeating things that truly and insanely endanger them.

Would my murdered comrades blame money and power and fame, and what it has done to the world's role models that contribute to our moral deterioration? Phil Rizzuto, the great Yankee shortstop, liked to tell a story, where upon having an MVP season, he was offered a contract the following year with a pay cut. Prior to society's insanity, money wasn't in the way to cloud the opportunity to serve a role, where young minds might follow. Things were done for a purer reason. People of influence were inclined to offer us things that were good for us and for the positive development of our young.

Would those who died cringe at today's role models, noting that their antics and lack of morality and values are continually on display? Such a joke that today's dads buy their kids sports star jerseys of holdout superstars, loyal to nothing but their checkbook and lifestyle.

How can we allow and support people like Doug Baldwin, a Seattle Seahawks' millionaire receiver, who, after catching a touchdown pass in the Super Bowl, performed his premeditated end-zone celebration by simulating taking down his pants and defecating on the ball. REALLY, DOUG? That's what you came up with? That's what, for you, punctuated the thrill that every kid dreams about?

Or just maybe those who passed would understand that for most, our solution to today's really serious issues has been to decrease the circumference of our circles to simply family and a few friends, spending our energies on our own enjoyment, our own health, our own financial stability, making all of us, YIKES, part of the problem.

Chapter 8

Buyout

It was now almost a week after 9/11. I got word that our new communication web site just got loaded with the complete list of those missing from my company. The total came to 87 human beings, incomprehensibly gone, now with very little hope left that any could still be alive. I sat at a computer and was afraid to click. Turns out, I didn't have to. My phone rang. It was BJ.

BJ is a guy I hired from one of the big accounting firms who was looking to improve his quality of life. He had recently become a father and, at the time, Big Six demands were taking its toll on family life. Moving out of public accounting was until then, the best move of his life.

He had a great job, a beautiful, caring wife and now sons. Like for everyone else, the 9/11 attacks were causing BJ to question everything. Eventually, he went out on his own and formed a thriving consultancy firm. A good guy and still a good friend, BJ was a technology expert, working closely with floor 97 and had established many

close relationships with the technicians and administrators of our company's technology unit.

His voice, high and panic-like, begged if I had seen the list. I could tell he was crying. While many knew the names of several of our missing friends and associates, seeing it in writing for the first time was devastating. Not only did the recording confirm what many had, up until that point, refused to fully accept, it disclosed the names of so many others, perhaps not previously thought about or that had been off of one's personal radar.

Sitting there going down the list brought memories into the forefront of so many men and women who were now gone. Plainly, it resulted in bringing back all the pain and took one right back to the scene of devastation and despair. Any small relief of grief naturally resulting from time gone by, a short week's worth of time, was gone.

Desperate attempts to heal, remain calm, or even breathe normally were back to square one. Many, of those continuing to work, were privately expressing doubt as to their ability to go on, to keep moving forward. The missing list was something that had to be put up, but it served to, at least temporarily, destroy any healing progress being made by any of us.

For me, every name was recognized and chilling, but some of them hit me like a sledgehammer.

There was MB, just a fun-spirited, regular guy despite his lofty company status, a golf lover, so proud of his son's college success, so enjoyable to be around. There was SL, a sweet-hearted, down-to-earth lady who took the time to make any visiting child feel special and welcome. She was the type of person that if your son or daughter was revisiting dad's office three months after his or her prior visit, they might ask, "Are we going to see SL?"

There was IL, a guy much like me, who held an important position but his time at the firm was relatively short compared to some. A reader, a father, a family man who often told me that if I gave him a good book and a beach to sit on, he would be as content and happy as any man.

There were BS and ME, two indispensable technology guys, both family guys, both friends, both fun, both funny. There was VA, a real good guy with a love and knowledge of cars that few could match. He also made it clear that he was in it for his family.

During my first few conversations with SE, the skeptic in me had privately questioned his authenticity, thinking that nobody on the level

could be that helpful and friendly, only to find out over time that he was the real deal, perhaps one of the nicest, most caring guys I have ever met. There was FT, a big laugh, a cowboy type guy, as down to earth a guy that ever sat on Wall Street's stage.

There were so many others, men and women, all ages, all types, all good. Each and every one of the 87 had something special to offer to the world, clearly something valuable to contribute to the firm and each caring for and loving their very own special and powerful circle of family members and close friends.

And of course there was DC, GA and MB, my friends who shared the 94th boardroom with me at the very moment that Tuesday's chaos erupted.
May they all rest in peace.

Rockefeller Center was chosen as the new home for our company. While different from the worldwide recognizable Trade Center structures, it represented its own upscale, high-end attractiveness to both our employees and our clients.

The next several weeks were both therapeutic and tiring. Routinely working 10 or

more hours a day, I truly began to understand the benefits and the by-products of keeping busy. Other than the funerals that had a way of taking you right back to the confusion that only grief and anxiety can bring on, I wrapped myself in an endless supply of details required to get our new facility up and running.

Fortunately, I had all the help I needed. People were bound together by a common cause and while we all knew that we might look back at this exercise someday as meaningless, for now it was just what the doctor ordered. We were crazy busy and thankful for our new found fatigue. But like everything positive on Wall Street, it didn't last.

Our firm's mega-management members who had survived 9/11 were quickly forming new in-roads with those of our new parent. Politics, the corporate kind, soon reared its ugly head. Personally, I knew that no one had forgotten, but on some days it sure seemed that way. My wife, and always my best friend, and I started to discuss if enough was enough and what would be best for our two children.

Earlier, prior to accepting the buyout offer from our new parent, the firm had distributed something called Change of Control contracts to a select group of its employees; just the people at

the top who they felt made a real difference. Essentially, this provided those lucky enough to receive one, a period to execute the contract subsequent to any future buyout of the company.

Mine called for a one-time payment of four times my management level annual salary and my agreement not to compete directly against what would then be my former employer. After the buyout in April of 2001, while I had occasionally thought about the very real and advantageous uses of such a payment, until 9/11, I never really had considered it.

I was happy in my work; my family was being well taken care of and even with new ownership, I was confident in my abilities to survive such a takeover. Also at the time, the new parent was saying all the right things about keeping our firm and its strategies independent, including keeping our well-known name.

While it may have seemed generous of our company to offer such a contract, nothing on Wall Street ever was what it seemed to be.

Since its inception back in the early 60's, our management had grown a small asset management start-up into a mid-sized, profitable entity and, as such, had put off numerous offers and attempts to be purchased. Now with the latest

line of mega-shots reaching retirement age, cash out was clearly the more lucrative option. Not that any of these men or woman were hurting, trust me, it was just the better hand to play.

Shit, if a mega-shot played his hand right, not only could he come away with the millions, pocketed through the premium purchase price paid for their company stock which they had been stockpiling as part of their bonuses for years, he or she could also be afforded a nice cushy job or consultant role along with a mega-money salary within the new integrated company. I mean it didn't have to be one or the other. These guys could have both, confirming the level of intelligence and guile it took to become a mega-shot in the first place.

For me, somehow I felt that my contract was mere shut-up-and-be-loyal money, so as not to be able to ever question the motives of their "it's really the best thing for our company" explanation upon buyout announcement time. Like most things on Wall Street, any roads traveled to get from A to B were usually meaningless and irrelevant.

What mattered were what B represented and the roads that would now become available to someday get to C. For me, that was four years' worth of damn good money. And for them, well

let's just say that we big shots would have loved to be behind those closed doors when the mega-shots discussed such a transaction.

For several days, my best friend and I weighed the pros and cons of such a move, always seeming to end the discussion with a revisit back to the all-to-fresh memory of 9/11 and an agreement to sleep on it. I think we both knew what was to become the inevitable, a chance to get out of the rat race, a chance to climb a bit higher on the prism of self-actualization.

In mid-November, 2001, I announced my intention to execute my Change of Control contract, effective year-end, December 31, 2001. Alas, not so fast. My request sent a few shock waves through the offices of the powerful ones and I was quickly summoned to what was to be the first of a number of meetings. Apparently, simultaneous to my announcement, the Comptroller, a wonderful lady who shared a similar background, had made a similar noise and with both currently manning active rebuild portions of our new company, the mega-shots had to act.

The first thing everyone learns on Wall Street, I mean once they get to a level where true education rights are granted, is that everyone and

anyone is replaceable. There are no exceptions. It's just a fact that sometimes one's leverage increases if the timing is right. Oh, they might tell you're indispensable but what they are really saying is can you give us a little time to figure it out.

Everyone in business knows that before you announce intentions to leave, one best you be sure, because the very second it leaves your mouth, you're really viewed as already gone. They will never look at you the same way again. Such was the case in hand, thus their offer to build my ego with compliments and my wallet with a few extra shekels.

While they understood my desire to execute my contract, (one guy who could buy me 10 times over actually said he wished he was in the position to do the same … I guess perspective is everything in life), they requested that I agree to another three months to complete what I started.

For that small concession, I would receive a handsome retention bonus payable immediately. Both the firm and I knew that three months was not nearly enough time to complete much of anything, but it was something. Hey, my family and I wanted out but I hadn't gotten that far by being stupid. Concession granted.

The days, then the weeks that followed were more of the same with a single but important exception. As the time grew closer to my final payout, now scheduled for March 30, 2002, my responsibilities unexplainably grew. With the deadline approaching, something had to give. Again, it was the only thing that really speaks on Wall Street; you guessed it, money. Another three-month request to continue my employment, another handsome retention bonus, another chance for me, like so many that kidded themselves long before me, to do the right thing.

We could have gone on like that forever and I think we may have if not for the parent's influence. Finally, with all extension contracts now exhausted, my big buyout check was hand-delivered and while perhaps pittance to some mega-shots, it represented a great deal of money to me and mine. Finally, financially in a place where few go, at least from where I come from anyway, I was ready to move on. Sorry, not so fast.

With check already deposited and simply stringing together a few final loose ends, I received a visit from the firms' Chief Financial Officer and Vice Chairman of the Board, yeah the guy who called from Switzerland the morning after 9/11.

MM was truly one of a kind. As fit an aging executive as Wall Street has ever known, MM and I had shared a little history. We had both worked for the same firm prior to joining our current one, although it was at separate times as he was a few years older than me.

Looking to move to a No. 1 division head spot, and thus applying for the job I was now about to leave, MM was the main contact during my two-month-long interview process. Sitting one day in the cafeteria, he shook my hand at the recent news of my hiring, a decision that we both knew could not have been granted without his approval, and said, "Congratulations, you're going to make a lot of money." At the time, it was music to my ears.

Over the years, I viewed MM as someone to learn from and learn I did. Honestly, I liked him a lot and would love to talk to him again, another thing unlikely to happen. In addition to his mastery of the world of finance, his bigger-than-life presence in any meeting or boardroom and his ability to maintain an unequaled stamina amidst a not-a-line-open schedule, his entertainment value was priceless.

Not that he was trying in any way to be entertaining; it's just the way he struck me. He was by far the nicest killer executives I have ever

known. Build you to millionaire status if he wanted to, or cut you so many times with little paper cuts that you bled to death, he possessed quite a repertoire.

He often acted like he was fond of me, like he respected my talents, and at times over some business lunch or dinner, even seemed to care for me personally. The following two things say it all. One, I didn't buy it for a minute. He couldn't have given a shit less about me and two, I didn't mind at all. If you knew it going in, you made quick peace with MM, always knowing it all could be over in, how do they say it? … a New York second.

MM's visit presented yet another opportunity to pad one's bank account. Always quick and smart as a whip, he sensed that I was not one to buy the "you're indispensable" bullshit rap, so as was his way, he cut right to the chase. "I want you to consider, now that your buyout is done, to remain on, as a consultant. Think about an hourly price. I'll be back in the morning. Enjoy your evening." And with that, he was off. My night? It was just another long ride home, lots to think about and yet another conversation to be had with my better half.

The next morning, I never had to open my mouth. As promised, MM passed by my now-

thought-of-as-perhaps-not-so-temporary Rockefeller Center office, stuck his head in, blurted the price per hour he knew would do the trick and said a contract would be ready in Personnel for my signature by the end of the day. So much for long drawn-out meetings. The man was far too busy for anything of the kind.

Not letting him get away that easy, prior to executing my new consulting contract, I explained to Personnel that my days on public transportation had officially ended on Sept. 12, 2001. As such, the parking spot that I had secured ground floor, Rockefeller Center, the one a few spots from the dudes from NBC's Today's Show, well it was getting a little too expensive. I wondered if they minded throwing in the monthly price for that spot, you know, as a kicker. They asked for a minute. Not having to guess who they called, they quickly and rather cordially agreed. Needless to say, while taking on a role with somewhat of a different flavor, I was, once again, back in the fold.

Quickly, and with the help of my accountant and good friend, I opened a Limited Liability Company and was off and running. The next two years represented a period in our lives where I earned more money than I ever had before and, as it turns out, more than I would ever again. As time moved on, the work became

routine, and although many of the old staff remained, the company took on a new feel, complete with new digs and both the parent's input and financial kick. 9/11 was still privately at the forefront for many, but publicly more and more unspoken and other than on its annual anniversary, in the rear-view mirror.

Finally, as with all consultant work, the projects and tasks eventually dry up, the company comes to its senses and decides that there is no need to any longer expend crazy money on consultants. Over two years since indicating that I was leaving, I finally moved on. With the mixed emotions of joy and sadness that accompany most forms of self-initiated change, I handed in my keys and access cards and tried real hard not to look back.

Who can change the world? Who can stem the tide, and move the pendulum back in favor of our world?

Most people would agree that, at times, the world is capable of amazing things. Despite the downward spiral of human values and respect for human life, the vast majority of this planet's inhabitants want peace, want opportunity, want progress that helps us all. Despite the

technological advancements that make weapons of mass destruction more feasible and more devastating, the majority of human beings consider use of such technology unthinkable.

Where do we go from here and who is to lead us for clearly we appear to be at the crossroads? The problems are not hard to find. They are not hard to see.

Our society is filled with brutally serious stuff, like terrorism -- murder fueled by differences in religion, by pedophile priests preying on those they should shepherd, by differences in political philosophy which threaten to ignite mass destruction, continued and unthinkable poverty and hunger and by racial tension, still remarkably an issue that continues to haunt us.

Less serious, there are also growing and annoying aspects of today's society which continue to exasperate our patience and call for common sense; everyday stuff, like misguided parents fighting at their kids' sports games, road rage and the declining church attendance, caused by the jelly-like foundation of out-of-touch sermons, collection baskets and rectories filled with cooks, maids and drivers.

Where will our solutions originate and who will lead us?

We spend great effort in this country talking about leadership. Our kids go to great lengths to involve themselves in noble exercises to develop their leadership skills, partially to evidence them on college or professional school applications. Big shots, with the power to accept or reject, hire or fire, quickly fix their eyes on applicants' leadership lines in efforts to separate the dime-a-dozen choices and select the ones with the proven experience that makes a difference. Often, our almost-an-adult youngsters lead the most humane of causes, maintaining objectives as pure and genuine as it gets these days. Their natural, youthful exuberance to help others and make things better, places the bar at levels that make us proud; where pretenders need not apply.

My question? Where the hell do they all go?

Our world's public servants, our so-called leaders -- political, religious, of race, of education and of family -- somehow have been populated by so many B-team individuals that it raises the most serious of questions. Those who have been empowered to impart fairness, common sense and righteousness now largely maintain the qualities and character that makes

us all want to take hot showers to rid ourselves of the smell.

Leading others has turned to agendas of self-service, corruption, and favors to select groups with equally less-than-noble intentions. Does something happen that drops the bar so rapidly, between the time one shows such promise and hope to that minute when it's their time to make a difference? It appears so.

One thing is for sure. Our nation's and our world's leaders are failing miserably. Decadence and human atrocities abound, racial tensions are alive and thriving and the common thread of goodness that used to permeate throughout all religious persuasions has headed for the hills and is nowhere to be found.

Is there no one left to convince the radical extremists of this world, or are they so far gone that the only answer is to murder them all?

My dad often used the expression tweedledee-tweedledum when discussing our choices that in the end were on the road to irrelevance. In other words, depicting the choice at hand as somewhat meaningless and certainly indistinguishable in comparison. When discussing politics, he seemed to know that any real differences among the candidates would eventually disappear, made futile by their one

common thread of succumbing to self-serving goals, clawing their way to larger roles, making decisions based more on their rise than ours.

Sometimes I wonder if the scrutiny that our public servants now must face, known as vetting in political arenas, has gone so overboard by rival parties that individuals with true and genuine ideals have turned to other less invasive-like careers. Has the opposing political party's tendency to rip and denigrate one's character, not for the sake of vetting, but for their own party's gain, resulted in potentially great leaders, (and their families), to conclude that it's simply not worth it?

Unfortunately, a look at our current political landscape discloses a cast of less-than-achieving Frank Underwood act-a-likes, rather than individuals who present and promote honesty and hope.

Is Hillary Clinton, an obstructionist to truth and transparency and clearly owning part of the responsibility for today's current mess, really the best that our nation has to offer for the Democrats? Is there not one fresh and inspiring man or woman within our free world to represent an alternative to a one-term failed Secretary of State and the abused wife of a prior Tweedledee? Doesn't her antics, lack of forthright discussion and incompetent assessment of the whole

Benghazi disgrace and email travesty immediately result in Jeopardy's wrong answer buzzer?

Is Donald Trump, a billionaire builder, entrepreneur and game show host on the Republican side, and a man who seems to care little about insulting and degrading anyone with a different point of view represent the best that the elephants have to offer?

Is Al Sharpton really the best that we have to represent the black communities? Does one have to be completely blinded to not see what is so obvious -- that this man does more to divide than unite?

And of our current Administration, once so hopeful, recruiting us with so many promises, can you explain your over seven years of Tweedledee? Is opportunity, moral fiber, safety from the world's insane terror, racial unity, political bi-partisanship, roads and infrastructure, education, world peace, energy sources, or the price at a GOD-DARN tollbooth any better? Like those before you, despite all the rhetoric and rallying, you too have truly come up small and empty!

Have we, once a nation leading the world toward life's freedoms, equalities and opportunities, now been reduced (and controlled)

by the size and amount of money in the respective campaign coffers? AAAHHHHH!

Where the heck did all the brilliant, fresh idea, honest and energetic young leaders go? Aren't they now mature, middle-aged, intelligent potential servants readying themselves to LEAD the world's tide for the better?

Has politics now taken on the pathetic trend of our religious leaders where we are left isolated and alone with no real guidance and leadership; left to figure out our society's remedies on our own, a possibility in which our success, without strong leadership, is in all likelihood lower than even our current political leaders' approval ratings?

So quiet and failing are our leaders in the need to speak on behalf of morality, they have miserably failed us, not finding a way to reach young people with relevance and motivation; failing also to impart a sense of responsibility on parents and guardians convincing them of their responsibility to impart a sense of goodness and accountability to those they are responsible to guide.

Today, the majority of our leaders are content to sit by and allow the machine to pick up, clearly out of touch and self-indulged. They are, in my view, a disgrace to their true mission.

Why haven't our leaders found a way to use every adult in the free and not-so-free world to once and for all rid our earth of the most barbaric and despicable among us? Stopping those who chop off people's heads, blow up innocent people; fly planes into buildings surely must be first on the list of priorities for all of mankind.

Shouldn't there be an outcry (of downright mob forming) from civilization, from the millions all over the world being asked to live in such insanity.

Can one of our world's leaders, in between their check-me-out behavior, begin to convince those so radically misguided and insane that there can be no God in favor of this madness?

It has become like reading fiction, too inconceivably insane to have been going on for so many years. So surreal and despicable is the concept of terror that it should inspire the thinking that, until it is eliminated, it is virtually impossible to continue with anything else.

You feel like screaming, "Are terrorists that offended by a Nordstrom storefront? Is there something unknowingly evil in a pair of Levi's? Are Joey, Rachel, Ross and Chandler really that bad? If we all raise our fucken right hand and

promise to pay an extra dollar a gallon, will they stop cutting off the head of someone's dad?"

Or will they force us someday to end it all, wiping away the breath of millions of human beings, dealing with their insanity in a way more serious than the world has ever known. It's becoming more serious than even the insanity of the holocaust or the atom bomb atrocities in Japan.

Will the barbaric among us finally cause the zillions who can think clearly to gather in the public square looking at a road map toward their terror so we can go and put an end to this madness?

And in relation, our higher institutions of education must get back to the mission of humanity and produce leaders who are not tainted, just clear in the call for human decency and co-existence.

These new leaders must understand the basic concepts of FIBER.

Fiber, whether you ingest it, chemically apply it or just plain live it, is the common ingredient that binds and keeps things together.

New leadership must symbolize that of a huge spatula, a massive butter knife to spread some fiber over all of us, to keep this world, our

world, from coming apart at the seams. Let's talk flavors, human values fiber, morality fiber, faith in goodness fiber, media fiber, family fiber, sportsmanship fiber, education fiber, race fiber, common sense fiber, and while we're now a society that focuses on such crucial things as gluten free and no transfat things, how about agenda free fiber and greed free fiber.

Maybe what we need are real leaders whose bar is set a little higher than those of the current leaders of our world ... those whose best unfortunately force us to take the bad with the good. Let's raise the damn bar!

Chapter 9

Robbed

I think that day in September, 2001, resulted in so many things for me, impacts that continually fade then resurface, help then hurt me, provide sharp thoughts and then at times numb any ability to find solutions.

Two things perhaps are certain. That day, its aftermath and the almost daily reminder through links to constant terror events some 15 years later, has changed me. And the second thing is that, for the most part, most would say it hasn't. I think I have done quite well at pretending to be in the vast majority for which that Tuesday has legitimately faded.

And while, if I were assessed by the many who know me, a wide and diverse opinion would surely exist. Most if not all however, would fail to link the event to the too often all too serious realist that I have become.

Chapter 10

Remembering

Memory is an interesting phenomenon. As my dad grew older, closer to dementia but still capable of carrying his awesome personality of optimism and faith wherever he went, he began to have trouble remembering the short-term things like this past Christmas or even events from a few weeks, or even hours ago. Somehow though, during this period, his long-term memory simultaneously got stronger.

If you wanted to have a great conversation with my dad at that stage of his life, all you had to do was bring up anything that happened years and years ago, even stuff from his young adulthood and he was engaging, accurate and miraculously razor sharp.

Such seems to be the way 9/11 works for me.

In a time that we were all hopeful that, for me, 9/11 would fade into the sunset, it seems to rekindle itself with each morning's sunrise. Frankly, I never maintained any illusions that it would completely disappear from memory just that it would eventually engulf less and less of my psyche.

Perhaps the event's freshness is a result of the daily news-line articles of terror that are so prevalent each day, especially for someone like me who feels compelled to read them. These daily reminders, these insane atrocities seem to force 9/11 memories to grow both more vividly and more frequently.

Perhaps it's the daily reminders from those who lead us, giving us the impression that nobody really gives a shit. Recently, I read an article that our President and his wife flew to L.A. but on separate planes, costing the taxpayers approximately one million dollars. That's egregious enough but really not the point that bothers me.

The President was flying to the west coast to appear live on the Jimmy Kimmel's late night comedy show. The First Lady went out west to appear on the popular daytime Ellen DeGeneres Show. Really! With all there is to do, with all that concerns us, our First Family is acting like Hollywood stars rather than even giving the impression that they are here for us working on solutions and a better way of life. And the world's problems just continue to roll down the hill, forcing us to find ways not to think about them.

Personally, and in stark contrast to the above, I am not beyond feeling humbly fortunate

despite the internal strife I endure. I have soaked in the miracle of watching and living my once little grammar school daughters' growth into gorgeous, intelligent and caring young women, more supportive and loving than any father deserves. I am blessed and grateful to be loved and to love back the most wonderful wife this earth has known, who privately will have none of any attempt by me for self-pity and self-concession.

I hope to come to peace with 9/11 someday. Perhaps it's possible. I hope it is. I wish hard for my mind to relax, for my late-night lungs to breathe easier and for my vision to see more of life's endless and God-given miracles.

I look forward to taking a long, deep breath and expend some time thinking about what I want to do in the last third of my life. I understand that filling one's bucket list may feel a bit too final.

Let's face it; few have the time or the inclination to have any such thoughts in the first two/thirds of their life. Through middle age, most are busy counting up, building their lives, working hard, establishing their mark.

But it's equally disturbing to never give it any thought. I don't ever want to count down, rather maybe just continue to have the courage to

step out of the box, realizing that leaving one's comfort zone may not only be reserved for the young.

After escaping death by a mere matter of seconds, then getting a few powerful, between the eyes life-kicks and all the time still maturing like a cellared wine, it is only the simple things, those with no relation to either money or ambition, that seem to be now worth my attention or desire. Friends have faded, the career moved to a means rather than an end, and my three girls' happiness has taken the forefront in most everything.

I hope to become more optimistic about our world and mostly to continue to do something that, in the end, is the only thing that ever really mattered to me … enjoying life with my family.

As for Wall Street and the hundreds of characters that it introduced to me, most times I remember it fondly. I'm even back from time to time to do a few consulting projects. Beyond the always-incredible money, which honestly and thankfully allowed wonderful opportunities to do things for the ones I love, I enjoyed much about it.

I was and still am good at it, I think. I'd like to even think, I was good to it, as least as much as it was good to me.

CLOSING

Some things that happen to a person almost 15 years ago are long gone. For other things, the memory has a way of dulling the details or even placing it in one's subconscious. And then there are those rare things that are so lasting in a person, those for which the clarity refuses to fade, things that maybe only death provides true separation or escape. These are events that leave an indelible mark that act as a constant reminder, too powerful to ever disappear, rather forcing one to learn to live with its memory, a difficult, lifelong and no-choice necessity.

Epilogue

I remember a year, many years ago, when my dad coached my brothers and me in baseball. We were bright-eyed enthusiasts looking forward to each Saturday morning when we would soak up the sunshine in our white uniforms with orange trim. If not the best year of my youth, it is the one that I remember most vividly. Our team was filled with friends and their parents, most always getting together after the game for hamburgers and sodas, each family taking its turn as host.

Their houses, like my dad's, were ordinary compared to today. But there was a warmth which was more powerful and more lasting than anything that a big deck or in-ground pool could provide. My father enjoyed coaching because he loved baseball, and because the community was filled with genuineness, so unlike the often-ridiculous environment of selfishness and inappropriateness that now permeates throughout most youth fields and leagues.

I remember we were 0-17 that year, the very best of experiences. We tried, just could never seem to end a game with more runs than the other team. Nobody called for my father's

head and nobody left with his head down. I am fairly certain that no kid was tortured by misguided parents in the car ride home. Everybody just looked forward to the barbecue, the kind where charcoals were lit on fire and took several minutes to heat up. No big deal. Nobody was in a rush. Everybody just simply looked forward to Tuesday night. That's the night our team had the field for practice.

My wife went to a good high school, one where kids grew up and got educated without the pressures so prevalent in today's schools. Today, kids from 9th grade on begin to prepare themselves for college entrance exams or their Division I college athletic scholarship.

They tell me that my wife was a free spirit as a kid. She decided that one day she would have some fun. She borrowed an old cloth housedress from her mom, the kind that grandma would wear as she did that day's laundry. She found an old gray wig that could hide her young brunette curls and borrowed a pair of granny glasses. She got her hands on an old mop that was lying around in her basement, a prop that would complete her devious plan.

In between classes, she readied herself in the school's hallway bathroom as her prank's

cohorts kept a watchful eye. Turning herself from a 16-year-old student with the plaid uniform skirt into an old cleaning lady, she walked in, unannounced, to her next class, which was already in progress. With head down eyeing only the floor, hiding her youthful complexion, she proceeded to mop the square tiles in and around the teacher and students' desks.

She responded to her instructor's shock with a mumbling and garbled voice of an old lady, making sure not to raise her head. The room was filled with student laughter as the teacher did her best to communicate that a class was in process and her tidy-up would have to wait. Pretending not to understand, she just kept mumbling and mopping.

Unable to take it anymore without bursting into laughter, my prankster wife picked up her head, and greeted her teacher with, "Good morning Mrs. Smit!" The class roared with laughter and the teacher, just being had, smiled. My wife leaned the mop against the wall in the corner of the classroom and took her normal seat, deciding she would finish the class, house dress, granny glasses and wig still in tow.

When the teacher finally got the students to stop laughing, the class proceeded, and then ended without further incident. There were no repercussions to be had from the school or my

wife's parents, no overreaction about the lack of sensitivity toward the aging, and no Huffington Post or TMZ story. It was just another funny tale to be told during the make-your-own-good-times, in someone's backyard.

When one of my angels, now a young adult, was a little girl, nearing the confidence of becoming a teenager, she performed in a dance recital at a local venue, well-populated by every parent, grandparent and friend. For her, this was huge, a culmination of several weeks of practice but somewhat different than the numerous other shows she had previously experienced.

On this day, she was to perform a solo tap dance, the reward from her dance instructor for her hard work and progression in what was her most treasured hobby. All 75 pounds of my little girl was, for the first time, to go it alone. I'm sure she felt that the whole world was watching.

The recital was one ninety-second, someone's angel routine after another, often with instructor standing off-stage providing support and encouragement to each dance group and in the case of really young performers standing in front of the stage doing the rehearsed dance routine so each little girl could follow. As would

be with all parents, this was a big deal because we knew it was important to our little girl.

The sound system, on cue, announced our somewhat stressful but much anticipated upcoming dance. Out from the pulled back curtain walked our angel, taking her place, center stage, and then freezing motionless awaiting the start of the music; little girl statues that preceded each and every dance.

The music started and angel began her tap-tap-tap, moving her little body to the sound of the song's melody, a scene that I had witnessed in various rooms around our house hundreds of times over the past few weeks. About halfway through the routine, the unthinkable happened. Hitting a slick spot on the stage floor, our little angel slipped, then fell, no doubt causing a nice bruise on, as my dad used to call it, her fanny.

Acting like the professional we all knew she was, she popped up and continued, an instruction taught over and over at all dance schools. The end of the dance was met with polite applause from the audience as I sat there knowing what was going through little angel's head. As my wife scurried from the theater seat next to mine to get back stage to deal with the anticipated tears of our daughter, I sat there feeling what any dad would, heartbroken for my baby.

As the recital ended, now several hours after arrival, I sat warming up the car waiting for mom and daughter to exit from the *dancers-only* door and make their way to the car. As my little girl climbed up the back seat, I turned, gave her a kiss and said, "You were great, honey, and especially the way you bounced right up after falling."

She gave me the smirk I knew she would but the elephant had clearly now just left the car. I continued, "Dad is STARVING, where are we going to eat?" Told to make my way to a local Applebee's, we dined on burgers, fries and ice cream sundaes. Seeing that mom and dad really did think she was great and hearing a few funny stories about how dad was the goat on a number of occasions throughout his illustrious youth sports career, our little girl felt back to normal.

Our car ride home was filled with our now chatty 11-year-old going on about numerous things, reminding mom that tomorrow was this and the next day was that and that I can't forget that I needed to drive her here and then there. Our angel was secure in our love and life's ups, downs and in-betweens. Her mom and dad's approach left little to no time for a stage slip to linger. There would be no Instagrams, no You-Tube videos, no way for the New Jersey dance

world to tweet about an 11-year old slipping during a dance routine.

Sometimes, I think back and try to remember who I was, how I became who I am. It's interesting for me, as it must be for you. We are all from where we came. Change occurs but, in the end, it's most difficult to alter our formation. For me, it was mostly good things, many of which perhaps don't fit snugly anymore in today's times.

I remember, as a boy, driving to The Bronx often, in one of the many broken-down cars my father drove. I remember there was a hole in the floor in the back seat where the kids sat. Swear to God, you could see the road flying by through the floor as we drove. No one seemed to mind; certainly no one made it into a big deal. Now? Shit, the Child Safety Division would bring charges against my parents.

Luckily, without seat belts, I could move around easily, away from the hole so as to prevent any of my little army men toys from falling through onto the road. Needless to say, on the very cold days, the back seat chilled up a bit. My father's parents lived in The Bronx, still in

the neighborhood where he grew up. I hated the drive but was given no choice.

As we would arrive, my dad would remind me to eat grandma's food, especially her meatballs; that it was important to her. I hated the meatballs. They were filled with raisins. Who the hell puts raisins in their meatballs? I hated raisins. I used to say, "But I like my other grandma's meatballs, not this grandma's."

My dad would hear none of it. He said that Grandma loved me and it was important to her. Guess what? I ate the damn meatballs. I even ate the gross Italian candy that she used to force on my brother and me; some kind of disgusting taffy with brown stuff in it … no, not raisins but something just as bad. When it was time to leave, I hugged her … we all did and, once again, I left believing I did the right thing. It was just the way things were in my house … you always tried your hardest to do the right thing. We all ate the disgusting meatballs. It meant a lot to grandma.

When my youngest daughter was in her early teens, she wrote a one-act play. Since 9/11, she became interested in history and particularly war veterans. I think my circumstances resulted in her developing a curiosity about those who dealt with war and terror and loss. I include it here because, while elementary and from the mind of a then youngster, I believe it says a lot about transformation and maybe even her daddy's mindset. It's called the Prologue to After and it won an award in the young writers club of New Jersey.

The Prologue to After

A one-act play, November 6, 2010

Cast of Characters

OLD MAN
An old homeless man, in his early seventies. He is missing his right arm.

YOUNG BOY
A young boy, age 7-9 from 1952. He has dark hair, slicked back. Bright-eyed.

BILLY
A young man in his early twenties from 1964. He is handsome and strong.

PATTY
A young lady in her early twenties from 1964. She is pretty and sweet and BILLY'S fiancée. She wears a yellow ribbon pinned to her shirt at all times.

MIDDLE-AGED MAN
A middle-aged man in his late forties, early fifties from 1995. HE is a powerful, strong, distinguished veteran. He is missing his right arm.

Scene
A New York Train Station

Era
The present. Although, the characters that greet the OLD MAN are obviously not from the present.

TIME:
Sometime in early afternoon.

AT RISE:
A train station. In the corner is a sign that reads TRAIN STOP. Center stage, is a common wood bench that would be found in any train station. The floors are dusty and littered with old wrappers and forgotten magazines. The background noise is random train chatter and sounds. Extras are in the dimmed background. On the bench is the OLD MAN. He is a disheveled man in his late sixties or early seventies. He is tired looking and unshaven. He is wearing an old, discolored baseball cap with a faded Brooklyn Dodgers insignia. His jacket is old and army green with its left chest a darker shade then the rest of the jacket, appearing as if a patch of some sort has been ripped or torn off.

His pants are non-descript, except for the bottom where they are tattered and worn as they cover a pair of scuffed boots without laces. His right arm is missing, his jacket sleeve tucked tightly into his jacket pocket. He lounges on the bench, looking obviously like a homeless man. He shakes a metal

cup with his left hand, sounding as if it contains a few coins. The can is bruised but somewhat reflective. He wears no expression, and does not verbally beg. He only shakes the can. At his feet is a folded newspaper. For a few moments, he is alone until a YOUNG BOY enters the stage from the opposite side of the train entrance. The TRAIN STOP sign goes dim. He is obviously not a young boy from the present, considering his attire (a plaid button down shirt tucked into his blue jeans, old sneakers and a Brooklyn Dodgers' baseball cap) He sits down right next to the OLD MAN and puts his baseball glove next to him on the bench. He begins to chat amiably. And the OLD MAN puts down his can of change.

YOUNG BOY
Well hey there, Mister. Whatchya doin? *(not giving him time to answer)* I'm goin' to a baseball game! My momma gave me 5 WHOLE DOLLARS so I could take this train to Ebbetts Field, buy me a ticket and a box o' cracker jacks!

(The OLD MAN looks at the young boy without emotion. He nods and the BOY continues)

YOUNG BOY (CONT.)
I'm hopin' this will get me excited for MY game tomorrow! It's the first little league of the season! Well, not little league… Street league, Momma calls it. All the boys in the neighborhood make teams and we have games every Sunday, till Momma calls for supper. Except not all boys. One

girl. Her name's Patty. She's real pretty, but she plays baseball, still. It's swell really. She's rough like us boys, but real nice to look at. A lot of the boys are stuck on her....Not me though, I'm there to play baseball.

(The OLD MAN looks at the boy, still expressionless. Excited, the YOUNG BOY continues)

YOUNG BOY (CONT.)
Well hey! I didn't even notice! That's a swell hat, Mister! You like the Dodgers too? I'm just itching to get on the train now. I bet one day I'm gonna play for them. Heck! I'd bet my bubble gum I'm gonna play for them!

(YOUNG BOY elbows the OLD MAN)

YOUNG BOY (CONT.)
And that's a big bet, considerin' I got me a big bubble gum blowin' contest next week.

(The OLD MAN moves over a little, clearly uncomfortable that the little boy touched him. Still, the YOUNG BOY continues)

YOUNG BOY (CONT.)
Oh I'm sorry, Mister! Did I elbow you too hard? Papa says I got me the strongest arm he's ever seen. My throwin' arm is my prize possession. On rainy days, Mama lets me lift her cans of vegetables at the kitchen table just to make my

arm stronger. The beans are the heaviest so I like them the best. My little brother always lifts the peas. *(Whispering)* Those are the lightest, but don't tell him I told ya. I don't think he's big enough for the beans yet. *(Not skipping a beat)* Have you ever been to Ebbett's Field? I haven't. This'll be my very first visit! But I can tell ya right now it won't be my last. I'm gonna mow everyone's lawn in my neighborhood this summer so I can go to another game this season. And then in the fall, I'll rake leaves! Then shovel snow! I'm gonna save up all the money I can and it will go right to my baseball fund. And once I have enough, I'm gonna buy me a new glove and all the tickets I can.

(The YOUNG BOY picks up the glove he put on the floor in the beginning)

YOUNG BOY (CONT.)
See! This is my glove. It's real old. It was Papa's when he was a boy and his older brother gave it to him. So it's real beat up. But let me tell you, it does its job well. Last season, I caught the game winnin' ball at the bottom of the ninth for my team. Everyone was proud o' me. Even Patty. And she's the best on our team!

(The OLD MAN, still expressionless)

YOUNG BOY (CONT.)
So I'll never throw this puppy away. But I think it's time he retire soon. Maybe he will catch a fly ball today! That would be swell. I think he's got one last great catch in 'em. Whatdya you think?

(The spotlight fades to black on the OLD MAN and the sound of a train roars. A single spotlight illuminates the sign that says TRAIN STOP and you can see the young boy running towards the sign, he is frozen then, still in view of the audience. And a dim spotlight is held over him.

The main spotlight shines again on the OLD MAN. Now a young man named BILLY and a young lady named PATTY accompany him. Dressed well, SHE has a yellow ribbon pinned to her shirt. They sit next to him on the bench with their backs to him. They are obviously fighting. BILLY has an unmarked duffle bag with him. Poking out of the zipper is a baseball bat.)

BILLY
Come with me. We can get married in L.A. Don't make me leave my dream.

PATTY
(Sad and angry)

Aren't I your dream? I can't leave my family behind to follow you to a city across the country. For what? Baseball? It's time to grow up, Billy.

BILLY
Grow up? I am grown up. I'm a draft pick for the Brook—I mean Los Angeles Dodgers. This will be my job now. I can make money following my dream as long as I move out there and move with the team. We can rent an apartment, save up some money, ship your whole family out there and have the wedding of your dreams, Patty.

PATTY
It's baseball, not a job. We grew out of this didn't we? We can stay here. And you can keep working in my father's hardware store and when he retires it's all yours. We're not married yet, Billy. I can't just move away with you. But if you leave without me, what's next?

BILLY
I have to go. I've been waiting for this day my entire life. Nothing's supposed to hold you back from your dreams.

(at this line, the OLD MAN blinks a few times, but continues watching expressionless)

BILLY (CONT.)
I love you and you love me, who cares if we're here or there. As long as we're together.

PATTY
I do love you, but I can't cross the country like this on such short notice. You have to understand. My brother was drafted into the army only last year, I can't leave my parents home alone. Please stay here. Try for a different baseball team! You'll make it. The Yankees? Somewhere in New York.

BILLY
I was born to play for the Dodgers. Whether they're in Brooklyn or LA I have to go. You know that, Patty. You're parents will be okay. This will all blow over, it always does. Your brother will come home. Besides, you can't be with them forever. But *I* want you to be with *me* forever.

(The OLD MAN winces at the line and rubs his eyes in anguish)

PATTY
(Starting to cry)

I can't.

BILLY
The next train is at six. Go home and pack your bags. I'll meet you in LA

PATTY
You don't understand –

BILLY
(The roaring of the train sounds in the background)
My train is here, Patty. I have to leave. This is my dream—

PATTY
Don't—

BILLY
(He looks at the OLD MAN sitting)

Nothing's supposed to stand in the way of your dream, right Mister?

(BILLY kisses Patty on the head and she embraces him tightly. When they break apart Patty shakes her head and cries harder. He runs towards the now illuminated sign that says TRAIN STOP. You hear the train pull away. The spotlight on the train sign is darkened. Patty holding her stomach runs toward where the YOUNG BOY is frozen and freezes. The lights fade for a moment on the OLD MAN who has an expressionless look on his face.)

(The lights rise again on the man now accompanied by BILLY. He now has a duffel bag with a stamp that says PROPERTY OF THE U.S. ARMY. BILLY sits down on the bench next to the OLD MAN.)

BILLY
Hello.

(The old man looks up, but doesn't respond)

BILLY (CONT.)
Uhh, may I see that newspaper near your foot , Sir?

(The OLD MAN reaches with his left hand to get the folded newspaper by his right foot. He hands it to BILLY.)

BILLY (CONT.)
(Reading the headline)

Violence continues in Vietnam… *(he turns the page)* I don't wanna believe I'm going into this.

I was drafted last week. I had to come home from LA. I only got to play for the Dodgers for a month. Actually a bunch of us players were drafted. The coach said we'd be out soon enough. He's worried we'll get hurt but if we don't we're all going right back to the team.

(The OLD MAN rubs his eyes)

BILLY (CONT.)
(Distraught)

But that's not all I'm leaving behind… When I got home from LA to say goodbye to my folks and

my fiancée, I found out she's pregnant. With my kid. I didn't even have time to marry her before I left. She was too sad to come to the train station with me. It's the second time I'm leaving her. *(He begins to cry)* I'm so worried I won't come back for her. I heard somewhere hundreds are hurt real bad every day or even, well, you know. If I'm maimed in war, I can't play baseball and support her. If I don't make it back… she's alone.

(The OLD MAN bends over and puts his elbows on his knees, holding his head in his hand)

BILLY (CONT.)
If I don't make it back I hope my kid learns to play baseball. I hope he has my throwing arm and my fiancée's talent.

(BILLY wipes his eyes on his sleeve)

BILLY (CONT.)
We used to play together on the street, when we were younger, ya know. She was better than me, but the high school didn't have a girl's league. So she stopped and I continued. If I make it back, I'll marry her in New York then move to LA and take her and my child to every one of my games. And after the games, we will stay later and teach our kid everything we know. I'll even admit that my wife is better than me at baseball.

(He stands up and takes a deep breath and throws his bag over his shoulder.)

BILLY (CONT.)
(Starting this line strongly, but loses confidence and trails off)

I will make it back for her. I got some will left in me, right? ...

(The OLD MAN just stares blankly at him. BILLY walks toward the TRAIN STOP sign, which is now illuminated; you hear the roar of a train. BILLY freezes next to where the other figures are frozen under a dim spotlight.

The main spotlight over the OLD MAN is illuminated again and the OLD MAN is accompanied by a MIDDLE AGED MAN in his fifties. He is well dressed and powerful looking. He wears an overcoat like a cape so that it covers some but not all of his medals and pins from the military on the left side of his body. The right side of his torso is completely covered.)

MIDDLE AGED MAN
Good afternoon, Sir.

(The OLD MAN doesn't respond. They sit awkwardly for a few moments. The MIDDLE AGED MAN notices the newspaper next to the OLD MAN)

MIDDLE AGED MAN (CONT.)
That today's paper? Can I see the, um, job listings?

(The OLD MAN hands the entire paper to the MIDDLE AGED MAN. The MIDDLE AGED MAN looks over the paper for a moment before remarking sadly with a chuckle,)

MIDDLE AGED MAN (CONT.)
I guess there's not too many jobs willing to hire a Vietnam veteran, right? Seventeen years o' service and a limb gettin' me nowhere, eh?

(He takes off his overcoat and obviously shows that his right arm is missing. He points at the OLD MAN's missing arm.)

MIDDLE AGED MAN (CONT.)
Lost mine not focusing in battle. You?

(The OLD MAN doesn't answer. Just stares at the MIDDLE AGED MAN.)

MIDDLE AGED MAN (CONT.)
Yeah, I know, it's rough. When I lost mine, I lost my ticket to the major leagues. Life's hard.

(There is an awkward pause, the MIDDLE AGED MAN continues reading the job listings.)

MIDDLE AGED MAN (CONT.)
I really don't need much of a job. I just got me to support… My fiancée passed when, uh, I was away. She was carryin' a baby…

(The MIDDLE AGE MAN is distraught)

MIDDLE AGED MAN (CONT.)
MY baby. Damn, I was gonna be outta the army by the time my baby was 15 months old, then I would never leave 'em again. But then I got that letter… that letter

(breaking down)

MIDDLE AGED MAN (CONT.)
…And I promised her… I promised. But really, what was to go home to after that? No family, no throwing arm… no career?

(He pauses for a while noticeably upset, somewhat sobbing. He puts his head in his hand. The OLD MAN is also noticeably upset, somewhat sobbing. He puts his head in his hand the exact same way. It is quiet for a moment with just the silent scene of the two men, bent over, in the same position. Finally, the OLD MAN sits up and then the MIDDLE AGED MAN)

MIDDLE AGED MAN (CONT.)
(Fighting now with himself)

No…..no. stop. Just keep going. I can do it….keep going.

(He takes a very large, stabilizing breath. Now sounding sad, but fighting for hopefulness)

I'll find something to come home to.

(He lifts the job listings page and shows it to the OLD MAN)

Plenty of new opportunities.

(Slightly believing himself)

My fiancée's dad… He had a hardware store if I remember correctly…I'm sure things will work out…Just keep going. I fought for this country, I'm sure it will repay me.

(Referring to himself)
I mean, this old pitcher's got another start left in 'em right?

(Asking again as if to convince himself)

Right?

(The train roars and the MIDDLE AGED MAN walks toward the now illuminated TRAIN STOP sign and freezes.)

YOUNG BOY
(YOUNG BOY, who was also still frozen, faces the OLD MAN.)

I think he's got one last great catch in 'em.
Whatdya you think?

PATTY
(PATTY, who was also still frozen, faces the OLD MAN.)

For me, he does.

BILLY
(BILLY, who was also still frozen, faces the OLD MAN.)

Nothing's supposed to stand in the way of your dream, Mister.

MIDDLE-AGED MAN
(MIDDLE AGED MAN, who is also still frozen, faces the OLD MAN.)

Then he does have some will left in him, right?

(The sign and dim spotlight goes dark as the three figures finally exit the stage. Now there is a spotlight on the OLD MAN. He picks up his silver can of change he was using earlier and looks at the side, using it as a mirror. He adjusts his hat in this makeshift mirror as if seeing himself for the first time. He leaves the can on the bench, still full of money. He's very shaky as he says this last line, but it is full of hope.)

OLD MAN
Yeah… I do think this old guy's got one last start in him. …He's got no other choice

(He stares out at the audience, for a short time flexing the arm he still has.

Finally the train roars and BILLY at age 73 in 2010 walks toward the illuminated TRAIN STOP sign. Lights fade.)

END OF PLAY

END OF BOOK

34454723R00118

Made in the USA
Middletown, DE
21 August 2016

Made in the USA
Middletown, DE
21 April 2021

38064425R00120